THE WEBS THAT BIND

BOOK FIVE
OF
THE RELUCTANT ASSASSIN
A HUNDRED HALLS NOVEL

THOMAS K. CARPENTER

The Webs That Bind

Book Five of The Reluctant Assassin

A Hundred Halls Novel

by Thomas K. Carpenter

Published by Black Moon Books

Cover design by Ravven
www.ravven.com

Discover other titles by this author on:
www.thomaskcarpenter.com

ISBN-10: 9781093962826

Other Hundred Halls Novels

THE HUNDRED HALLS

Trials of Magic

Web of Lies

Alchemy of Souls

Gathering of Shadows

City of Sorcery

THE RELUCTANT ASSASSIN

The Reluctant Assassin

The Sorcerous Spy

The Veiled Diplomat

Agent Unraveled

The Webs That Bind

Be kind people

THE WEBS THAT BIND

Part I – The Wish

Chapter One

On the train from Atlanta to Invictus, August 2017

Prophecy comes in strange places

"Sometimes even the best plans fail."

The words hung in the dim air of the Magtrak elite privacy train car as the North Carolina countryside flew past in a dark green blur.

Zayn, who'd been leaning his head against the cool glass trying not to think about the fact that it was their last year at the Academy, glanced over to his cousin on the opposite seat.

Keelan sat straight and tall as if his inner thoughts had made him rigid. When they'd met up at the station in Atlanta, he'd worn the dark sunglasses of a Watcher, but those were stuffed into his jacket pocket, revealing his brown eyes.

"Sometimes even the best plans fail," repeated Keelan.

The words had a chilling effect on Zayn. Had Keelan somehow listened in on his thoughts?

Zayn pulled himself away from the comfortable armrest, stiffening to match his cousin's posture. He checked the runes along the walls for signs of an active spell, but they were dull gray, signaling that the car was completely devoid of active magic.

"What are you talking about?" asked Zayn.

For a moment, they locked gazes and Zayn's hackles went up, which simultaneously twisted his guts because it felt so unnatural to look at his best friend that way. The intensity of their matched gazes broke when Keelan looked outside at the hazy morning sky above the fields.

"Remember the day of my daddy's funeral?" asked Keelan, his Alabama accent coloring the edges of his words. "When I wanted to do nothing but get away from Varna?"

The memory came back easy for Zayn as if it'd been waiting there for him, but so did other memories from those times. Memories with more at stake to them.

"You were throwing rocks at some old junk," said Zayn, feeling the heat from that day as if he were back in that vine-choked forest. "Called me an ice zombie, or something like that."

Keelan's forehead bunched at the center as if he were working on a mental knot. His mouth twitched before he spoke. "I'm sorry about getting your ass kicked."

"It's okay," said Zayn. "I understood why it happened, plus it got me that job with the Goon. Eventually, anyway."

Zayn glanced at the dull runes and the train car, and thought about the other memories from that time—namely that he'd made a promise to himself in front of Keelan that he would end the Lady of Varna.

Sometimes even the best plans fail.

Was that a coded warning to stay away? Zayn wanted to ask his cousin, but those Watcher glasses were sitting right there in plain view, a reminder of his new responsibilities. Sometime during the summer, Keelan had started wearing them. Zayn had caught a glimpse of him without the glasses when they were BBQing on his deck. A wasp had flown around his head, and he'd knocked them off trying to swat it away without spilling his beer. It was only a glimpse, but his brown eyes had glints of purple to them.

But they weren't purple now. Last year when Watcher Sabrina had come to see him in Invictus, she'd kept her glasses off. Was that the purpose of the runed train car, so they could have a conversation in private? Or was it a warning for him not to make an attempt on the Lady's life?

A strained silence made the next few hours uncomfortable. Zayn watched Keelan fidget in his seat, looking like he was going to say something else, but he never worked himself up to it.

Zayn went back to watching the countryside fly past, but his thoughts never left his cousin. He'd spent his whole life with Keelan, getting into trouble together, joining the Halls. But now that their paths were diverging, he didn't know what to say.

It wasn't just Varna. Zayn suspected if they'd grown up in a normal town, that this awkwardness would be the same. As much as he loved his cousin, they had different interests in life after school.

"What's O'Keefe going to have you work on for your final project?" asked Zayn, trying to dispel the mood

Keelan looked up from picking at his fingernail. He blinked a couple of times. Quirked his mouth to one side. "Nothing exciting. What about you?"

"I haven't the faintest idea what Priyanka will get me into this year. I'm just glad that she's still my mentor," said Zayn, regretting it as soon as he'd said it.

Because Keelan was a Watcher, Zayn hadn't told his cousin about everything that had happened last year, including why he'd had the headaches. The only events he'd explained were the same ones that he'd told the Speaker about, which kept strictly to the final battle with the dragon Akhekh.

Keelan frowned, as if he knew Zayn was withholding information. Zayn looked out the window, catching a glint in the sky.

"Hey, I can see the Spire. We're almost to the city," said Zayn, relieved that the trip would soon be over.

Since the Spire was over twice the height of any other building, it could be seen from far distances, especially since the morning cloud cover had cleared away.

"Last year, cuz," Keelan said wistfully as he pressed his face to the window.

"Last year," repeated Zayn. "How'd it go so fast?"

"A lot of things happened," said Keelan, who suddenly looked gravely serious. "Remember when we nearly got killed by that cave full of magic-eating spiders?"

"That was a close one," said Zayn, remembering the claustrophobic feel when they were surrounded in the pool.

"It's weird that you found another colony in the Undercity," said Keelan.

"Not that weird. Plenty of faez for them to snack on," said Zayn.

"They actually don't like faez," said Keelan. "While it makes them grow, they die not long after. It's more like a defensive mechanism, like a bee sting that kills the bee. Otherwise the world would be overrun with giant spiders."

"You're just like your dad when it comes to animals," said Zayn, instantly regretting it when Keelan flinched. He put his hand to his forehead. "Sorry, man. I put my foot in my mouth. You're nothing like Uncle Jesse."

It'd seemed like whatever Keelan had to say was lost to the reference of his father, which was a burden his cousin could never get rid of. It was hard to acknowledge the good parts of a shitty human being, especially one related to them.

When they pulled into the station, Keelan grabbed his arm before he left the runed car. He had a look of quiet desperation in his eyes as if there were many things still unsaid.

"Zayn," said Keelan, his face bunching with emotion. "Whatever happens this year and afterwards, remember that I've always got your back. Always."

"You too," said Zayn.

They hugged briefly before continuing out of the train. When Zayn stepped outside, he could smell the hotdog vendors outside the station, hear them hawking their wares and the impatient honking of taxi cabs maneuvering for customers.

Keelan stepped out next to him, backpack slung over his shoulder, a contented grin lingering beneath his eager gaze. The tension from the car had been dispelled by the onion-scented air and the bustle of the station.

When they stepped out of the glass station building, Priyanka was waiting for them. She wore a white shirt with a black leather jacket over top and dark jeans. Her hair was in a ponytail, and despite being one of the five original patrons, no one noticed her.

"I didn't realize we warranted special greetings," said Keelan.

Priyanka raised an eyebrow. "Sorry, Keelan. You're going to have to go on to the Honeycomb alone. I need to speak with your cousin."

As he headed the other way, Keelan, said, "No problem. I much prefer blowing stuff up with Instructor O'Keefe than putting my life in danger on a regular basis."

The smile on Priyanka's face didn't match the heaviness in her eyes. She led Zayn to a black SUV. He thought she was going to climb into the driver's seat, but she motioned for him to get into the front.

Zayn was expecting an instructor at the wheel, or maybe a fellow fifth year. He wasn't expecting the second most famous man in the world, the patron of the Dramatics Hall, Frank Orpheum.

Chapter Two

Sixth Ward, August 2017

A different side of celebrity

Zayn had never been much for celebrity, but as soon as he realized who was next to him, he found that his mouth didn't work. After Invictus, Frank Orpheum was the most well-known individual from the university, and one of the most liked in the world due to his extensive charity work, and of course, his beaming star power.

He'd sung for every pope and president, done improv with the Dalai Lama in a Tibetan temple, performed a magic trick that made the moon disappear for everyone in the northern hemisphere, slept with every actress or actor who ever made the Most Sexy lists, once hypnotized a stadium full of people into believing they were statues and not one of them blinked for over two hours, created the iconic Magelings series about a fictional Hundred Halls, and done a billion other things. Before he'd stopped performing, people jokingly called Hollywood Frankie-wood due to his utter domination of every aspect of entertainment.

"It's nice to meet you, Zayn Carter," said Frank, clasping his hand in a hearty handshake. "Pri has told me a lot about you. You're an impressive young man."

He glanced into the backseat to see Priyanka watching him closely. Was this a test?

"Not as impressive as you are," said Zayn, feeling stupid as soon as the words came out. He was probably sick of fawning sycophant fans.

"I have a knack for showmanship," he said with a wink, "but it's nothing compared to the work you do in the Academy. I only get to do my job because you're really good at yours."

A train station security guy in a blue blazer waved his light baton at them. Frank gave a friendly wave and pulled the SUV into the station traffic.

"I assume I'm not here for fashion tips," said Zayn.

Frank tilted his head to one side as he turned the wheel. "Black jeans and a black shirt. It's a good look. Sometimes simple is best."

Zayn had expected Priyanka to say something, but she was abnormally quiet. She wasn't a verbose person, but she usually commanded a room. Maybe Frank's star power was outshining her, or she knew that he needed to be the center of attention.

"Pri, dear, you can explain what's going on, and why we need his help," said Frank.

"Hmm...yes," said Priyanka. "I'm afraid I have no other way of saying this. We've discovered a terrible magic in the city that could upset the fragile balance of power."

"Balance of power? Are we talking Hall politics?" asked Zayn.

"Very astute," said Frank with a wink.

"There's a way that someone could take Invictus' position

as head patron," said Priyanka as if she were giving a lecture in front of a class.

"I thought that required agreement of the original five," said Zayn.

"Theoretically yes, though it's never been tested. But that's not what I'm talking about. This is about a wish spell," said Priyanka.

Zayn glanced between the two patrons, then he flipped down the visor, looking for a camera. "This is a joke, right? For a prank show or something? Wish spells are impossible. There are just too many variables."

But neither of them cracked a smile.

"That's what we thought too," said Priyanka. "Besides being a powerful mage, Invictus was a tireless researcher, always trying to divine new magics. We believe that he was successful in this endeavor."

"He created a wish spell," said Zayn, incredulous.

"It's hard to believe, but it's true," said Frank.

"What do you need me for? And excuse me for asking this, but why is he involved?" Zayn asked Priyanka.

"A fair question," said Frank as they came to a stop at a light. They were somewhere near the center of town.

"There are complications that only Frank can solve," said Priyanka. "And the other patrons want the spell for themselves."

"They know about it?" asked Zayn.

"A few," said Priyanka, glancing to Frank.

"I'd rather Pri get it than anyone else," he said, smiling at her with his eyes.

Their unspoken communication left Zayn a little bewildered. He'd never seen Priyanka so deferential.

"Then what do you need me for?" he asked.

"We need you to keep an eye on someone for us and tell us

if you notice anything unusual," said Priyanka.

"Of course, I'm happy to help. Who will I be spying on?" he asked.

"Invictus' son," said Priyanka.

"What? I didn't know he had a kid," said Zayn.

As Frank turned the SUV down an alleyway, he said, "He didn't. Technically the kid's not his son, but his ward."

"And this kid knows about the wish spell?" asked Zayn.

Frank refocused on his driving, so Zayn glanced into the backseat. Priyanka looked like she was deciding how to explain.

"It's doubtful that he consciously knows anything about the spell, yet he's the key to its discovery," she said.

Zayn knew obfuscation when he heard it. She was hiding something from him, but he was in no position to ask.

"Right. Follow the kid. See if he reveals anything. Should I look out for anything in particular?" he asked.

"You'll know it if you see it," said Priyanka. "Especially if anyone else starts watching him. They don't know about him, and if they start, then it means they've figured out that their current guess is wrong."

"Where do they think it is?" he asked.

"A prize of the Second Year Contest. This year is the one-hundred-year anniversary of the games. The patrons have been speculating for years that there would be a special prize given to the winning team, and some went so far as to break in to view the recording gem that Invictus made years ago for the event," said Priyanka.

Zayn's forehead wrinkled with thought. "Invictus made the recording years ago before he died? Does that mean he knew what was going to happen to him?"

"No one knows," said Priyanka, though she said it in a way that suggested she had more than educated guesses.

"But regardless of what they think, we know better. Which is why you need to be watching Ernie."

"That's his son, or ward, whatever he is," said Zayn.

"Correct," said Frank.

Priyanka's mouth pinched together. "His name might be Ernie, but he goes by Echo. He's autistic, and can be surprisingly observant under the right circumstances, so do not underestimate him."

"Anything else I need to know?" he asked.

Priyanka gave him the address of the group home he was staying at. Then she added, "I want you to report back about any friends he might have, acquaintances. We need to understand his social circle."

Zayn nodded. "I'll report back as soon as I have something."

At that moment, the SUV lurched to a stop. Zayn looked up to see they were near an Academy portal location.

"I take it this is my stop?" he asked.

Frank nodded.

"I'm getting out here too," said Priyanka, and then much to Zayn's surprise, she leaned into the front seat and gave Frank an intimate kiss that made Zayn feel a little awkward being so close.

As the SUV left them, Zayn found himself not meeting Priyanka's gaze.

"Despite my position and responsibilities, I'm still a normal human being beneath," said Priyanka, clearly picking up on his discomfort.

"I guess I just didn't see him as your type," said Zayn.

"I don't have a lot of opportunities in my line of work. He's one of the few people in the world that understands," she said.

"I'm sorry," said Zayn, holding up his hands. "I'm not trying to judge. I was just surprised, and that's all me. Like you said, I forget that you're a normal person."

"You do better than most, which is why I'm your mentor," said Priyanka, then she glanced at her watch. "Speaking of disappointments, I have a thing I need to get to. Will you please tell Carron to take it easy on the first years and that I'll be along later."

Priyanka headed back into the streets, while Zayn ducked into the back of the laundromat. He paused before he went into the janitorial closet where the portal was located, listening to sloshing washing machines and whirling driers, processing what they'd told him on the ride.

A wish spell. An honest-to-Merlin wish spell.

If he hadn't known how serious Priyanka was he might have thought it an elaborate joke.

A wish had to be the most powerful spell in the world, capable of doing just about anything. He could understand why Priyanka would want it so she could become head patron. It would solve a lot of problems that came her way.

But that wasn't the only problem it could solve. There was one other problem he could think of that it would fix.

The Lady of Varna.

He could use it to fix the poison problem that protected her. If no one had to take her poison, then she would be powerless. Everything solved with one simple spell.

Which meant that he would have to steal it.

Chapter Three

Eighth Ward, September 2017

Putting your best face forward

When Frank Orpheum stepped into the circular auditorium, a gasp went up in the room. He wore one of his trademark three-piece suits, but had his hands shoved into his pockets casually. There was a relaxed arrogance about him that seemed familiar from the years of watching him in the public eye.

Zayn didn't know what to make of his appearance, and neither did the rest of the class. The listing had stated their instructor would be a special guest, but no one could have guessed at how special they would be. A few of his classmates looked ready to throw themselves at his feet. The only person who didn't look excited was Vin, who had a suspiciously neutral expression.

Keelan elbowed Zayn in the ribs, whispering, "Is that really?"

"I don't know," said Zayn, thinking back to meeting with

him in the SUV last week.

"Hello, students of the Academy," said Frank. "As probably most of you know, I'm Frank Orpheum. Priyanka asked me to say a few words to you today."

As Zayn watched the famous mage, he had a sense of wrongness, as if something were different from when he'd met him. When he realized what it was, he knew what was happening.

"You're not Frank," said Zayn. "You're Instructor Pennywhistle."

Frank Orpheum turned to face him, forehead furrowing. "Excuse me, and who are you?"

The moment Frank addressed him, Zayn had sudden doubts that he was correct. The fact that Frank hadn't recognized him didn't mean anything since his involvement with the Academy was supposed to be a secret.

"Zayn Carter. And you *look* like Frank Orpheum, but you're really Instructor Pennywhistle."

The rest of his class shook their heads incredulously. They believed in Frank.

Portia whispered behind his back, "Zayn, that's him. I know it. I've watched every episode of the Magelings, in English and Spanish."

"Excuse me, son," said Frank, gesturing towards Zayn. "Would you come up here."

Doubts rushed in, bringing warmth to his face. He was sure he was right, but the long, drawn-out reveal was making him a little crazy.

When he reached Frank, the celebrity put his arm around his shoulders, presenting him to the class. As Zayn looked across the faces of his fellow classmates, he saw barely contained sighs, because they thought he was wrong. Even Vin, who'd had an odd expression before, now looked exasperated by his interruption.

Frank patted him on the back. Up close, he smelled like what he thought Frank Orpheum should smell like: a hint of whiskey and aftershave. He was a 1950s-style movie star who'd lasted into the modern age.

"You're a cocky young man, aren't you?" asked Frank.

The up-close examination put a stone in Zayn's gut, doubled by the gazes of his classmates. If there was one thing he knew he had to rein in at times, it was his arrogance. Zayn reluctantly nodded his head in agreement.

"I know this is a strange beginning to class, but Mr. Carter has helped demonstrate a valuable lesson today," said Frank, addressing the class while he patted Zayn on the shoulder. "And that is that you can never trust anyone."

A gasp went up for the second time in the short class as the form of Frank Orpheum morphed into the shorter and prettier Instructor Pennywhistle.

She quirked a smile at him as she pushed him back towards the rest of his classmates.

"I'm a little ashamed that you figured me out," said Instructor Pennywhistle. "What gave me away?"

He couldn't bring up that he'd met the real Frank a week before, or that Vin hadn't reacted the same way the rest of them had. Since he was her mentee, he'd probably known about the subterfuge.

"I don't know," said Zayn, shrugging his shoulders. "I remembered in years past hearing about a class on face changing, and assumed it was this one. A lucky guess."

Instructor Pennywhistle clearly didn't believe him, but she clapped her hands together.

"Either way, kudos to you, Zayn. You're the first student to ever blow my cover. But now that the fun is over, we're going to get to work. A good spy, or assassin, must be able to get into places they're not supposed to. You won't always be able to sneak in or use the Veil. That's when face changing comes into play.

"Today we're not going to make big changes. You need to get the hang of minor adjustments before you tackle full-fledged transformations involving height and body type. Vin and Charla, come up here. You're going to help your classmates with the lessons, since this is familiar ground for you both."

They came up to the front and stood to either side of Pennywhistle. Charla gave a demure curtsey, while Vin made a formal bow.

"The lesson for today is on how to change one small thing on your face. This will be much harder than you think, because no matter the magic, the mind doesn't want you to change. To encourage your subconscious cooperation, I've brewed up a potion that will help relax you, make you more malleable. The spell itself is simple, but the state of mind is the challenge. I'll break you up into three groups."

There were only fourteen students left in their year. With two helping Instructor Pennywhistle, they broke into groups of four. Zayn ended up with Eddie, Keelan, and Skylar.

Pennywhistle gathered them on the far side of the room next to a table with four vials in a stand.

"As I explained a moment ago, there are three stages of the process. First you must relax your self-identity. The potion will help with that. Second, you must cast the spell. It will help create the framework for your mind. And finally, you must visualize the change. So let's get started. Drink up."

The vial was icy cold, as if it were chilled. Crystals floated around in the pale blue water, sparking when they bumped into each other. When the liquid touched his lips, it burned for a moment, but the heat dissipated quickly, leaving a lingering warmth.

After drinking it, he didn't feel any different. He noticed a slightly glassy-eyed stare in the other three, and wondered if he looked the same.

The spell, as Pennywhistle had said, was simple. As they spoke the incantation, they traced lines across the flesh that was to be modified, literally creating the scaffolding for change. Zayn drew lines across his face, filling his touch with faez.

As he finished, he remembered seeing the imbuement lines on Vin's face. Their purpose was revealed in the spell.

Pennywhistle faced them, looking them straight in the eyes. "This is the hardest part. I want you to find a quiet place in the room and concentrate on your change. Make your nose bigger, change the color of your eyes, give yourself full lips, whatever you want to do.

"But remember, your sense of self is locked up in your appearance. You must not only imagine the change, but also respect that the change is still you. Come back to me when you're finished."

Skylar punched him in the arm as she headed to a corner of the room. "You're probably going to get this first try."

"Loser buys dinner tonight," said Zayn.

He climbed the steps, heading to the upper portion of the auditorium, excited by the prospect of the task. If he could master face changing, it would give him another way to get into the Lady's mansion. He found a seat by himself. His fellow fifth years were doing the same, settling into quiet locations.

Zayn started with breathing exercises to calm himself, pulling in air through his open mouth for eight seconds, then slowly exhaling until he had voided all air from his lungs, repeating the process until he felt at peace.

He knew right away what he wanted to change. He planned to modify his ice-blue eyes to a subdued brown, as they were the most striking thing about him. Plus, that seemed easier than making his flesh change shape.

Time seemed to slow down as he focused on the idea. He imagined looking at himself in a mirror, seeing his eye color shift. After a few minutes of effort, he pulled out his cell phone, switched to selfie mode, and checked his reflection. His eyes were still the same ice-blue that they'd always been.

Focusing more on the change did nothing for his eyes. He bore down as if he were lifting something heavy, but when he checked his reflection, it wasn't different. By this time, other students were approaching Pennywhistle at the center of class.

Eddie had given himself a ridiculous Pinocchio nose, which brought praise from the instructor, while Portia had given herself a more masculine version of her face.

Frustration grew as more and more of his class completed the task, while he felt no closer. When he was the last one, Instructor Pennywhistle asked them to change to a new face, preferably something non-human, and she climbed the steps to see him. She plopped down next to him.

"Not working so well, Mr. Carter?"

"I'm focusing all my energy into changing, but it's not happening," he said.

"You can't think of it as something you force. You must imagine yourself with those features, and let the magic flow through the spell," said Pennywhistle. "Remember, this change is still you."

"Okay," he said, not feeling confident.

"Why don't you try while I watch."

Zayn closed his eyes, bringing forth the image of his new reflection.

"Picture yourself doing mundane tasks with this change already in place," she whispered.

He did as she suggested, imagining shopping for cat food

for Marley, making a peanut butter and jelly sandwich, and then juggling knives.

When he was finished, he opened his eyes and looked at Pennywhistle.

She held herself tightly. "What change were you attempting, Zayn?"

"My eye color, to turn it brown," he said.

"I see. That should be an easy one," she said as she searched his face for clues to his failure. "Can you tell me what you're doing?"

"I'm imagining myself doing things with that change in place, trying to focus my mind on it. I feel like I'm doing exactly what you said, but it's not working," he said.

Pennywhistle made a noncommittal sound in the back of her throat. "I see. Sometimes certain individuals cannot do this type of spell because they have too strong a sense of self."

"What does that mean?" he asked.

Pennywhistle gestured at Vin, who was across the room, laughing with Chen as he was getting his skin tone to change to a light blue as if he were turning a dial.

"Your friend Vin, he's a natural at face changing, one of the best students I've had in years. His ability to change comes from his past, the non-acceptance of his parents, the other fluid factors of his life. He hid himself from everyone for most of his life and probably in some ways still does," she said.

Zayn glanced to his cousin, who had given himself a pig nose.

"So I have my parents to blame for not being able to face change?" asked Zayn sardonically.

Pennywhistle chuckled, patting his knee. "In a way, yes. But I suspect it goes deeper than that. For as long as you've been at the Academy, you've had a singular purpose to you, some great task that seems to be burning inside you."

Zayn froze up inside at her words. She was seeing right through him.

"Don't worry," she added with a soft smile. "I don't want to know what it is, but it's this purpose that is interfering with the face changing. You cannot imagine yourself as anyone else, doing anything else."

"I didn't realize face changing involved therapy," said Zayn.

"Any good study, no matter what the subject, has a certain amount of self-reflection involved, this one more than others. It might be that you have to determine why, even under the weight of this task, you cannot change," she said.

Zayn rubbed his forehead. "So what do you suggest?"

When she looked away, he didn't have much confidence that there was going to be an answer.

"I will think on it. I have a feeling you're going to be a harder nut to crack than most," she said, looking back at him.

"Great," he said, shaking his head.

"Don't be sad, Zayn," she said, her smile turning wistful. "A sense of self is a gift. Most people don't have that. We're all wounded souls trying to make sense of the world, and ourselves."

"I guess."

"Believe me, Zayn. I know this from experience," she said, her gaze haunted. "Next time, I'll have some ideas for you. I promise."

"Thank you, Instructor Pennywhistle."

"Oh Zayn," she said, a mischievous grin rising to her lips. "You should know by now in the Academy that special help from an instructor is not going to be easy, and in fact, it will likely be much, much worse."

Chapter Four

Thirteenth Ward, September 2017

Dungeons and Spiders

Finding out where Ernie lived wasn't that difficult, since he was listed on the internet. The group home was on the south side of the thirteenth ward in a rather sketchy neighborhood. Zayn witnessed at least two drug deals on the way from the train station, but luckily no one messed with him, so he didn't have to break out any magic.

Finding Ernie had been one thing, but learning anything about him was another. For three days straight, Zayn watched from the roof of the apartment building across the street. Ernie mostly sat in his room reading Dungeons & Dragons adventures, which he kept in a pink My Little Pony backpack on his wall.

After the third day, Zayn snuck into the home and checked their records, finding that Ernie had been there for three years. Before that, he'd been in various children's homes, but thankfully they kept all his records. The file was thick, detailing weird events that seemed to happen around Ernie. It wasn't hard for Zayn to determine that the kid could do magic.

Zayn realized he wasn't going to learn anything without seeing Ernie outside the home. He found a service that taught autistic kids social skills by playing roleplaying games and signed him up. A few days later, a broad-shouldered girl in roller skates arrived from the autistic social services group and hung out with him for the afternoon before talking to the home administrator about taking him out for a day.

A few days later, Zayn followed Ernie when he traveled into the city. He was a quiet kid, around his age, Zayn realized, but he seemed younger because of the way he held himself. He had messy blond hair, a non-ironic wolf shirt, and thick limbs.

Ernie went into the fifth ward, which surprised Zayn, eventually ending up outside the drawbridge at Arcanium Hall. It was the hall dedicated to books and learning.

Zayn was confused about the meeting location, since the girl who was helping him, Hannah, was from the Tinkers Guild. So he was looking for her tall blonde head gliding through the tourist crowd, when he saw Aurie.

He didn't know her name at first, but he learned it quickly afterwards. Aurie had dark hair, soft brown skin, and an intensity to her gaze that reminded him of Priyanka. Before she greeted Ernie, she'd been talking to a group of fashionable young women that were clearly Hall students by the way they held themselves. There'd been some disagreement, and Aurie had stalked away to help Ernie avoid a pushy trinket salesman.

Unlike the other women, Aurie dressed comfortably as if she were too busy studying to worry much about clothing, wearing torn jeans and a plain black T-shirt, a look that Zayn could appreciate.

He turned up his senses to catch what they were saying:

"What is your class?" Ernie asked her.

"I'm...in Arcanium. We study a lot of things," she replied.

"What class? What class?" Ernie said while making an awkward face.

"I...uhm...I don't know—oh wait, you mean in the game. I don't know. I didn't have time to read the stuff Hannah sent me. What do you suggest?" she asked.

"Every party always needs a cleric. You could be a cleric."

"A cleric? Like I'm leading a congregation? Church thing?" she asked.

"Cleric like a doctor. Like Golden Willow. A healer."

"Did you know I worked there?" she asked.

"Hannah told me. I like Golden Willow."

"A cleric it is. Let's get moving. The rest of the group is at Freeport," she said.

Even before the gaggle of young women approached Aurie and Ernie, Zayn sensed the impending result by the way they looked over at them making snarky comments under their breath.

"Am I witnessing a date? Look at this, girls, we have a first date," said the lead girl.

Ernie froze as the squad of girls surrounded him.

"This isn't the time for games, Violet," said Aurie, standing her ground as if she were going to fight the lot of them. The way she rose to protect Ernie against overwhelming odds made him fall for her.

Violet ignored Aurie and put a finger under his chin to make him look at her. His lips writhed from her contact, but he didn't pull away.

"Is something wrong with him?" asked Violet. "Are you so desperate to have a date that you'll pick someone who's this stupid?"

"Violet. I know we haven't always gotten along. But please, step aside. This is my friend, and we're going to play some games," said Aurie, reaching out to pull Violet away.

Violet smacked her hand, and her friends snickered. "What's your name?" asked Violet, getting into Ernie's face.

"His name is Ernie," said Aurie, trying to step between them, then under her breath to Violet, she said, "Please. Let this go. We're leaving now."

Violet latched onto Aurie's arm. "Why should I? Last year, you tackled me, enchanted me with sleep, and after failing miserably in the *verum locus*, still got top grades in the class. I know your *kind*, and I know how you're getting by, and I won't stand for it."

"We're leaving now," said Aurie calmly.

Zayn watched as one of the other girls squirted something on the back of Ernie's backpack. He thought about interfering, but Aurie moved to intercept before he could make a decision. Even from fifty feet away, Zayn could feel the tension in the air.

"Back the hell up, or I'm roasting the eyebrows off you skinny bitches," said Aurie, bringing a chuckle to Zayn's lips.

Then a sloppy wet sound, like a plunger in a toilet, was followed by Ernie's backpack crashing onto the drawbridge in a pile of goop. His gaming books, loose papers, and other materials were covered in a green slime.

A horrible wail exited his lips as he fell to his knees. "Noooo! Noooo! Noooo!"

A chorus of laughter rose, and Zayn felt a stone in his gut that he'd done nothing. He was about to step forward when Aurie, fists at her sides, inexplicably yelled, "Ragged!"

The sharp tint of faez hit his nose as if he'd been stabbed. Clearly the spell had come from Aurie, though he'd not seen her move a finger.

He didn't know what to expect when a thread on the strap of one of the girls' purses jumped off as if it were a tiny worm springing to life. Then other threads fled from their purses in a spray of confetti.

The initial burst was followed by a condensed silence, before a final explosion of fabric. In an instant, the remaining threads exploded off their clothing, like fibrous fireworks, tiny strands floating in the air afterwards as if a cloud of insects had descended.

The other women looked ready to kill until their clothes just fell off, collapsing around their naked ankles. Foot and automobile traffic stopped cold. Suddenly a throng of tourists had cell phones held high and set to record. The other girls screamed and ran from the scene.

Zayn had seen a lot of things in his four plus years at the Academy, but he'd never seen such a raw display of power, especially from a student. He followed at a distance as the pair headed to Freeport Games.

The whole way, Zayn's thoughts trended towards Aurie, even though he knew he should be thinking about Ernie. He was the one Priyanka wanted him to watch, yet he felt like he'd witnessed something special in her.

Part of him knew that he thought she was attractive, but he knew it was more than that. And then there was the nature of his curse. Even if he were interested, pursuing her would end badly, and he didn't want that on his conscience.

Getting into Freeport Games unnoticed was easy since the gaming store was packed with people. Most of the customers were in high school, though there was a wide range of ages. As he wandered around the store he felt a pang of jealousy, wishing that he'd had an opportunity for such carefree fun. He didn't know much about the games everyone was playing, except that they had smiles in their eyes, even when they were intensely staring at the game boards.

Aurie and her friends were crowded around a table with the girl in roller skates standing behind a screen. Dice, papers, and pencils were scattered across the table, and like the rest of the groups, they were laughing and having a good time.

He didn't want to be caught spying, so he thought this would be a good time to try out his fifth-year imbuement. Zayn slipped into the janitorial closet. He was surrounded by mops and cleaning supplies. He stripped out of his clothes, setting them and his latest dose of poison from the Lady on a shelf.

Feeling a little weird about being naked while he could hear the laughter from the main lounge, Zayn closed his eyes and concentrated on his imbuement.

A tingle started at his spine and radiated outward, leaving his body prickly as if new hairs were growing out at a rapid rate. He focused on a shape, letting the imbuement do its work. As the faez kicked in, his senses scrambled as if the wires were crossed. His knees sank towards the floor as the spider detached from his side. It was modeled on the *achaeranea magicaencia*, but had none of their abilities.

The moment his awareness shifted into an external part of his body, his mind nearly fractured. Adele had warned him that this would be the most difficult part, splitting his mind into two, one in his body, the second in a scouting spider.

Being inside the spider wasn't as simple as seeing through its eyes. He felt the way the breeze from under the door tickled the hairs along his abdomen, the tremors of fleeing insects in the walls, the differences in temperature along the tile floor.

It was overwhelming, and it took him a moment to orient himself (and push away the thoughts of hunting down a bug for food). Once he managed to contain his hunger, he scurried under the door, thankful that the imbuement translated his desires into movement.

He was a small spider, maybe only half an inch in diameter—he didn't want to frighten anyone and get stomped—but he could see just fine. Adele had told him that a spider's vision was different than a human's, and an inexperienced brain just couldn't handle it, so she'd translated it into regular sight.

There were other forms that he could take, but he had no need, and after his failure at face changing, he wondered if he'd even be able to change himself into a spider. Thankfully, he only needed to covertly monitor Ernie and his new friends.

Inside the main area, he found moving through the tables relatively easy because everyone was so focused on their games. The only danger was accidently getting squashed by an errant shoe.

He found a good spot by a table leg, far enough to the center that he was safe, and observed the group of students. Ernie seemed in his element at the gaming table, talking too loudly, rolling dice with enthusiastic glee—a much different kid than the one he saw in the group home. Whatever happened with the spying, Zayn was glad that his subterfuge had gotten Ernie out of his room.

Of the others, he watched Aurie the most. She was clearly distracted, he guessed from the incident outside of Arcanium. After a time, he realized one of the other members of the group was Aurie's sister, a girl named Pi. She had short dark hair, rich blue eyes, and a youthful face that clearly hid her age. He could imagine that she was frequently mistaken for twelve or thirteen years old, and like her sister, Pi had an intensity to her, though hers was more out of control.

Zayn was busy trying to figure out what Priyanka might be looking to learn from Ernie when he realized he'd been spotted. Aurie glanced in his direction a few times, trying to be covert, but he saw right through her deception.

As quickly, and as spider-like as he could, he scurried his

scout back through the tables and beneath the janitorial door. It was a little weird seeing himself kneeling on the ground, eyes rolled into the back of his head, but as his spidery senses detected the approach of squeaky sneakers, he jumped onto his side and absorbed the spider into his flesh.

As the door flew open, Zayn shimmied back into his jeans. He was face-to-face with Aurie, who smelled like jasmine. She took one look at his mostly naked body and mumbled, "Speller."

"Speller?" he asked, quirking a grin at her embarrassment.

"Spider or hello, or both, I guess," said Aurie, staring at her shoes. "I'm an idiot. I meant spider. I saw one come down this hall. I thought it might have run under the door."

"Spider?" he said, feigning concern by looking all around. "I hope it didn't come in here."

"What about your web tattoos? Don't you like them?" she asked, clearly staring at his stomach.

"I just like the way they look," he said.

"So...uhm, why are you in the closet with your clothes off?" she asked, scratching the back of her head.

His mind raced with ideas until he spied the travel bag of poison on the shelf. He pulled out the syringe, which had been made to look like an EpiPen. He didn't use the needle, it was all a ruse, but it was the best way they'd found to ship it through the mail.

"Diabetic?" she asked.

"Two shots a day leaves a lot of marks," he said.

Aurie's eyes widened. "I'm...I didn't mean to..."

"Hey, don't feel sorry for me. Everyone has their burdens. This one is mine," he said.

In the moment of silence afterwards, they locked eyes. Zayn found himself imagining what it'd be like to tuck the strand of hair hanging into her face behind her ear.

"Once again, I'm an idiot. You're trying to put your clothes back on and I'm just standing here with the door open. I'll leave you to it," she said, and started to close the door.

"What's your name?" he asked, hoping to keep her from leaving.

"Aurie," she said, pausing at the open door while she blushed.

"Zayn," he said.

"Nice to meet you, Zayn," she said, before she returned to the others.

He finished dressing and, content that he wasn't going to learn anything more about Ernie, left Freeport Games. The kid was exactly what he'd expected: autistic, kind, and enthusiastic. It didn't make sense why Priyanka and Orpheum wanted him to watch Ernie, even if he was Invictus' ward, unless there was more that they weren't telling him.

He planned to continue his surveillance, hoping that the interactions with Aurie would continue. He couldn't help but think about her, even if any attempt at a relationship would be doomed to fail.

Chapter Five

Eleventh Ward, September 2017

Never saw the clinic

On the following weekend, when his Academy friends were headed to the coast for the afternoon, Zayn stayed behind in Invictus. His initial plan had been to observe Ernie again, but he'd decided he would learn nothing new about the autistic mage.

Frank Orpheum had been lingering in his thoughts. While the famous patron's involvement with Priyanka bothered him, it was the prize of the wish that made Zayn change his plans.

If he were going to double-cross Priyanka—a thought that filled him with dread—he had to know what they were doing. There was no way he was going to be able to monitor her—Priyanka's paranoia and foresight was legendary—but Frank was a weak link to be exploited.

Frank being in the public eye made it easier to track him. He had an engagement at Ashnod's Theater, a charity event for the Children's Floor at Golden Willow. Zayn waited outside with a No-Look enchantment on his hood, to keep people from examining him. It wasn't difficult since a crowd of onlookers waited outside, hoping to get a glimpse of the famous mage. When he finally exited the theater, the throng surrounded him. The good-natured celebrity greeted everyone on his way out, shaking hands and signing books and body parts. When he finally slipped into the backseat of a ghost taxi, the vehicle was surrounded, which made it easy for Zayn to attach a tracking beacon.

There was no magic involved with the beacon. It was an off-the-shelf brand that mundanes used in domestic disputes, but sometimes the simpler methods were best. Ghost taxis abhorred extraneous magics—attempting to put a spell on it would have incited an attack—and Frank was sure to utilize anti-scrying spells.

After the ghost taxi left, Zayn pulled up his cell phone and watched the little dot meander through the city, headed southwest. As it crossed through the third ward and into the boundaries of the eleventh, Zayn jogged to the nearest train station and hopped onto the Green Line.

By the time the train got moving, he'd watched the dot pause in the Enochian District, before heading back out of the ward. The location seemed odd to Zayn, not only because it was one of the poorer parts of the city, but because of what he thought was nearby.

Zayn's worries were confirmed when he made it to the Enochian District, which was the old historical section of the city. Most of the buildings were over a hundred years old, three-story shotgun style in brick. Many fronts were boarded up or had graffiti on them. The houses that looked lived in had metal grating on the doors and windows as if they expected an attack at any moment.

But more importantly, the Enochian District was home

to a well of power. The dragon fountain sat at the center of a large square, surrounded by empty buildings. A dull green patina had formed on the copper dragon. It looked innocuous, but Zayn knew better. Deep beneath the substructure, in the Undercity, was a well of power. It probably wasn't a coincidence that Frank's place was nearby. Zayn had learned from Akhekh's attempt to wipe out the Hundred Halls that the wells were a source of excess faez for great magics. If the wish spell was real and as powerful as advertised, it would need the wells to work. Zayn assumed it was easier and safer to reach the well from above, rather than travel through the Undercity. But maybe it didn't have anything to do with it at all.

Frank's place looked like any other in the district, except that it was surrounded by a few more occupied houses than the others. The shades were drawn over the windows, which made observing Frank difficult, but the fact that he was in the area was enough.

Sitting inside the third floor of a nearby deserted building, Zayn pulled a piece of paper from his back pocket and folded it into a cone. After settling the cone against his left ear, Zayn used his sensing imbuements to listen for the vibrations of Frank's speech against the windows.

Zayn didn't hear anything at first, except for the rattling around of pots and pans, as Frank was cooking in his kitchen. It wasn't until later, when the telltale buzzing of a cell phone announced an incoming call, that he finally heard Frank speak.

"...that's my price. I'm not a charity. Tell them it's not going to get any better. The next offer will be considerably lower. If they want to get out with any value whatsoever, they better do it now..."

As Frank walked into a different room of the house, his voice faded from hearing, but what Zayn had heard was important enough. Gone was the smooth, inviting voice that Zayn knew from the TV and his brief ride in the SUV. Zayn knew from Academy teaching how important tone was in a negotiation, and clearly Frank was past the initial stages. But what was he buying?

It annoyed Zayn that Frank had moved beyond hearing, but it was still daytime, and he didn't want to be seen sneaking around the neighborhood.

When evening fell, Zayn expected a normal evening in the city, but right away he knew something was very wrong. At first, he thought there was an event going on in the district square, maybe a small festival or something. But no lights came on, and no one headed in that direction. Instead, the residents of the district ambled around the streets, shuffling their feet and staring vacantly into space. Zayn didn't have to get down to street level to see that they were acting like mindless zombies.

Except he knew that *zombies* was the wrong word for them. They'd been perfectly normal city residents only a few hours before, taking out the trash, cooking supper in their tiny kitchens, but now they'd lost their humanity. They had blank, empty stares and meandered around the neighborhood like homeless people with nothing to do.

Was it a virus or something else?

Zayn had been so focused on the walkers that he'd forgotten about Frank Orpheum. He couldn't see him, but could detect that he was somewhere deeper in the house, so Zayn approached the building with great care, weaving his imbuements to remain unseen and completely alert. Once he found a hidden spot behind a dumpster near the back, he did the trick with the scouting spider.

It was trivial for the critter to sneak under the back door, maneuvering through the house to find Frank. Zayn climbed the stairs, following the sounds of feet scuffing carpet. Around the time he made it to Frank's location, he heard the buzz of his phone again.

Zayn kept his scouting spider behind the corner as he listened to Frank's half of the call.

"Hey, beautiful," he said. "I was just thinking about you."

Zayn internally cringed. He didn't want to hear the conversation if Frank was talking to Priyanka. And if he was cheating on her, he didn't want to hear that either. Their private lives were none of his business.

"No, no," Frank said, replying to an unheard question. "But I wish you were here. I hate that you have so many responsibilities. You know, you got the short end of the stick when it came to Halls. Yours is all duty and no fun."

Frank paused again, listening to what the now confirmed Priyanka was saying.

"Nope, still holding out. Do we really need to get all of them?" A pause. "Yes, yes. I get it, we don't know what we don't know, but I feel like this is a lot of expense to avoid a few casualties. My expense, if I might remind you. Pri, please. I understand. *Pri, please.* I don't mind. Anyway, it's quite fun letting the bad part of me loose, but we need to get more information on this damn kid. I'm not sure why you don't think I can just hypnotize him and be done with it. I can't imagine the old bastard thought of that." Another pause. "Yeah, fine, but be careful. We need him on our side...okay, bye, love."

The new information tumbled through Zayn's head, unlocking new ideas about what was happening. He was about to send his spider back, thinking he'd learned everything he needed to for the moment, but decided to take a quick peek before he left.

When the spider crawled into Frank's room, Zayn nearly lost consciousness at what he was seeing: a seven-foot-tall demon with reddish skin and black leather wings that brushed the ceiling.

Zayn brought the spider straight back, lurching to his feet the moment they were reunited.

Frank is a demon?

The news threw everything he'd learned into doubt. Why was Priyanka working with him, and what did it mean for her motivations?

Zayn was so shaken, he almost missed the back door opening. He threw himself into the Veil, sprinting away as the big demon ducked through the open door.

He only took one glance backward before he turned the corner, but there was no doubt in his mind that the demon he saw was Frank Orpheum.

Chapter Six

Seventh Ward, September 2017

Not what he was expecting

A few days later, Zayn caught up with Keelan at their house. He was walking out the door wearing a suit and carrying a briefcase.

"Decided the life of a notorious assassin was too much for you?" joked Zayn.

"Hey, cuz," said Keelan, gesturing to his suit. "I'm headed into the first ward for my face-changing homework. You already done with that?"

"Oh, right," said Zayn sheepishly. "I'm still working through some technical difficulties."

After the second class, which had remained a complete failure for Zayn, Instructor Pennywhistle had given them homework to sign up for a job interview using a different face and a manufactured identity.

Keelan gave him a sideways look. "You need something? Or just headed inside?"

"I'll walk with you to the station," said Zayn, who'd been weighing whether or not to have this conversation for weeks. "I need your advice."

Normally that kind of opening received a cutting barb, but Keelan narrowed his gaze and made a *go-on* noise.

"What do you think about Priyanka?" asked Zayn.

Keelan's face went through contortions. It clearly wasn't the question his cousin was expecting.

"I don't know. Aren't you the expert on her? You're her mentee, after all," said Keelan.

A drizzle of rain started, receiving a skyward glance from both of them. It wasn't coming down enough to warrant a spell.

"I *think* I know her, but do I really?" he asked.

"What's this about? You learn something you didn't want to know?" asked Keelan.

"Something like that," said Zayn with a sigh. "You know, when I came to the Academy, there were a lot of things about it I didn't know, like its responsibilities with the other realms, stuff like that. It made the morally ambiguous techniques we employ easier to swallow."

"Morally ambiguous techniques," said Keelan, laughing and shaking his head. "You got a way with words, cuz. No wonder you're her mentee."

When Zayn shot him a look, Keelan shrugged his shoulders. "Sorry, Zayn. But you know I'm right. We're not in the ice cream business. This shit is real."

"What about motives? What if it's not about protecting the Halls? What if it's just self-preservation, or the advancement of her own agenda?" asked Zayn.

Keelan stopped and faced Zayn, his gaze searching. "You know you're not asking me because you think I have an answer. You're asking me hoping that I'll give you permission for whatever it is you're planning on doing. And whatever it is, I think it's best I don't know anything about it."

The clarity with which his cousin saw through his questions unnerved Zayn. How could he keep a double cross from Priyanka, if Keelan could unmask him from a brief conversation?

"My question still stands. Do you think that Priyanka is a good person?" asked Zayn.

Keelan resumed walking, but said nothing for a while. As they neared the station Zayn began to wonder if he was going to answer at all.

When they reached the end of the sidewalk, Keelan grabbed him by the arm and leaned in close.

"I don't know if this is what you're looking for, but whatever, you'll figure it out. This summer, when I was at the plantation, helping some other Watchers package the poison that was to be sent to those alumni who have permission to live elsewhere, I saw a package without a name addressed to a PO Box. When I asked, no one would say a word, but later, one of the others told me it was for Priyanka."

A chill traveled through Zayn until he felt encased in ice. He had the sudden realization that if Keelan were truly compromised, the Lady could be using him to keep her enemies divided. Sowing mistrust would go a long way towards that, making Zayn regret his question, but it was hard not to ask his cousin for counsel.

When Zayn said nothing, Keelan pulled away, frowning. He checked his watch. "Gotta go. Can't be late for my interview."

As a train rumbled past the station, every interaction Zayn had ever had with Priyanka came into focus. If Keelan were being truthful, then he couldn't believe that he'd never seen it before. Why else would she tolerate the deal with the

Lady if she weren't also compromised?

It made him wonder how it'd come to be in the first place. Had the Lady tricked Priyanka? Or had she gone willingly? It also explained why she wouldn't allow discussions about the poison in her presence. Was Priyanka like the Speaker, who was clearly linked to the Lady, but didn't wear the glasses?

Maybe the purple eyes were something that went away over time, or perhaps Priyanka was allowed her freedom because of her position.

By the time he turned back towards the house, he'd made up his mind that he had to treat her as his enemy, just like the Lady. Not only was she in league with her, but the events with Frank Orpheum showed that she had ulterior motives as well.

Which meant that no one was safe. He couldn't trust his cousin and he certainly couldn't trust Priyanka. Whatever he planned to do, it would have to be just him. It was the only way to be sure. If he had allies, they had to be unwitting, otherwise they could compromise everything.

He was alone.

Chapter Seven

The Spire, September 2017

Cheaters prosper

Every fall semester, the Second Year Contest was revealed. It was a time for the various Halls to come together in a task that taught them teamwork through competition. The winning team, made up of members from separate Halls, was awarded a valuable prize that could only be found in the Halls.

In Zayn's second year, the winning team had earned an assortment of potions brewed by Celesse D'Agastine, body armor enchanted by Bannon Creed, and an all-expenses paid week at the exclusive Ice Hold. Tracking the scores and progress would consume the *Herald of the Halls* and other news organizations around the world, especially since this was the hundredth anniversary of the games.

Like with the Merlin Trials, fifth years were required to support the administering of the contest. It was going to be Zayn's duty to help with the team-choosing trials, which were being held in the Spire.

After helping with the revealing ceremony, in which the rest of the school learned what Priyanka had already told him, he was sent to an office for instructions, only to find Frank Orpheum seated on the desk chewing on a toothpick and thumbing through his cell phone.

"Mr. Carter," said Frank with a smile in his eyes. "It's excellent to see you."

The image of Frank with reddish skin and leathery bat wings flashed through Zayn's mind, followed up by the mindless walkers. He hadn't decided if the two were connected.

"I assume this is not a coincidence," said Zayn. "Will Priyanka be joining us?"

Frank's eyes creased at the corner with pleasure. He pulled out his toothpick and pointed it at Zayn.

"Priyanka told me you were quick, but it's good to see it in person. No, she won't be joining us. She has other duties. Which is why you're here," he said.

At first Zayn thought this was a ploy by Frank, but he decided it was too easy for him to check with Priyanka, so anything he was told had to be on the up and up.

"Are you going to tell me or do I have to guess?" asked Zayn.

"Since I have a prior engagement I must attend to, I'll skip right to it. I got you assigned to the choosing trials because we need to make sure we get the right people on the right team," said Frank.

"I thought you said the big prize wasn't at the end of the contest rainbow. Hedging your bets, or did you get it wrong?" asked Zayn.

Frank's lip twitched in annoyance. It was clear he didn't like the suggestion that he was wrong. Zayn filed that away for later use.

"Neither," said Frank, pulling a folded piece of paper from

his shirt pocket and handing it to Zayn. "See the name on that paper?"

It read Raziyah Johnson.

"Yeah? Who's she?"

"No one in particular, but you need to make sure she's on the same team as Ernie," said Frank.

"Ernie?" asked Zayn, his voice rising from the shock of hearing his name. "What's he doing in the contest? He's not even a student."

"Technically yes, he has no Hall, but to protect him when he was younger, Invictus bonded him, so he might not be in a Hall, but he's eligible for the contest because of his link to the head patron," said Frank.

Zayn's stomach sank with the thought of the games. They were not for the faint of heart. His year, they'd involved a deadly obstacle course that required the whole team to bypass. While the danger wasn't real—they used some magical holodeck-like device to create the illusion—the impact of the blades and crushing weights had felt real. It'd been a blessing that his work with Priyanka had kept him busy enough that he'd missed most of his team's attempts.

"You can't be serious about putting him in there. He's just a kid," said Zayn.

"He's older than you are," said Frank.

"You know what I mean, and it still doesn't make it right," said Zayn, raising his voice. "Why do you need him in the contest?"

Frank crossed his arms. "Pri told me you wouldn't be a problem on this."

His gut twisted. If he started opposing the things she wanted, then she might start doubting his loyalty. But on the other hand, was it fair to use Ernie like this?

"No, I'm not going to be a problem, but this just doesn't

feel like something Priyanka would sign up for," said Zayn.

"Then maybe you don't know her as well as you think," said Frank.

Zayn swallowed the rest of what he had to say. It wouldn't do any good. If he didn't put Ernie on the team, Frank would find another way.

"Where do I go?" asked Zayn, and when Frank bunched his forehead, he added, "To fix the teams. Do you want it done or not?"

"You're more drama than I expected," said Frank.

And you're an asshole, thought Zayn, but he said, "We get our drama out of the way early, but once the mission starts, we're all business."

Frank gave a curt nod. "Good. Here's your paperwork. The admin group on the twenty-fifth floor will give you your assignment."

"How do I make sure they're in the same group?" asked Zayn.

"You'll have to figure that out. I'm sure you can improvise something," said Frank dismissively as he knocked a piece of lint from his shirt and moved towards the door. "Don't screw it up."

After Frank Orpheum left the room, Zayn growled under his breath. "To think I used to admire that guy."

The elevator took him to the correct floor. A woman with her gray hair in a bun, poked through with two pencils, sent him to a room down the hall with more instructions. He felt like he was working through some bureaucratic maze, and almost expected to find a minotaur in a suit when he went through the door.

Instead it was a control room with dozens of video monitors. A large attractive woman in a bright red dress and matching lipstick sized him up as soon as he walked through the door.

"You're Zayn? I'm Meg," she said, shaking his hand.

"Nice to meet you, how can I help?" he asked, craning his neck at all the monitors.

"This is the central nervous system of the group testing. See those little rooms on the other side of the camera lenses?" He nodded. "Each of the second years will go in those rooms, try to figure out the timed puzzle, and then based on their score, get placed on teams."

"Sounds simple. What's my job?" he asked.

"Most of the work has been automated. Our tech wizards, literally, have the rooms wired to our monitors. Whatever happens with their spells, it'll translate directly here. The biggest thing we have to do is sort them, which should be easy, since we're doing score groupings. Top scores with top scores, bottom scores with bottom scores."

"Great, just point me to the computer and I'll be ready to sort," said Zayn, rubbing his hands together.

"Oh," said Meg, her red lips pursing into a bow. "You're not doing the sorting. Elizabeth over there is doing that." A woman in a blue blouse at a terminal waved her hand. "You're keeping the information flowing through the portal box. Those tech wizards did a miracle on the test side, but they mucked up the connection to the control room. You'll be standing over there on the other side of her, pushing faez into that box to keep the connection running."

The black box was ten feet away from the terminal, not even near the screen. Not only was he not the person who would be doing the sorting, but he also had no way to know when Ernie or Raziyah's scores would come through. He'd initially thought he could make their scores the same, guaranteeing they'd be on the same team, but there was no way to do that now.

For the next six hours he had nothing to do except keep a low level of faez shunted into the black box. He didn't even get to peer over shoulders to see how anything was working. His position was surrounded by a tangle of wires that went in all directions across the floor of the control room.

A few times he tried to strike up a conversation with Elizabeth, but she was hunched over the table, face illuminated with glowing blue light.

When the last scores came through Elizabeth looked over to Meg and said, "I think I'm ready, are we good to upload?"

He was about to lose his chance to fix the teams. In a burst of inspiration, Zayn pulled a smoke pellet from his pocket and threw it into the corner where the wires came out of the wall. Within seconds, a trail of smoke lifted into the air. It only took a moment for everyone to notice.

"Shit, smoke," said Meg, rushing over to the fire extinguisher on the wall.

Chaos erupted in the control room as everyone ran towards the expected fire. Zayn joined them, and as everyone crowded around Meg blasting the source of smoke, he kicked loose a couple of wires, making it impossible to complete the upload until it was fixed. He didn't know how he was going to change the teams, but he hoped to take advantage of the disorder.

After the smoke died down, Meg picked through the wires in the corner. "Doesn't look like anything got burnt. I guess we got to it fast enough."

With the excitement over, everyone returned to their stations.

"Problem here," said Elizabeth. "The connection is lost. I've got no way to upload."

Meg looked to Zayn. "You see any wires over there that are loose?"

Zayn feigned checking the area. "No, nothing, but I'm not a tech guy."

Elizabeth looked up and sighed, clearly exasperated. "Fine. Come over here and tell me if you see it reconnect."

Zayn took position behind the monitor while Elizabeth went digging into the wires. He waited until everyone had gone back to their work before poking around in the lists. Thankfully, the program was drag and drop, and everyone's names were in groups. He scrolled to the bottom, finding Ernie in the DNF, or Did Not Finish pile. There were quite a few who hadn't finished the timed puzzle, maybe fifteen percent of the students.

He found Raziyah's score at the very top with a time that seemed impossible. It wasn't until this moment that it finally occurred to him why they wanted Raziyah in Ernie's group. Raziyah was Priyanka. He knew it as soon as he saw the nearly flawless score. She'd already known the answer, but had expected that the groups would be fixed. Zayn quickly slid her into the group with Ernie.

"Connection back?" asked Elizabeth.

The little bars at the corner of the screen had filled in, and Zayn was about to answer in the affirmative, when he thought about poor Ernie in the games. If he was going to be stuck in a group with Priyanka, he wanted him to have allies.

"No, not yet, it blinked on for a second. Keep wiggling those wires," said Zayn.

He scrolled through the lists and found Aurie and Pi, throwing them onto Ernie's team. He didn't even care that Aurie had a high score, and that she was from the same Hall as her sister. He hoped that would be a clue to them that something was unusual about their group. At the last second, he threw their roller-skating Tinker friend Hannah in the group too. Maybe between the three of them, they would counter

Priyanka's influence.

Zayn looked up with a smile on his face. "Yep. Right there. You got it."

Elizabeth shook her head. "Finally. I swear I didn't do anything different, but glad it worked. Time for upload."

Zayn moved the list off the bottom and returned to his spot. The upload went as planned.

He hoped that those girls would be enough to protect Ernie from the deadliest patron in the Hundred Halls. Otherwise, things might go very wrong.

Chapter Eight

Fourth Ward, October 2017

A wish in one hand

As the school year approached the end of October, Zayn took a free weekend to head to the City Library. The leaves wore bright autumnal colors and there was a festive air with Halloween nearing. Oestomancium Hall threw a giant parade and festival that went on for weeks, culminating in the last night, which always reminded Zayn of the Wild Rumpus. He'd made it out once in his earlier years, but having a hangover during Instructor O'Keefe's explosives class convinced him that he was better off avoiding it.

The librarians were dressed up for the season. The lady behind the front desk had gray skin and a morbid expression as she scribbled in a notebook.

"Maetrie?" he asked, on approach.

"Finally, someone gets it," she said with a sigh as she broke character. "Everyone keeps asking if I'm a zombie, or wingless gargoyle."

"You might try a touch more derision in your expression. They think our world is filled with idiots," said Zayn.

The librarian's eyes roved around as if she were considering his suggestion. Then she bunched up her lips and gave a disapproving scowl.

"Yes, that's it," said Zayn.

"Thank you," she said with a very unmaetrie-like smile. "How can I help you?"

"I'm doing some research on a project. I'm looking for any books about wishes," said Zayn.

The librarian went straight to her computer, typed in a few sentences, and handed him a paper fresh from the printer.

"These are all the books on wishes," she said with a pleasant smile.

He scanned the list, seeing titles like *The Mythology of Aladdin, Wishes in Fairytales,* and *The Parable of the Wish.*

"Hmmm," he said.

Her forehead scrunched. "Is that not what you're looking for?"

"Is there anything about the spell craft of wishes? Any hypothetical or research documents?" he asked.

She gave him a long look before diving back into the computer. A minute later, she looked back to him, shaking her head.

"I'm sorry. When I did searches with those notations, nothing came up, not even in our restricted section. I'm not a mage, but I thought that wishes were impossible," she said.

"They are," he replied.

Even though he knew Priyanka and Frank were looking for the spell, he didn't really believe it was possible. Spells were like computer programs, they had to be constructed to solve a particular problem. A wish spell that could theoretically do anything would have to be so vast, and so powerful, that no individual person could cast it.

"You might try Arcanium Hall," said the librarian. "Sometimes they let students from other halls use their resources, or maybe the rare book market in town. If there's any practical knowledge about wishes or other valuable magics, it's unlikely to be here in the City Library."

"Thank you," he said as he left, bringing up an internet search on booksellers in the area on his cellphone. He spent the next hour making calls around the city, receiving mostly laughter for his questions. When he got down to the final shop on the list, he found that it didn't have a phone number listed.

"Seppi's Rare Books and Tea House," said Zayn. "I guess we're making a visit."

He didn't bother with a train ride, since it was about six blocks down into the fifth ward, right on the edge. It was such a nice day, it seemed criminal to sit in a taxi or train car. Though the Carnival was in the seventh ward, he could hear the barkers and smell the cotton candy as if it were a block away.

The front of Seppi's Rare Books and Tea House looked plucked from a previous century. It was jammed between an electronics store and a chain bakery that sold sugary donuts in the shapes of runes.

The doorbell rattled upon his entrance into the dimly lighted store. His first impression was not that it was a proper bookstore, but that it was owned by a book hoarder. Not only were the shelves full, but piles of books had been stacked in every empty space. Zayn was afraid to move beyond the entrance for fear of causing a chain reaction of books falling.

He sensed the approach of someone from the back, expecting a diminutive man with spectacles to match the bookish vibe of the store. When the creature stepped into the light, Zayn unconsciously shifted into a defensive posture, faez bristling at the ready.

"Greetings, mortal. I am Seppi. How may I help you?"

It took Zayn a moment to register what he was seeing due to the multiple contradictions. Seppi stood nearly seven feet tall and probably weighed four hundred pounds, with most of it being muscle. He looked like a bodybuilder in a three-piece tweed suit with more buttons than necessary. Zayn almost thought what he was seeing was an illusion, or a costume for the season, until he used his imbuements to verify otherwise. Seppi was ogre-ugly with scars and a snaggletooth that showed off his inhuman origins, but his keen gaze looked like it was coming from the mind of a theoretical physicist.

"I'm looking for books that I'm not even sure exist," said Zayn.

"What kind of books?" asked Seppi, his muscular forehead bunched with interest.

"On the spell craft of wishes," he replied.

Seppi, who looked like he was ready to burst out of his tweed suit at any moment and leap into battle, said in a thoughtful tone, "Then let us converse over a cup of tea and find a solution to your problem."

The large non-human went into the back, miraculously avoiding knocking down any stacks of books. Zayn followed, weaving his imbuements in case trouble arose.

In the rear of the store was a sitting area with ornate high-backed chairs and tables. Seppi motioned for Zayn to have a seat while he went through a curtain into the back.

When Seppi returned, he carried a tray with a teapot and two cups. The porcelain set had underglaze blue designs that appeared both familiar and otherworldly.

With the tea set sitting between them, Seppi leaned forward.

"I gather..."

"Zayn."

"I gather, Zayn, that this is not a typical problem, which means that you are enlisting my expertise," said Seppi, his hands clasped before him, elbows resting on knees, watching him with focused interest.

"You're correct," said Zayn.

The corner of Seppi's lip twitched in a snaggletooth smile. "Then I must ask for your consent that we might do business."

Suddenly feeling out of his depths, Zayn hesitated before he responded, but eventually decided he needed the help.

"I consent."

"Very good," said Seppi, reaching out to pour the tea. "This is a lemongrass tea. I find it does wonders for solving thorny problems."

Zayn accepted the warm cup, cradling it in his hands. He moved to take a sip when he caught an unusual aroma. He was versed enough in poisons that he knew something was added.

When Zayn set the cup down without drinking, Seppi seemed delighted.

"Oh, a real competitor," said Seppi. "I have not had one in quite some time."

The ogrish bookseller grabbed a new cup. After pouring, he handed it to Zayn, who took a tentative sniff to confirm it was free of additives.

"What did you try to give me?" asked Zayn as he savored the citrusy flavor of the tea.

"A simple suggestive. Had you sampled that first cup, I would have sent you back into the street with nothing," said Seppi. "Long past are the days when I disemboweled my customers. It seems to have an effect on repeat business."

Zayn couldn't tell if he were being serious or not, but decided to treat it as at least partially true. It was unfortunate that he couldn't determine where Seppi was from. While their studies in the Academy included knowledge about many realms, he couldn't recall any stories about bookish ogres that liked to poison their customers.

"Excuse me, but may I ask as to the rules of this game," said Zayn, trying to match Seppi's formality. "It appears I have consented without truly understanding the stakes."

"A fair question, and one that I will answer since you defeated my first inelegant forward thrust. I am a Brodarian. I was born a warrior. In my home realm, I was known as Battle Leader Seppitarius Prime. My people believe in the glory of conflict. While I do not practice their conquering ways anymore, I do enjoy a challenge, and it appears one has walked into my store today."

"You still haven't explained anything," said Zayn.

"But I have," said Seppi, his eyes twinkling. "You desire knowledge, something valuable that I have, but you will have to pry it from me in verbal combat. But you must offer something in return, something equal to what you seek, but which you do not want to give up."

Zayn shifted in his seat, suddenly wishing he hadn't come to the rare book store.

Seppi spoke again in his rumbling voice. "I see you have many secrets which you do not wish to give up. That is good."

"My secrets are dangerous," said Zayn.

"And so are mine," replied Seppi. "Without danger our conflict would be meaningless, a simple mercantile transaction, and no one would be the better afterwards."

The beastly humanoid pulled an opaque stone from his pocket and handed it to Zayn. The smooth stone fit comfortably in the palm of his hand.

"A recorder stone," said Zayn, recognizing the magical trinket. The stone could hold thoughts, which was useful for passing information.

"These have been modified slightly to indicate the importance of the thought to the wielder," said Seppi, who placed his stone against his forehead.

He closed his eyes, and the coloration in the stone turned from smoke trapped in amber to a vibrant blue that swirled like mist in a cauldron. When he was finished, Seppi set the stone onto the platter next to the teapot.

After retrieving the recorder stone, Zayn set it against his forehead. It was cold, but soothing.

There was only one thought as valuable as the information about the wish, and that was his plans for the Lady of Varna. Seppi could sell the information to her for a price, and since it was connected to the wish, it was of equal value.

When he pulled the stone away from his forehead, it swirled with two colors, bright blue and crimson, equal in their vibrancy. Zayn set the stone next to the teapot.

"It seems we have a contest," said Seppi. "The game is thus. We shall take turns telling stories, as long or brief as you'd like, and the other must decide if it is true or false. You may ask questions afterwards. If you are wrong, then the other gets a chance, and if they are correct, then the game is over."

"I see," said Zayn. "Why don't you go first so I can get the hang of it."

As Seppi took a sip from his cup of lemongrass tea, Zayn amped his imbuement so he could pick up any telltale signs from the Brodarian. He didn't know if the techniques he'd learned at the Academy worked for all non-humans, but it was a place to start.

"When I was a young Brodarian," began Seppi, "before I had made my name in the Justified Conquests, before I'd earned the honorific of Prime, or bled the gannish root, I volunteered for the gladiator pits so that I might rise above.

"Now these were the civilized fighting arenas of the Altarius, not those wasteful holes in the outer regions like Spagot or Baudaian. We followed certain rituals and rules, meant to maintain the proper balance of honor.

"We were not thrown into battle as feldars to the slaughter, but trained under the watchful eye of the pit captain. Once we could show that we knew how to wield the chain-whip and the angerblade without embarrassing ourselves, we were sent into the pits.

"In my first battle, I drew an unlucky stone. I was set against the current Champion of Altarius. She was a titan in the arena, using twin angerblades, wielding them as easily as if they were whispers.

"Our match lasted for over an hour, not because of my skill, but because she toyed with me. Angerblades are beastly weapons, tearing off limbs if they connect cleanly. But they are also a chore to carry. At first, she wanted to draw the match out, for a quick slaughter meant the crowd had nothing to cheer for. I allowed myself to be put in mortal danger during the first moments, and she chose to give me only ritualistic cuts, rather than deathblows. But once I saw in her eye the determination to end it, I changed my tactics, keeping away from her, letting her swing those heavy weapons until she tired. The crowd jeered, bringing the possibility that the pit captain might add another fighter on her side to end it quickly—matches were usually over within five minutes. But that would have brought great dishonor to the champion, which I had also counted on. So it remained a battle between two.

"In a regular battle, I wouldn't have lasted thirty seconds against her. I had not the bulk that I enjoy now, nor knew the proper way to hold a weapon or how to cut someone to bring them down hours later. But it wasn't a regular battle, it was the gladiator pits and certain rituals had to be followed.

"In the end, once she had tired beyond frustration, I killed her to the sound of silence. The arena had become her tomb. Everyone knew she would die, even her. After that, no one else fought with twin angerblades again."

When the tale was finished, Zayn found he was sitting on the edge of the seat, completely enraptured. Seppi was a masterful storyteller. Zayn could feel the imposing silence at the end of the match, when the champion had been felled by the upstart. It brought the hairs on his arms to attention.

Seppi leaned back in his chair, crossed his leg over his knee, and set his muscular hands in a prayerful position.

"What is your conclusion? Was there falsehood, or truth?" he asked.

Speared to the moment, Zayn searched his thoughts for clues. Seppi had been engaged during the tale, his heartbeat reacting to his story as if he'd been there. He could even imagine the warrior's own sadness at having to cut down the champion, even though it meant he lived.

Zayn swirled the remnants of the tea in his cup. Glanced up to find Seppi smirking at him.

What else did he know about the Brodarian? He liked conflict, and games, but he was also clever, and enjoyed the same. He'd seemed genuinely pleased when the subterfuge around the poison had been discovered.

That matched the story about the gladiator pits. He'd beaten his opponent by being clever, which meant Zayn had to be doubly careful. Zayn felt like he was sitting down with a Grandmaster of chess having only just learned the game.

"What was her name?" asked Zayn.

"Athatarius, the Lady of Carnage," he replied with fondness in his gaze.

"What weapon did you use?" he asked.

"A hook blade and shield," said Seppi.

"And did you eventually become champion like her?" asked Zayn.

"I did," said Seppi, "and when I fought my final battle before I joined the Core, I used the twin angerblades on my banner in her honor." He paused, letting a smile grow on his lips. "I cut down my opponent in the first minute."

"Is this common, the path to the Core through the gladiator pits?" asked Zayn.

"It is but one path. Common, it is not," said Seppi.

Zayn mulled what he knew about the Brodarian. Honor in battle was important, but not above winning. He worried that the story felt true, which almost made it false. Should he take the skillful deliverance as proof that it was an illusion? Or was this a double switch?

In the end, Zayn decided that he had to trust the skills that he'd learned in the Academy. The story seemed true both in the telling, and in the logic of it. Zayn could imagine that if Seppi had earned the title of Battle Leader, which he assumed came with expectations of strategic thought, that he could win a gladiator battle through clever exploitation of the rules.

The only thing keeping Zayn from answering was that he felt a burr somewhere in the story. A tiny bit of doubt that plagued his surety. But after reviewing the story in his head from beginning to end, he could determine no point in which he had doubts.

"I have come to my conclusion," said Zayn. "I believe your tale true."

When Seppi gave no immediate reaction, he thought he'd chosen correctly, but then a wide, snaggletooth smile formed on his opponent's face.

"You are mostly right, but mostly isn't enough. There was one part of my tale that wasn't true. A small part, but false nonetheless."

As soon as Seppi said it, Zayn knew the answer. He should have seen it the first time.

"You didn't draw a stone for the champion, you volunteered. You picked her because you knew how to exploit her in ritual and in weapon," said Zayn, a sinking hole opening in his gut.

"Now you see it, but unfortunately for you, your answer came too late," said Seppi.

Zayn put aside his anger, even though he wanted to rage at himself. Seppi had put all the clues to his falsehood into his story. Much like the battle in the gladiator pit, he'd won by being diabolically clever.

"Now," said Seppi. "Tell me your tale. If I choose correctly, then I am the winner."

The recorder stone sat on the tray, swirling with his and Seppi's thoughts. If he couldn't deceive the Brodarian, he could lose everything he worked for. But on the other side was knowledge about the wish, a final tool that would help him defeat the Lady, by eliminating the threat of her poison.

He thought he had a way to defeat the Brodarian, to flip his strengths upon his head, but feared he might be too clever in his tale. But since he had no other ideas, he went with what felt right in his gut.

"When I was a young boy," began Zayn, drawing a lip twitch from Seppi at the mirroring of the story, "before I'd broken into the Bastille of the Black Council, before I'd plumbed the secrets of the Eternal City or danced with the mystdrakons, I volunteered for the Academy of the Subtle Arts."

The Brodarian grunted with pleasure, clearly enjoying the spectacle.

"But this is not a tale of carnage and battle, of honor and pride. This is a tale of doing what is necessary to survive. For I come from a place called Varna. It is unlike any other place in the world.

"This place is unique, not special, for that would give it too much credit, because no one in that city is allowed to do what they choose. Everyone in Varna gives their fealty to the Lady, and she, in turn, decides what they might do."

Zayn had started his tale with lightness and humor, but as he continued, he'd let himself become somber, until his tone sucked the air from the room.

"But what is most unique, not special, is that despite this abdication of power, the city of Varna has produced more mages than any other place in the world, and they pledge themselves to her time and time again."

He let his conclusion sink in before he spoke again. "Is my tale true or false?"

Seppi pressed his hands together in semblance of prayer, setting his fingertips against his lips. He made noises in the back of his throat that Zayn best interpreted as pleasure.

Zayn waited quietly, staring at Seppi without making the slightest motion.

"Why does everyone let this Lady decide what they can do? Is she royalty?" he asked.

"No," replied Zayn. "And they let her because it has always been that way."

He knew he was being coy with the truth, obfuscating when he could clarify, omitting when he should include, but he knew that this conundrum would vex a creature of honor like Seppi. Zayn hoped that the Brodarian would reject the idea of Varna because he could not conceive of a place that would allow it to happen. But that was the truth about his kind. Humans would always tolerate injustice as long as they were given the convenient illusion that it wasn't a choice.

The Brodarian's mouth wrinkled, as if the thought of Varna tasted foul to him. He shifted on the high-backed chair like a toddler after too much sugar.

"Any why do you stay? Why do you not rise up?" asked Seppi.

"Because of family," said Zayn.

Seppi tapped on his chin.

"Why did you break into the Bastille?" he asked in a way that suggested he thought he was defusing a trap.

"To steal the Word of Annihilation," said Zayn.

The inbreath between his teeth suggested that Seppi had heard of that terrible magic.

"Were you successful?" asked Seppi.

"Of course," said Zayn, daring a grin.

"And the Eternal City, why were you there?" he asked.

"To stop the Diamond Court from taking over the Hundred Halls," said Zayn.

Seppi slapped his hand to his chin, growling in frustration. "Either you're the greatest liar of all time or the greatest thief, neither of which I can believe. How can a whelpling, not yet graduated from these Halls, have broken into the infamous Bastille *and* wandered the streets of the Eternal City and survived? But yet come from a place that does not allow its citizens to choose their lives?"

Seppi snapped his fingers. "I see where you went wrong, Zayn Carter. You said you volunteered for the Academy, yet this Lady does not allow you to choose. Which is it? You can't have both. Which means that you are a liar. All of it, or at least most."

"Is this your answer?" asked Zayn, trying to convey a hint of disappointment.

"It is," said Seppi, eyes alight with the promise of victory.

Zayn paused before delivering the blow. "I'm sorry. It's all true. Every last bit of it."

"But it can't be," said Seppi with excited exasperation.

"But it is," said Zayn. "And I'll tell you why it is. The Lady controls what people decide because to kill her is to kill everyone in the town because they are dependent on her for life. Thus she controls what people do."

"Then how did you volunteer?" asked Seppi.

"Because we are still allowed that much," said Zayn.

"And the Bastille, and Eternal City?" asked Seppi.

Zayn winked. "I can provide references should that become necessary."

Seppi slapped his knee and guffawed. "That will be highly unnecessary. Boy, I haven't been bested like that in a long, long time. It makes me want to meet you in the gladiator pits. I have a feeling you're feistier than you look."

"I prefer my fights unfair," said Zayn.

"Ha! Well said," said Seppi, eyes alight.

"About that information?" asked Zayn.

"Yes, yes. The book on wishes. I know of one book, and only one that contains spell craft on the construction of wishes. It is a tome that I have long desired to lay my hands upon, mostly because it is a unique property.

"The author of that tome is one Invictus, the head patron of the Hundred Halls. It is called *Impossible Magics*, and the current owner of it is Semyon Gray, the head of Arcanium Hall. It resides in his personal library."

His relief that he'd won the challenge with the erudite Brodarian turned to cold disappointment at hearing the news of its location.

Seppi clapped him on the shoulder. "Come now, if those tales are true then sneaking into Arcanium shouldn't be that much of a problem. Or do I need to take back my thought stone?"

"No," said Zayn, letting excitement fill his gaze. "Just thinking about the challenge."

"Wonderful," said Seppi. "I'd hate to think that I overestimated you. Now, I will have to add that if you can acquire this tome for me, I will pay you a hefty sum. And by hefty, I mean the kind of money that can buy a small empire."

Zayn rose from his chair, carefully setting down his teacup.

"I will keep that under advisement. Thank you for the information. It's been an enlightening and instructive afternoon," said Zayn.

"Come back anytime," said Seppi. "I would swap tales more with you."

When Zayn left, he wasn't thinking about tales to share with the Brodarian. He wasn't even really thinking about the tome, *Impossible Magics*, either. He was thinking about someone he knew at Arcanium, and how he would like to see her again.

Chapter Nine

Eighth Ward, October 2017

Always a bridesmaid

"Nine classes."

Instructor Pennywhistle pushed her stylish glasses back onto her nose with a sigh.

"Nine classes, Mr. Carter, and still you have made no progress."

Zayn glanced around the room at the rest of the fifth years. The challenge was to take the face of a celebrity. He saw a Marlon Brando, a Luke Skywalker, and a Simone Geldhart in the room.

"I'm sorry," said Zayn. "I'm doing the breathing exercises. Every day, without fail. And without clothes, as you suggested."

Pennywhistle rubbed her temple. "I know, I know. I'm afraid I'm failing you as a teacher. I've never had a student I couldn't crack."

"I'm willing to try anything," said Zayn.

He hated the idea that he couldn't do this one thing. It wasn't that he expected to be the best at it, but he'd at least always been able to be fairly good at everything he put his mind to.

Instructor Pennywhistle crossed her arms, giving him an exaggerated stare down.

"I don't understand why it's not working. The ability to face change is connected to sense of self. But didn't you act in a play last year to get into the Diamond Embassy?"

Zayn lifted one shoulder and scrunched his face up. "I was the narrator. Vin said I was a terrible actor."

"You did fine your first year, what was it, with Uncle Larice? The Jamaican bodega?" she asked.

"Yeah, Uncle Larice. But you know, he was a nice guy, and I was just changing accents. I barely had to change a bit about myself, except where I came from, and even that rarely came up," said Zayn.

Pennywhistle tapped on her chin. When her eyes lit with an inner fire, his stomach flipped because he sensed he wasn't going to like it.

"I have an idea," she said. "Meet me at the Carnivorous Coffin in the third ward at nine o'clock."

"Do I need to bring anything?" he asked.

"Wear something nice, as if you were going out on the town," she said.

After class, Zayn went looking for his teammates, but none of them were around, which was strange since it was during the week, and on the occasions they went clubbing, it was a weekend.

He arrived at the Carnivorous Coffin at the appointed time. The bar had a jungle theme. It was a bit touristy. He could hear karaoke in the back and a small bachelorette party was at the bar. The maid of honor was handing out shots to her girlfriends, who were yelling at the top of their lungs.

Zayn was standing at the entrance, checking the time and wondering where the actual bride was, when he realized the four girls in the bachelorette party were staring at him. He was about to turn his back on them when he realized their stares were predatory, but filled with mischievousness.

"Oh, no," he said, "you've got to be kidding me."

When the tallest blonde girl flipped him off, he recognized Keelan's body language.

Zayn joined them while shaking his head. "I'm getting the feeling that tonight will be a night to remember. But what I can't figure out is who is who, except for Keelan. Nice job, by the way. You look like you could take a selfie with the best of them."

The Keelan-blonde yanked out his phone, tilted his head just so, and snapped a selfie as if to prove the point.

The maid of honor said, "It's me, Portia, but tonight you can call me your maid of honor." She pointed at the rest. "That's Skylar in the pink dress with the penis shot glass, and Vin has no sense of proportion."

"Great," said Zayn, shaking his head. "Where's Instructor Pennywhistle? I thought she said she was meeting me here."

The bartender, a girl wearing a Hawaiian shirt, brought another round of shots.

"I'm here," said Instructor Pennywhistle. "But you'll be going on without me. I'm just here to give you the instructions."

The bartender held up a frilly white dress. "Once we get your inhibitions down you'll have no problem making the magic work."

Zayn took the dress. "I got no problem wearing this. When my sister wanted to produce horror movies, she liked to cast me as final girl."

"Well, then go change into it. It's not about the dress, but the face changing," said Instructor Pennywhistle. "We want to help get you in character, so they're going to treat you as if you look like the rest of them. As the night goes on, I want you to try and face change."

When he returned in his dress and high heels, they applauded at his balance. The maid of honor ordered a round of shots before they moved on to the next bar.

It took Zayn no time to get into character, screaming and whooping along with the rest of them.

Every few bars, Zayn tried to face change. He couldn't manage to modify even one lash, but that didn't keep him from having a good time.

The drinks piled up, and around the seventh or eighth bar, Portia got them kicked out when she turned some guy's clothes to ashes when he made a rude comment.

By the end of the night, they were stumbling down the street, arm in arm, singing the latest pop song by Blue Crush at the top of their lungs. Somewhere around the tenth bar or so, he'd given up trying to face change.

When it came time to head home, they stopped by the first bar. Instructor Pennywhistle was still working behind the bar.

"Zayn, it is my professional opinion that you are a complete failure."

"I'm sorry, Mari-Lyn," he said, pronouncing her name as two names. "I guess I suck at this."

"No, no," she said with heavy-lidded eyes while patting his shoulder. "Don't be sad. You have something inside that won't let you change."

"I have a baby tiger inside me," he said.

She laughed. "Yes, yes, baby tiger. And because of it, you cannot change." She tapped on his temple. "But maybe someday you can. But not today, and probably not tomorrow, nor next week, but eventually you'll be able to. Unfortunately, I have to turn my resignation in to Priyanka."

"Wha...? No, it's not your fault," he said, suddenly feeling sober.

A mischievous smile rose to her lips. "I am kidding. You're fine. But it's time to go to bed."

Walking back to the train station, Zayn said, "Sorry I let you all down. If I was anyone else, it would have worked."

Skylar punched him in the arm, the penis shot glass hanging around her neck by a string. "You may have failed face changing, but we did not fail at having a good time."

"Yes, we did have a good time," added Portia. "But now I must sleep."

The tall blonde put his arm around his shoulders. "It's okay, cuz. I know you didn't face change because I look way better in a dress than you."

Zayn laughed. "Truer words were never spoken."

Chapter Ten

The Spire, November 2017

Next-level deceptions

As the city of sorcery turned towards winter, Zayn refocused his attention on Frank Orpheum and Priyanka. He spent time in the Enochian district, watching Frank when he spent his time there, or the walkers who made the night an unwelcome place. It wasn't difficult to spy on the patron of the Guild of Magical Dramatics because of the location. Zayn hadn't yet figured out the connection between his demonic form and the walkers, but he knew they were linked. He'd seen Frank leave the house at night and not be bothered by them.

His patron was more problematic, only because he didn't know about her comings and goings in the Honeycomb. His best opportunity to spy on her was when she was disguised as Raziyah heading to the Spire for the Second Year Contest. Or at least he hoped that was the best time as he hadn't completely verified that it was really Priyanka beneath that guise. If it weren't her, then he had to factor a third conspirator in their plan to acquire the wish spell.

Zayn waited in the parking garage that fed the Spire near the student entrance. He'd positioned himself near the entrance, using a series of mirrors stuck to concrete pillars to keep an eye out for Raziyah. The mirrors were important because he didn't trust that she wouldn't catch him spying on her if he did it directly, and he didn't dare use magical means because of her insane precautions.

He sat on a concrete barrier with his hood up, feigning that he was thumbing through his phone, while keeping watch on the four mirrors. When Raziyah appeared as a tiny shape in the reflective surfaces, he hopped down and crept through the parked cars towards a pillar.

As soon as he saw her striding through the concrete garage, he was fairly certain it was Priyanka. She walked as if she were a coiled rattlesnake ready to strike. But he knew he needed to verify it somehow. It wasn't like he could go up and ask. He needed a way to get her to break cover.

An idea floated through his head, but it was dangerous. It would require putting himself at risk of being caught. His only hope was that her reluctance to expose her disguise would keep her from coming directly after him, because the real Priyanka could catch him with her eyes closed.

Backing towards his spot on the ledge, Zayn stretched his fingers against his palms before beginning the spell. It was a scrying enchantment that non-Academy students would unlikely detect, but would be like a blaring beacon to anyone from his Hall.

Almost as soon as he finished the spell he heard faint scuffs against the concrete, so light that a butterfly could have made them, but he threw himself into the Veil, leaping over the ledge and sprinting away. To his surprise, he saw the dark-skinned girl leaping over a red sportscar and landing near where he'd been only moments before.

His heart leapt into his throat.

It *was* Priyanka.

He hadn't expected her to switch back into her patron form and come after him.

He leapt fifteen feet straight up and grabbed the concrete barrier on the next level. He crouched behind the edge, emerged from the Veil, and listened for her approach. When he could only hear the beating of his own heart, he knew he was in trouble. It sounded like a drum in his ears. The look on her face when she leapt the car had made him feel like she would have shown him why she was sometimes called the Mistress of Knives.

Zayn caught movement out of the corner of his eye. Before Priyanka could make the turn, he shifted back into the Veil, dropped over the edge, and ran full out across the parking garage.

After he threw himself behind a wall, he glanced back, only to see her stalking through the cars with a murderous look in her eyes.

He almost gave up the game and stepped out from behind the wall, hoping that his position as her protegee might keep her from putting a knife between his ribs, when he heard someone enter the garage on the other side humming under their breath. He caught a glimpse of her between the pillars.

It was Aurie.

He quickly formulated a plan, dropping back into the Veil and racing to the other side before returning to the mortal realm. He fell in behind her, staying out of view but making sure to step loud enough that she could hear him.

A bright blue Beetle passed her, and when she looked back, he stepped out of sight. The whole time his back bristled, knowing that Priyanka was somewhere behind him, but he knew that if he looked over his shoulder, he'd give away the illusion that he was here for Aurie.

When she hurried forward, Zayn ran to catch up, only to be surprised when she stopped and yelled, "Entangle!"

He was shocked when his shoelaces untied themselves and wrapped around his ankles, throwing him to the concrete.

"Who are you and why are you following me?" yelled Aurie. "I'll turn your underwear into leeches if you try anything stupid."

Zayn groaned and moved cautiously to his knees. He hadn't expected her to disable him so easily, though he knew it was fortunate that she had. From his kneeling position, he sensed that Priyanka was standing about thirty feet away to his left, watching. He only knew it was her because he smelled the light floral perfume that she used when she was "Raziyah."

"Be a good trick, considering I'm not wearing any," said Zayn, grinning as he looked up at her.

Her cheeks turned bright red as her eyes widened. "Oh shit. I'm so sorry, Zayn. I thought you were a stalker."

He rubbed the back of his neck as he climbed to his feet. "Technically, I was. I saw you through the columns and was coming up to talk to you."

Standing face-to-face with her, he couldn't help but feel a gathering warmth invade his body. It wasn't like she was his type either, which made it harder for Zayn to navigate his feelings. She was beautiful for sure, but almost as if she were chiseled from stone and placed in a museum. The girls he enjoyed were a little rough around the edges like Katie or Tally.

If it weren't for the look in her eyes, he didn't think he'd take two glances at her. Within her gaze was both fragility and fierceness. She had deep wounds, but a desire to overcome them by any means necessary. It was something that spoke to him primally.

"Do you normally sneak up on people when you do?" she scolded.

"Probably?" he said, sort of laughing. "Habit I guess. Honestly, Priyanka would kill me if she knew that you surprised me like that. I was purposely not trying to be quiet."

"Priyanka?" she said, and he heard a tinge of jealousy, followed by a brief widening of the eyes that suggested Aurie realized the tone of her voice. If he'd had any doubts that she was interested in him, they were gone in that moment. But then the memory of his curse came crashing through his desires. He could play this brief game with her, but he couldn't get romantically involved. Not for real. It would only end in tragedy.

"She's the patron of my Hall," said Zayn, when he realized that Priyanka had left the parking garage. She'd probably headed into the Spire in her Raziyah form. He hoped that meant she didn't think he'd been spying on her. "She's why I was down here anyway. I'm her assistant."

He climbed awkwardly to his feet and indicated his entangled sneakers. "Could you?"

"Yikes. Sorry," she said. The shoelaces returned to their previous positions. "So what did you want?"

The naked display of power made him do a double take. Normally spells required molding and shaping with voice and gesture, often with material to help grease the faez into the necessary forms. But she'd changed the world with a simple word. He hoped he never had to go toe-to-toe with her.

Zayn crossed his arms, thinking about how he might turn this chance meeting into an advantage. "Do you...do you think you...could help me with a project?"

"Oh," she said, then made a face at her reaction. He sensed she was hoping he'd ask her out. "Um, I don't know? I mean, why would you ask me? I'm a second year."

Zayn pulled his shoulders back as he thought of the best

way of broaching the subject. His face went through a few contortions before he answered. It was best that he not come straight out and ask about *Impossible Magics*.

"My Hall has a narrow focus. The problem—project—I have requires a broader knowledge base. You're in Arcanium, and I saw you in action at Trials last year," he said.

To his surprise, her shoulders deflated, and then a slight blush rose to her cheeks. He caught the way her hands clenched and unclenched as if she were deciding whether or not to punch him.

"So?" he asked tentatively.

"No," she said.

He startled, not expecting her answer. "No?"

"Not entirely no," she said, her lips twisting deviously. "We'll call it a maybe. Take me on a date. Nothing normal. We don't even have to eat, but it has to be something unique to you."

The reversal stunned Zayn. She'd turned his subterfuge into desire. He worried that his feelings for her were so strong he wouldn't be able to safely navigate any future interactions. "I'm, well, I mean, yes, of course." His brow furrowed. "Is this a date or a test?"

"I'll let you know afterwards," she said.

He chuckled lightly.

"Well, alright. Something unique to me. I'll work on that," he said, looking forward to the challenge.

"Saturday," she said.

"I'm not sure—"

"Saturday," she repeated emphatically.

He held his hands up, laughing. "Okay, okay."

"I have to get going. We're practicing at sucking in the contest," she said.

"I could help you. I've heard a few things."

"That'd be cheating," she said.

"Do you really think the other teams are playing fair? Especially with that whole special prize thing from Invictus. Some teams have rich backers that are actively funding research into the contest," he explained.

"We don't need it," she said.

He raised an eyebrow. "Really? I've seen your score. You need help."

"You're keeping track?"

He realized he'd slipped up. He was watching because of Ernie and Raziyah.

"Everyone does. There's huge bets placed on the contest every year. This year is worse," he said.

"Did you place a bet?"

"I'm not saying," he said.

"Goodbye, Zayn," she said, and started walking away.

"I'll see you Saturday, Aurie," he said.

After she was gone, he didn't know what to feel. Part of him soared amongst the clouds at the thought of spending time alone with her. Other parts worried about his self-control. If he had any feelings for her, then he couldn't get involved, otherwise her life would be in danger. But he needed to find out about *Impossible Magics*, and she was the best way to do that.

In the end, he knew he would have to chance it. If he were going to be an effective member of the Academy of the Subtle Arts, he had to learn to put his feelings away. She was a piece of important business, nothing else.

"Something unique," he muttered.

She'd requested a date like no other, which was perfect for him. It might seem weird during a normal date to suddenly bring up a book he needed, but if the date were out of the ordinary, it wouldn't seem so strange. If Aurie wanted something unique to him, then he knew exactly where he would take her.

Chapter Eleven

Harmony, December 2017

Not a good place to be lost

Two days after the encounter with Aurie in the parking garage near the Spire, he was studying disarming runes in the lounge when Eddie interrupted him. The New Jersey mage had lost his accent, but his attitude always came through his posture as if he were always ready to get into a bare-knuckle fight.

"What the hell you do to the big boss?" asked Eddie, leaning on the table.

"What?" asked Zayn, his thoughts swirling with the pictograms from the tome.

"Priyanka. She sent me to get you. Said it was urgent, for you to leave your stuff and meet her at the portal. I was afraid she was going to stick a hot poker through my eye when I suggested it was a date," said Eddie.

"You always say the stupidest things, Eddie. Ever think about that?" asked Zayn.

"No," said Eddie, shaking his head. "I know when she's mad at me. Trust me, I'm an expert. But this was different. Dunno, but you'd better hurry. Who ever she's pissed at, I wouldn't want to be them."

His stomach dropped to his knees as he thought about the encounter in the garage. He hoped she hadn't figured out that it was him.

When he met her at the portal room, she was standing perfectly still, her thoughts held close to her chest. But when her eyes flitted up like daggers being whipped at him, he went cold down to his toes.

"Come on," she said, holding out her hand.

He took it, almost expecting ice, but instead it was burning hot as if her anger were literally boiling her blood.

They came out in a sweaty jungle. Harmony. It was the last place that he'd expected. She released his hand and marched down the path towards the Aerie. He had to hurry to keep up, and when they reached the house, she went straight through, heading down the winding stairs that led to the top of the valley.

"Is something wrong?" he asked.

He got no answer, only her stiff back as she hurried down the path.

When they reached the training area, he was surprised at the chill in the air. The thicker mist had come up from the valley, and it felt like his skin was being kissed with cool drops of water.

"Pri...yanka," he added the second half of her name when she glanced at him with a murderous glare.

There was a moment, right after he imagined that she could stab him, that he saw a strangled cry for help in her eyes. But then it was gone behind a mask of intensity.

"Try to keep up," she said.

Priyanka leapt onto the pole path that led into the valley. She ran across the poles in full stride, each step fifteen feet long. Zayn had to push himself to keep up with her, but since he had full capability of his senses, unlike last year, he was able to stay on her heels without too much trouble.

The maulapines screeched when their territory was breached, but speed and use of his fourth imbuement kept the spiny tree dwellers from mounting a serious defense. Before long, they'd passed into the lower regions of the valley where the mist strangled the air.

Zayn almost expected Priyanka to burst through the jungle cover into the open areas beside the river, but to his great relief, she paused at the tree line and stared into the mist as if she could see through it clearly.

They stood on a massive branch as wide as a train car that had become entangled with the nearby trees, making it an ideal observation platform. Zayn noted scuff marks on the bark, which suggested Priyanka had visited this place many times before.

"Are we here for moondew?" he whispered.

Priyanka stared straight ahead, laser focused on whatever she seemed to be seeing in the mist. Zayn could barely see the river, so he turned up his senses, feeling his way forward with hearing and smell.

The water gurgled softly as it meandered through the jungle. Insects buzzed at a distance, searching for food. He smelled the rich and rotting vegetation, its plant life in constant turmoil.

"Do you smell that?" she asked, head tilted slightly toward him.

Zayn knew better than to ask. He focused on what he could smell, digging deeper into the array of scents, looking for something unusual. After a minute, he found a sweetness at the center of the rich foliage.

"Something sweet? Like cotton candy," said Zayn.

Priyanka gave one long nod. "There's a mystdrakon down there. They must eat a lot of calories, fats and sugars especially, to be able to fuel their speed. It makes their breath sweet."

Using that knowledge, Zayn pinpointed where he thought the sweetness was coming from. Though it was hard to make out the mystdrakon form through the blinding mist, he could see the rough edges as the beast crouched along the river.

Zayn extended his arm, indicating the place where it lay, to receive a brief nod from Priyanka.

They kept watch on the mystdrakon as the insects buzzed through the jungle around them. They were far enough away that Zayn dared to swat the annoying insects feasting on his flesh.

The sounds of something large crunching through the jungle reached him long before he could see it.

"Hellarmor beast," said Priyanka. "Like a big angry dinosaur in full plate."

"Can a mystdrakon take one down?" asked Zayn.

"A single one, no, but a group working in concert could, not easily, but wait and watch," said Priyanka.

The hellarmor beast was too far away for him to directly see it through the mist, so Zayn had to rely on his imagination by the way the plants and small trees crunched beneath its feet. He thought of it as a triceratops or a stegosaurus, but when he saw a tall tree shake when the hellarmor bumped into it, he revised the scale.

Zayn caught a faint squeal only moments before the mystdrakon burst from the water's edge. It sounded like one of the pig-creatures he'd seen before. The mystdrakon was barely a blur before it disappeared ahead, followed by a louder tortured scream as it found its mark.

When the cries had silenced, Priyanka nodded at last.

"We can safely move now," she said.

Beyond the tree line, there were no more poles to keep them elevated. They traveled downstream, moving along the river's edge, padding across the spongy soil and dodging round prickly bushes.

A mile down the river, a floating dam had formed on a giant tree that had tipped into the water, funneling it to spill over its opposite bank. Priyanka cautiously crossed the shifting bridge. The tree was newly fallen, and the river tugged at it as he climbed over the branches and limbs.

They had to make imbuement-added leaps to make it across the final gap, splashing into the shallows. The noise combined with the claustrophobic mist had Zayn glancing over his shoulders, expecting an attack from every direction.

With the river behind them, they headed deeper into the jungle, moving through the undergrowth at speeds that unnerved Zayn. They traveled so quickly that he had a hard time sensing danger ahead.

A half hour later, the jungle turned to a rocky moss-covered plain. It looked like an old volcanic region that was being reclaimed by the jungle. The moss was at least a couple of inches thick, making the plain seem carpeted as they walked across it. The moss was unblemished, except for one section that had scars across the rocks, as if something heavy had passed over it.

Priyanka slowed their pace, moving with caution through the pale mist. Even she seemed set at a hair trigger, head scanning as if she expected danger everywhere.

He was climbing a rise when a baritone hooting cut through the fog. It sounded like a hunting call. Zayn froze when he saw Priyanka do the same. She motioned for them to crouch down. He got as low as he could without losing his feet, feeling that it was more important to be ready to sprint than to hide.

The hooting sounded a second time, like a great ship blaring its horn in a fog, or a whale echolocating. Zayn felt the reverberation in his feet before he saw the hellarmor beast. A massive shape moved to their left, at least the size of two double-decker buses.

The mist hid most of the creature, but he could see its lower half outlined. Two smaller, though that was a relative term, hellarmor beasts moved behind the first in a slow procession.

From deeper in the mist, a faint hooting reached them, another group of hellarmor beasts he assumed, calling for their brethren. Zayn imagined the hooting was a form of communication that cut through the ever-present fog.

After the hellarmor beasts left, they continued for another ten minutes until Priyanka held up her hand.

Rather than speak, she motioned ahead to a little depression in the rocky ground that was about ten feet across. She tapped on his side where his fourth imbuement had been tattooed, suggesting that he would need to use it. Reaching out with his imbuement, he caught the sweet scent in the air, though it was lighter, suggesting something different about this mystdrakon.

Together they crawled towards the depression. The spongy moss was cool against his hands. When he peeked over the edge he understood the change in smell.

Two small mystdrakons, each no bigger than a large iguana, lay curled amid a pile of small bones and refuse.

When Priyanka pulled out a blade and advanced towards the mystdrakon younglings, Zayn grabbed her arm. She scowled and shook him off, then in exaggerated slowness pressed the blade against her arm until a line of blood formed.

When she was finished, she shoved the blade back into its hiding place, then massaged her arm until it was dripping. She let her blood fall amid the bones, waking the two mystdrakons, who bleated soft cries into the mist.

Zayn's senses went on high alert. He imagined the parent mystdrakon or mystdrakons, he didn't know how they reproduced, couldn't be that far away. While they were in a depression, to his faez-imbued hearing, the bleating sounded as loud as the hooting from the hellarmor beasts.

Together, they backed away from the depression. She dripped blood the whole way. They stopped about fifty feet away, on the other side of a small ridge, where the ground had been pushed up and split apart.

Priyanka held out her arm and concentrated, and the wound closed of its own accord. Then she pulled out a small gun and placed a needle dart into the barrel.

While they waited, Priyanka leaned close and whispered, "When the mystdrakon comes, I want you to still it so I can get a good shot. If it runs, I'll follow, but you stay here. I'll come back for you. Whatever you do, don't try to kill anything. Run or hide in the Veil if you have to."

"Why not?" he asked.

Her lips bunched. "Even if you could move fast enough to stab a mystdrakon, they're filled with glands, the fuel source for their speed. If you nick one and it gets on you, that mystdrakon or any nearby would go into a frenzy trying to get at you."

"That sounds dangerous," said Zayn.

"They don't try to kill each other, but if one goes down, the rest will consume it because those glands are filled with hypernutrients," said Priyanka.

When the youngling mystdrakons stopped their bleating, they both froze. Zayn peered over the ridge, looking for signs of an approach. He slowed his breathing and fanned his senses out. Between the moss and the fog, the place seemed muted, but he could sense something moving their direction.

Priyanka tapped on his shoulder a few seconds before he saw it. A mystdrakon was following the trail of blood. It was hard to believe that it could move so fast, or that it was such a deadly hunter based on its uneven gait. But he imagined it normally didn't hunt by tracking. As he'd seen at the river's edge, the mystdrakons let their prey come to them, using surprise and speed to kill.

At first when Zayn opened up his imbuement, the intensity of the mystdrakon's pheromones almost made him drop it. It was like picking up a pot and finding out that it was still hot. The supercharged fuel that coursed through their veins also made their essence potent.

The mystdrakon was about fifteen feet away, moving towards the ridge in a bowlegged march, when Priyanka nudged him again. He reached out with his imbuement, concentrating on holding the creature fast. The mystdrakon didn't fight him, but stilling it was like holding a hot rock.

Priyanka lifted her dartgun, aimed at the motionless mystdrakon, and squeezed the trigger. A feathered dart appeared in the neck of the pale creature, and a moment later, Zayn lost control of it. In a surge of energy, the mystdrakon shot into the fog.

She sped after the mystdrakon, moving in a blur, until both were swallowed by the swirling mist, leaving Zayn alone. The brief action followed by imposing silence left him wired with his heart pumping in his ears.

Time slowed down after Priyanka left. Zayn kept checking his phone to find only a few more minutes had passed. She hadn't said how long she might be gone, but after two hours, he began to worry. Especially when he realized it would be night in a few hours.

It also became exceedingly harder to keep his focus up. The mist dulled his senses, made staring into the fog like staring at a blank wall and expecting to see something.

When a familiar reverberation tremored through his shoes, he felt relief at the interruption until he realized that the hellarmor beasts were headed his way. As the massive shapes breached the fog like a ship coming into a harbor, Zayn backed away from his ridge, padding softly the other way.

When he'd been stationary, he'd felt relatively safe, because he knew mystdrakons didn't appear out of nowhere, they waited and attacked like a coiled snake. But back on the move, he felt exposed, especially without Priyanka.

He planned to move back to the ridge so Priyanka could find him, but he heard a scuff from thirty feet ahead. Reflexively he slipped into the Veil and leapt to his left. His caution saved him, as a mystdrakon flew past him, the sound of its powerful jaws snapping like a trap closing, right where his leg had been moments before.

Still in the Veil, he sprinted as far and fast as he could to get distance between him and the mystdrakon. When he stopped, he stayed crouched to the mossy rocks, scanning in all directions.

His heart thundered in his ears at the brief encounter. He waited and watched, feeling at any moment that the mystdrakon would attack again.

Once he realized that it had either moved on to cool itself, or had given up entirely, Zayn planned on leaving, but he'd gotten turned around in the fog and didn't quite know which direction he was facing.

When he'd been with Priyanka, it'd felt like she knew exactly where she was at all times, but he didn't have the sense that she had.

Not good.

He gave it a few minutes before deciding that he couldn't stay where he was. She wouldn't randomly find him in the fog, and it'd been so long since she'd left that he couldn't know for certain that she was still alive.

Or there was another possibility that had been silently gnawing on him.

That she'd taken him into the depths of the valley so she could leave him. The anger at him that she'd clearly displayed had been a sign that something was wrong. He'd tried to dismiss it as his imagination, or that it was really meant for someone else, but because of the events in the garage, he worried.

Or maybe he'd misjudged her allegiance to the Lady of Varna, and she'd been instructed to quietly kill him. Leaving him in the jungles of Harmony would be an effective way to do it and have the least culpability. His family would be sad, but they would understand as danger came with the choice of hall. While Priyanka was immune to prosecution, he had a sense that beneath her title she had morals—shifting morals, but morals nonetheless. She wouldn't kill him outright, but letting him get "lost" in Harmony amounted to the same thing.

Realizing that he couldn't rely on Priyanka, and that he was exposed on the mossy plain, he headed in what he hoped was the direction of the jungle by following the slight slope upward.

He traveled with extreme caution, walking with senses alert for a dozen paces, then pausing to check the way ahead. When he saw the jungle rise up he felt a sense of relief, even though he was still lost and had a long way to go.

After the void of the foggy plain, the jungle seemed overwhelming to his senses. He went from staring at a white wall to being dropped into a psychedelic maze of senses. He kept traveling upslope, hoping that once he ran into the river he could find his way back.

But when darkness fell and the thick jungle canopy turned his world black, Zayn found a place to hide for the night. He climbed a massive tree, one tangled with cable vines, and found a hollow in the crook of a massive branch.

During the day, the jungle was a noisy place. But at night, that festival of sounds turned into a raucous nightclub. It sounded like a war of life and death. Once during the night, he heard a creature get chased up to the base of his tree, scream, and then go unnaturally silent.

At another time, he sensed something crawling across the limbs above him. Zayn pulled his knife, keeping it in a defensive posture, and watched while the creature moved past his hiding space.

The night was long and he slept little. When finally, the world around him started to draw in, and the noise had calmed as the night predators returned to sleep, Zayn moved out.

He found the river a half hour later, and after following it for a few miles, made the natural dam. Once he reached it, he realized his path out of the mossy plain had been off by about thirty degrees.

Tired and hungry, Zayn made his way back to the pole path. The journey through the maulapine territory seemed anticlimactic compared to the ever-present terror of the jungle and mossy plain.

When he finished his climb back to the Aerie, he found Priyanka waiting for him in the kitchen. Her lips stayed flat, and her forehead bunched.

"Why did you leave the spot where I told you to stay?" she asked.

"A group of hellarmor beasts came through, and when I tried to go back, I got ambushed by a mystdrakon," he said.

Without giving any indication to her thoughts, she nodded once.

“Did you ever catch the mystdrakon?” he asked.

She patted a pouch next to her. “She ran further and faster than I expected, but eventually I tracked her down.”

“May I ask what it was for?”

“No,” she said. “But I’ll tell you anyway. We were taking a sample of mystdrakon glands for Adele.”

But the way she looked at him suggested that there’d been more to the trip.

“Are you well enough to return?” she asked.

He was exhausted and hungry, but he really wanted to get back to the Honeycomb and away from Priyanka, so he nodded.

“Good,” she said, frowning. “I can’t wait for disobedient students all day.”

Chapter Twelve

Undercity, December 2017

Accident squared

When Saturday came Zayn was relieved to be going on a date with Aurie. The events in Harmony weighed on him, leaving him to question everything he knew about Priyanka and the Academy of the Subtle Arts.

He'd known right away he wanted to take her to the Undercity to visit the *achaeranea magicaencia*.

Zayn met her near the statue of Invictus. She wore jeans and an aqua sleeveless light hoodie.

They chatted about innocuous topics until they reached the portal. She didn't seem surprised by the Garden Network, which most students were unaware of. When they reached the Undercity, he gave them both darksight.

"Better that we not announce our location," he explained.

He led them until they reached the cave with the spiders.

"What is—" she started to ask, but he put his finger on her lips and shook his head.

He whispered, "We can speak, but quietly. We don't want to disturb the nest."

Her eyes went wide, so he pointed into the cave. Covering the far wall was a glistening white sheet, gently moving in an unseen wind.

"That's a web," she said with both awe and horror. "There must be hundreds of spiders."

"Thousands, maybe more," he said as he searched her face for a reaction.

"Are they dangerous?" she asked.

He didn't want to tell her the whole truth about them. The spiders could be used as a weapon by the wrong people, so he gave her a half-answer.

"Only in swarms, though I suppose if you're a cave cricket, even one is dangerous. *Achaeranea magicaencia.* One of the few colonies left in the world. They live near heavy faez usage, which is why they're in the Undercity. Which reminds me, don't use any magic. They're drawn to faez and can absorb it, making them deadly to mages."

"Wonderful," she said.

He looked back at her, touching her leg. "Don't worry. We're safe up here. I come here all the time."

"I thought you didn't like spiders?" she asked.

The answer he'd given her when they first met came back to him. He calibrated his answer before speaking. "Back in Freeport Games? I was afraid it might be poisonous."

She touched his elbow, running a finger along a line of web tattoo. The caress sent shivers up his spine.

"I don't think you were being completely honest with me that day," she said.

"You caught me half naked in the closet. What was I supposed to say?"

"Why do you come here?" she asked, her fingers still on

his arm.

The tension grew between them until he found the will to speak, looking away from her so he didn't kiss her.

"This is going to sound weird, but it reminds me of family. I have a lot of aunts and uncles and cousins back home. Everyone lives in the same town, so it's kinda like that spider colony, with everyone pitching in to help, swarming over problems no matter how difficult."

"You miss them," she said.

"Yeah," he said wistfully. "I'd never been outside of my town until I came to the Halls. It's lonely."

"What about your other classmates?" she asked.

"My hall isn't like most of the others. It's best to keep to yourself," he said, to keep up the illusion that the Academy liked to project.

He couldn't help but notice that they were mere inches from each other. In the cool cave, he felt the warmth radiating off her skin.

"What was that project you needed help with?" she asked.

Oh, that's right, he thought.

"We don't have to talk about that now if you don't want," he said, hoping his reluctance would prod her to inquire more.

"It's okay," she said, the corners of her eyes creasing. "I don't mind. After all, you showed me a unique part of yourself."

He feigned that he didn't know what to say. "I feel like an ass asking. There's a book in Arcanium's library that I was hoping to get a look at. I have this thing, and it might be able to help me."

"What's it called?" she asked, lifting her chin.

"*Impossible Magics*," he said.

Aurie twitched, sitting straighter, slightly away from him. Her reaction twisted his stomach.

"You okay?" he asked, hoping to steer the conversation back to safer subjects. He knew he should have waited to ask her. But since she'd brought the subject up, he'd thought it was acceptable.

When she turned her head towards him, he thought she was going to ask another question. Instead, she jammed her lips against his. A little noise came from the back of his throat in surprise and then he felt himself melt against her.

Forgetting about the reasons why he'd brought her, he relished in the kiss, letting their lips and tongues dance playfully across each other. She ran her fingers down his neck, eliciting quivers of electricity. When she switched to a firmer clawing, he let a moan escape.

He felt himself fully and irrevocably falling for her. *No, Zayn. You can't.*

Amber's prophecy about his love life swirled through his head. It was dangerous to have feelings for her.

He needed to stop kissing her, but didn't want to pull away, because he needed that book if he wanted to help his family. Trapped by his feelings, he searched for a way out, sending out his senses for solutions.

When he felt the soft claws of an ordinary rat, Zayn took hold of the creature with his imbuement and sent it into the cave where the spiders clustered.

A frenzied squeaking broke their kiss, and Aurie peered over the edge at the rat. But it wasn't just the one—a smaller baby rat had fallen all the way down to the floor. The spiders, sensing a meal, mobilized towards the youngster. A pang of guilt shot through his gut.

"We don't have to watch if you don't want," he said.

"It's okay. I'm not squeamish," she said.

"Once they get enough venom in the rodent, it won't feel anything. It's a powerful paralytic. Then like ants, they'll drag it back to the nest for feeding," he said.

The swarm of spiders came on rapidly. The young rodent was only moments from death when its mother darted in from above, grabbed its baby by the scruff, and bounded away from the incoming spiders.

"Yay!" Aurie exclaimed.

But then the rodent mother carrying her injured baby sprinted up the cliff, right between them and out of the cave through the ravine. Like a carpet of living earth, the spider swarm moved after the rodent.

"Oh, shit. Run," he said, pushing her towards the crevice that led them back towards the portal.

On the way down, they'd been able to take their time. But now a host of magic-eating spiders were after them. Aurie was a powerful mage, but her magic wasn't physical like his. She moved slowly, banging her knees and elbows on the jagged rocks. To her credit, she kept going, but he sensed the spiders were catching up.

"Keep moving," he said, glancing hurriedly over his shoulder.

She slammed her boot into a rock, ripping the sole away. Aurie paused, leaning down to repair it with a quick spell.

"No magic!"

But it was too late. Her spell repaired the broken boot, but it incensed the spiders. He could hear their many legs stabbing across the rock, sounding like needles on stone.

"Let's stop and fight," yelled Aurie over her shoulder. "We can burn them."

"No. It won't work. They eat magic." The swarm was almost upon them. "I have one thing left to do. Keep going, don't look back. There's a white line painted on the rock in the place you have to climb up."

"Don't be an idiot. You can't face them alone," she said.

"I'll meet you at the portal," he said. "Just promise me you won't look back."

"Don't be a hero," she said, eyes rounded and lips white.

"Don't worry, I never am. No looking, and keep running! I'll meet you at the portal!"

He didn't have time to take off his clothes. Zayn used his fifth imbuement, the one that would change him, before the spiders arrived.

His senses stretched and distorted, as if he were a piece of taffy. Arms shrunk, legs bent and shifted, limbs grew where nothing had been before. Within the span of a few seconds, his body morphed until he was seeing from a much lower position. He shuffled his body through his clothes, scurrying forward, his eight legs dancing across the rocks.

The swarm of *achaeranea magicaencia*, drawn by the magic of his changing, scurried after him as a living blanket. Zayn could have escaped on foot, but he needed to know if he could avoid them in spider form.

He fled over the ravine—leaping, jumping—landing easily. As a two-legged human, he constantly had to adjust his balance, keeping himself upright and protecting his head. But as a giant spider, it felt like he had an internal gyroscope keeping him upright at all times, and with his body at the center of his many legs, he felt completely protected from the normal dangers of free running in tight spaces.

But unfortunately for him, his changing had taken too long, and a side-stream of spiders had cut him off. He came over a rise, expecting a free shot through the cavern, only to land in the middle of two dozen magic-eating spiders.

The smaller spiders leapt onto him as he scurried away. They clung to him, injecting poison with each bite. Without hands to punch them away, he forced himself into a roll, crushing the smaller ones and knocking away the rest.

Free of the spiders, he moved across the cavern floor at great speed, but the poison coursed through his veins, bringing pain and quivering elation. Zayn could feel his body slowing with each stabbing step.

Zayn tapped into his faez, hoping his imbuements would work in spider form. The burst of energy and the wide cavern, which favored his long legs, helped him put distance between him and the swarm, and he ran until his limbs started to freeze up from the poison.

Before the pain immobilized him, he changed into human form, which left him naked and shivering on the cavern floor. But the changing had an unexpected benefit, as the agony from the poison lessened, as if his human body was more tolerant, or the morphing had cleansed it.

But try as he might, he couldn't move. He didn't think he would die right away, but he couldn't stand either.

Waves of shaking burned through him. His skin was on fire, and his gut felt encased in ice.

It went on for at least twenty minutes until his shaking had reduced to a light quiver. Knowing he had to get back to Aurie, he stood carefully and made his way back the way he'd come. He paused frequently, holding his stomach back.

When he reached the place he'd transformed, he found the spiders had returned to their cave, which allowed him to retrieve his clothes and head to the portal.

"Zayn!"

The look she gave him suggested he was worse off than he thought, which only made him fade into unconsciousness. But Aurie muttered something, and he felt momentarily awake, enough to give the password, and bring them back into the upper city.

He barely registered stumbling through the streets, and then he was surrounded by the glaring lights of a hospital emergency room. A squeaky gurney took him away.

When he awoke, he was in a hospital bed, body achy and sore, surrounded by his anxious teammates and his patron, Priyanka, who stood in back, silent as a grave.

"Hey...you're all here," said Zayn in a hoarse voice.

"Well, you tried to die on us," said Keelan, who stood beside the bed. "Which you're only supposed to do in our company, not on a date."

"No dying before graduation, Zayn," said Vin, patting his foot beneath the covers. "I have a bet with Portia."

"I'll do my best," said Zayn. "Have you seen Aurie? She was my date. She brought me here."

"You really need to learn how to have a normal date," said Skylar. "She left. She was on the couch asleep when we got here, but she was gone about a half hour ago when I used the bathroom."

"Oh," said Zayn, wondering what it meant that she hadn't stuck around.

"Your doctor tells me you were bitten by an *achaeranea magicaencia*. They're supposed to be extinct," said Priyanka with her forehead hunched.

"I guess not," said Zayn, catching a look from Keelan.

Her comment confused him, because he couldn't remember if he'd told her about the spiders when he'd gotten lost after the earth well last year.

"So was it a good date at least?" asked Portia.

"I don't know. Since she didn't stick around, it's hard to tell," said Zayn.

"She saved your life," said Skylar, punching him in the arm.

"What I'm trying to figure out is why you haven't told any of us about this new girl. Did you say Aurie is her name?" asked Portia.

"Yeah," said Zayn, catching a brief twitch from Priyanka out of the corner of his eye.

When he turned towards her, she clapped her hands softly to get the attention of the group. "Alright, everyone. Now that we know he's alive, we should let him rest. At least for the evening. But we will expect you in Maggie's class tomorrow."

"Will do," said Zayn, saluting her.

After everyone left, he couldn't help but worry about Priyanka. Her alter ego, Raziyah, was in Aurie's contest group. The coincidence of dating her was far too convenient not to make Priyanka suspicious. Maybe it was why she'd acted so strangely in Harmony. She was trying to determine his loyalties, which would make further deceptions harder. He would have to assume that she was watching him, and he didn't have the benefits of all her resources.

Or did he?

Chapter Thirteen

Seventh Ward, Jan 2018

A new problem to face

In the city of sorcery, the New Year celebrations made Independence Day look like a kids' party. Sleeping was nearly impossible, even if you weren't partaking of the festivities, which meant the days afterwards were some of the quietest in the city.

The students of the Academy were no exception. Since it was their last year, Zayn's team had spent the night on the town, then slept through the next day.

When he awoke at the seventh ward house, Zayn washed his face, threw on a pair of shorts, and headed downstairs to find Keelan sitting on the couch eating a bowl of cereal with Marley asleep in his lap.

"Some party, eh?" asked Keelan.

Zayn rubbed his jaw. "Did I get punched by a goblin?"

"I don't know what he was, but you bet him he couldn't knock you out with one punch. I've never seen anything shorter than a trashcan that could hit like a truck," said Keelan.

"It seems vaguely familiar," said Zayn, squinting as if that could help him remember. "How did he hit me if he was so short?"

"He climbed on a table. You even showed him your jaw so he could clock you one," said Keelan, chuckling as he shoveled another spoonful of cereal in his mouth.

"Not my brightest moment," said Zayn.

After crunching through his cereal and swallowing, Keelan said, "Honestly, cuz, it was good to see you cut loose like that. You were partying like it was your last night on the planet."

"Everyone else crash here?" asked Zayn, stretching.

"Nah, Portia went home with some girl early in the night, and Skylar helped Vin back to the Honeycomb when he drank too much and fumbled the spell to make him sober again," said Keelan.

Zayn wouldn't have much time alone with his cousin, so he took the loveseat across from him.

"Can you do me a favor?" asked Zayn.

"Of course, you don't even have to ask," said Keelan. "But I'm hoping this favor is that we get to hang out again before the year is up."

Zayn grimaced. "Sorry, cuz. And you don't get to ask why I need it."

Keelan wrinkled his nose as if he'd smelled a fart. "O-kay."

"You remember that bracelet you borrowed from O'Keefe when we talked to that pretentious Animalians guy with an alamus?" asked Zayn.

"Alex Malice," said Keelan with a mouth half full of cereal. "And the bracelets are called Blankers. Why? Do you need 'em again?"

"I need something stronger," said Zayn. "The alamus

worked passively, but I need a trinket that will protect me from active scrying measures."

Keelan raised his eyebrows. "That's a big ask. Even if O'Keefe has something like that, I doubt she'd let me borrow it."

"I don't want you to borrow one, I want you to make it," said Zayn.

"Make it? I don't know," said Keelan, scrunching up his face. "That's beyond my ability."

"I doubt that," said Zayn. "O'Keefe thinks you're her most gifted student in a long time. I bet you can make one."

"I can try," said Keelan.

"That's all I ask," said Zayn.

"When do you need it?" he asked.

"The sooner the better. Thanks, cuz," said Zayn as he got up to return upstairs. He hadn't visited Frank's demon house in the Enochian district in a few weeks, and he wanted to check on it before class resumed the next day.

As his foot touched the first step, Keelan said, "Oh, hey, I've been meaning to ask you. What were you doing at that maetrie bar?"

Zayn stopped and faced his cousin, who had his head turned. "What?"

"Yeah, a few weeks ago. I thought I saw you going inside. The Glass Cabaret," said Keelan.

"I've never been there," said Zayn. "Seriously. You sure it was me?"

Keelan faced back to the front. Shrugged his shoulders. "I guess not."

Zayn frowned a moment before heading upstairs. "Weird."

Chapter Fourteen

Honeycomb, Feb 2018

Mini-heist

A few weeks later, Zayn had class with Instructor O'Keefe. They worked in a huge laboratory, each student at their own table, with Bunsen burners and titration sets lined up in organized rows as if they were soldiers in formation. The space didn't look much different than an industrial chemistry lab, except for the preserved head of an exodemon above the wipe boards and the commonly used runes written on a huge board as if they were kindergarders at their first day of preschool, but no one minded because the wrong runic character for a complicated trinket could result in unexpected results, or worse, the compact magical device could just blow up.

"Alright, lads and lassies, today you're going to make a delayed spell detonation device. This project will challenge your attention to detail as it is a mix of electronics, runic work, and advanced chemistry," said the instructor from the front of the class.

She wore her lab kilt with a white coat overtop. Her steel gray braid had been looped behind her neck like a noose to keep it from getting singed by open flames. Outside the lab, O'Keefe's bluster and oversized personality suggested recklessness, but inside, she treated minor violations as if they deserved the death penalty. During their first class, Eddie had tripped a sparker, a common item found in fireplace lighters, and O'Keefe had made him clean the glassware after class by hand. Their experiments that day had involved miniature mud golems that left everything caked.

So when she mentioned the task would require attention to detail, Zayn's stomach tightened. He saw a room full of squeezed lips and furrowed foreheads. Three weeks ago they'd made avian messengers: origami birds that could take a message to a designated target, even across town. But the folding had to be precise because the runes were internally constructed from separate lines. Half the class' paper birds attacked them until they crisped them out of the air.

"Alright, Keelan here is going to explain the trinket, and then you'll want to read the papers I left at your stations. I broke the project into eighteen different steps. Do *not* go to the next step until you have my or Keelan's approval," she said.

Keelan stood at the next table, his lab coat fitting comfortably around his wide shoulders. He'd been growing his hair out a little, and Zayn thought it looked stylish.

"Hey, everybody," said Keelan as he held up a small glass cube filled with wires and two vials of bright blue liquid. Runes covered the inside surface. "Today's task is to make a Distractor Cube. When this little beauty goes off, she puts out enough obscuring smoke to fill a small auditorium, sends illusionary versions of yourself through the fog to draw away your pursuers, and then really gets the heart pumping with a few minor, nondestructive explosions."

"Nondestructive, a word that makes my poor Scottish heart weep," quipped Instructor O'Keefe.

The class chuckled.

"There are three fail modes on this project, none of them above a six, but you won't have eyebrows and you'll smell like raw cabbage for a few weeks if you screw them up," said Keelan.

"That'd be an improvement for Eddie," said Skylar from the back of the class.

Eddie, who was in front, raised his fist and extended his middle finger towards Skylar, then turned and gave her a playful wink. Five years of classes together had worn the edge off Eddie's demeanor, though no one gave him any room for backsliding.

Instructor O'Keefe's failure scale went from zero to thirteen. Around eight was the threat of limb loss, ten was death, and thirteen was having your soul trapped in another dimension for all eternity while you were in complete agony. The regular trinkets class never went above a five, since it wasn't their focus area in the Academy, but Keelan and Skylar had told him about projects that had reached as high as eleven, including her shadow cloak, which continued to stymie her due to the thorny nature of imbuing pseudo-intelligence into the fabric.

Keelan went on to explain each step, which took a half hour. Everyone took detailed notes, then they dove into the work. Zayn was on the third step—wiring the trigger mechanism—when his cousin stopped by his table.

"Hey, cuz."

Zayn nodded, but didn't speak, as he was threading a wire into a screw hole and had to make sure not to touch the sides, operation-style, to keep foreign matter from contaminating it.

When he was finished, Keelan leaned close and spoke under his breath.

"Remember that thing you asked for?"

Zayn nodded.

"There's something I need from O'Keefe's special stash. This is the best time to get it, while the room is open and everyone including her is distracted," said Keelan.

"What is it?"

"A shaving of bone from a Gamayun bird," said Keelan.

"Merlin's great hairy ass, how'd she get that?" he asked.

"Dunno, but your trinket won't work without it," said Keelan. "I'll set up a distraction to get you back there, but you need to do the dirty work. Watch out for traps—she's more paranoid than a suburban mom in the city with her kids."

"Got it."

Keelan grabbed his arm and squeezed tightly. "Don't let her catch you. She'll kill you if she does. I'm serious."

"I wasn't planning on it," said Zayn, showing his cousin a confident smile even though his gut roiled like the sea in a storm.

When he'd gone against the Black Council, or the Diamond Court, he'd been nervous, but not abnormally. But going against his own Hall, spying on his patron, and stealing from an instructor made his lips go numb. It wasn't just the price of failure to contend with, but the shame of betrayal if he were caught.

Keelan continued to meander around the classroom, while Zayn threw himself back into the work. He didn't want to be stuck on a step that required completion, so he prepared the later materials and reread the notes.

When a flock of curse words rose from Eddie's station, along with a ball of billowing smoke that summoned Instructor O'Keefe to barrel in like a bull after a mate, Zayn knew it was his time to act.

"Eddie Lynn, you utter cockwobble, you worthless wank-stain of epic proportions," began Instructor O'Keefe as she boiled up a cauldron of insults. "Eh had wallpaper smarter than you..."

As the smoke obscured the back of the class, but not the look of sheer terror on Eddie's face, Zayn used the distraction to slip through the storage area in the corner that led to her private stash.

Zayn was familiar with the next room from retrieving supplies for class. The rows of shelves were expertly labeled, each space noting the contents, both quantity and quality so deficiencies could be quickly rectified. When they removed a reagent from the room, they had to write it down and sign a log so the instructor could replace it.

But Zayn wasn't interested in the front room.

He paused, catching the Scottish-tinged diatribe still rolling from O'Keefe's lips before addressing the door. It was open, the room beyond a copy of the organization of the first storage area, but with exceptions. Many of the higher-end reagents required special conditions like a liquid nitrogen bath or the breath of a living nightmare to be stored safely.

Basic security theory stated that a proper system should be safeguarded with an overlapping layer of three different systems: electronic, magical, and physical. This narrowed the possible people who could effectively break into a place, since few burglars know how to bypass one, let alone all three.

Zayn checked the area for latent faez, which might indicate the location of a trap, but the whole place gave off signs, which meant O'Keefe had expected that as the first step. Next, he studied the interior of the doorway, finding small holes that indicated a detection device. He saw no visible runes, which meant it was likely an electronic-based protection system that would require a key to be punched into the panel to the right of the door.

Rather than attempt to guess at her password, Zayn popped the key panel from the wall after loosening some screws and levering it from the tightly fitting hole.

He sighed in relief when he recognized the make of the security system: WitchWard Security. They'd studied this brand in their third year. O'Keefe had probably just grabbed one from the class to use as her security system. The inside had multiple braids of wires in blue, red, and green. He knew exactly which wire to reroute to keep it from activating.

With a steady hand, he grasped the blue wire and prepared to pluck it from its home when a pang of danger went through his head.

"She used this brand on purpose," he whispered to himself. "Because who else would try to steal from her than her students, who would be primed to disable it."

As a quiver of uncertainty made his hand unsteady, Zayn took a few moments to examine the innards closely. When he found the signs of scuff marks around the wires, slight indentations from being previously crimped, he knew he was correct in his paranoia. O'Keefe had switched the colored wires, so disabling it would actually sound the alarm.

When he switched to the green wire, a second wind of uncertainty blew through him. He took a deep breath, held it, and pulled.

The silence afterwards was as sweet as a symphony. Zayn pushed the green wire into a secondary hole, tightened it, and slipped the panel back into the wall in case she returned while he was inside.

Before going through the entrance, Zayn tried to decide if the locked door—the only key hanging around her neck—was a subtle physical protection, which would only leave a magical one to disarm.

Seeing nothing obvious, Zayn stepped inside only to hear the click of a pressure plate.

"Not good," he said.

A row of tiles had depressed a millimeter, but nothing had happened, which suggested that it would activate on release. Usually traps like that were meant to keep the perpetrator in place until they could be captured. He doubted releasing the pressure would trigger an explosion, as that would damage her priceless supplies. Probably it would fill the room with knock-out gas or something similar.

Zayn had to set aside his thoughts of escape when something incorporeal came rushing up from the back of the room setting all the hairs on his arms and the back of his neck standing. His first instinct was to look in its direction, but the faintness of its being warned him away, so he kept his head down. He was rewarded for his caution when he heard distant wailing in his head. The creature was a guardian banshee, and its voice would only work if he met its gaze.

"Let green exist as spokes on a disk, while blue and red may never mix," said the banshee.

The nature of the trap became abundantly clear. The pressure trap kept foolish thieves nailed to the spot while the banshee gave its riddle. He knew better than to run, but if he didn't answer soon, it would gain power, dominating him until Instructor O'Keefe returned.

What has red, blue, and green in it? he thought, quickly dismissing the wires in the security device because that would be too easy.

The tendrils of the banshee's supernatural abilities intruded on his mind. The longer he delayed, the more it would take hold of him. Already his fingers twitched in response to her tugging on his strings.

Red, blue, and green. Think dammit.

He was distracted from the riddle when he heard heavy steps entering the storage area. He'd know Instructor O'Keefe's footsteps anywhere. The open door was hidden by shelves, but as soon as she came around the corner, he'd be caught.

Think.

His thoughts grew hazy. It was hard to remember why he was there.

Red. Blue. Green.

The footsteps grew near.

"IMT. Invictus Metro Trains," he whispered, releasing himself from the banshee's grasp. Those were the three colors of the city's trains and the blue and red lines never crossed. The incorporeal creature quickly faded back into the room.

Then, before Instructor O'Keefe came around the shelving, he slipped into the Veil, reflexively holding his breath as he shifted to the edge of the pressure plate so she wouldn't run into him when entering the room. The fleeing shape of the banshee returned to the edge of his sight, but the rest of the world was dipped into the hazy twilight of the Veil.

Zayn caught the hitch in her neck when she paused at the threshold to punch in the code as if she suspected something was wrong. With a frown hovering on her lips, she glanced in both directions, before stepping over the pressure plate and continuing.

When she was further into the room, he dropped out of the Veil. Staying too long was dangerous, especially with a guardian banshee nearby.

Using his sensing to detect when she returned, he slipped back into the Veil. As she marched past the shelves towards him, a sinking feeling in his gut told him that she would notice the depressed tiles, or catch his faint body odor, or some other taletell sign.

But then she was past.

Zayn returned to the mortal world, heart thundering in his ears. His palms had grown sweaty, so he wiped them on his black jeans.

For the pressure plate, Zayn pulled a thin sheet of sugarwood from his pocket and clipped away a half dozen shims. With the little tabs in his hand, he breathed faez into them, which would activate stiffness for around two hours.

Then he slipped them into the gap between the tile and the rest of the floor. Once they were in place, he stepped off the plate, breathing another sigh of relief that it'd worked. The sugarwood shims would eventually dissolve, activating the trap, but Zayn would be long gone.

Feeling like he'd been absent too long, Zayn hurried through the shelves, looking for the Gamayun bones, but thankfully, O'Keefe's organizational system made them easy to find. He popped open the container and threw a couple of slivers into a plastic baggie.

Outside the private storage area, he fixed the wires in the security system and hurried to the class, finding the smoke mostly dissipated and everyone back at their desks. Instructor O'Keefe was in back with Eddie, who looked as pale as snow. Zayn grabbed a handful of crimping locks for his device before heading back to his desk.

No one gave him a second look except for Keelan, who let a hint of a grin color the corner of his lips. It took Zayn about twenty minutes before he could earnestly work on his project, because his hands were still shaking.

When Keelan came by his desk, he slipped him the baggie.

"I thought you were toast when she went in," said Keelan under his breath.

"Me too," he said, glancing around the room. "I'll tell you about it later. How long will it take?"

"A few weeks, not much longer," said Keelan.

Zayn paused, glancing back at Eddie, who looked like he was having his worst day ever. “There’s one other thing we need to do.”

Keelan wrinkled his nose. “Get together for sparring again?”

Zayn flattened his lips. “We should get something for Eddie. A nice fruit basket or a bottle of wine. Completely anonymous, of course.”

“I’ll take care of it,” said Keelan, matching his conspiratorial grin.

Chapter Fifteen

Eleventh Ward, Feb 2018

Didn't listen to IT

With the warding bracelet on his wrist, Zayn felt more comfortable returning to the Enochian District to spy on Frank Orpheum. The patron of the Dramatics Hall came and went at odd times, sometimes in his demon form, sometimes as a human.

Zayn still wasn't sure which one was real. He couldn't imagine that Invictus would allow a demon as a patron of the Halls, especially due to the danger that beset the wells, but he had no reason to think otherwise either since Priyanka employed many non-humans in her hall.

What he did know from his investigations was that people had been moving out of the district in record numbers, and that a dummy corporation—which Zayn suspected was owned by Frank or Priyanka—was buying them up. He suspected they needed the property because of the wish spell. If they were going to draw on the power of the well, they needed privacy. Which made sneaking into Frank's place a priority.

Thankfully, Frank was a public persona with numerous celebrity events on his schedule. He wouldn't be out of the city anytime soon, but he had a charity dinner in the first ward on the third Saturday of February. Zayn made sure he was ready and in place when Frank left his house in a black tuxedo with long tails, which it appeared was the latest fashion, to climb into a black SUV that glimmered under the dim streetlights.

There were only light wards on the house when Zayn checked, nothing difficult to disarm for a member of the Academy, which suggested that Frank didn't suspect him. The door creaked when he opened it, leading him into the kitchen.

In contrast to whom he portrayed in public, Frank was a surprisingly messy person. A pot in the sink had a dried yellow mush plastered around the edges, the counter was covered in old take-out boxes from the local Chinese restaurant, and the brown tile had crumbs and old dirt scattered across it. As best as he could tell, Frank had never lived alone. He was probably used to maids and live-in help to smooth away the rough edges of life.

Zayn made it to the second floor without making a single sound. As he was about to move into Frank's bedroom, he glanced through an open door to see an obsidian pillar in the next room. He recognized the Garden Network node as soon as he saw it. The room had no windows.

So that's why I never saw Frank come or go.

He crept into Frank's room to find the king-sized bed still occupied. A curvy shape with voluminous hair sticking from the covers suggested a female form.

His first thought was to tell Priyanka, hoping to drive a wedge between them, but then he realized that was a foolish thought. Both of them had lived far beyond the normal life span of humans. He had no business judging Priyanka's choice of Frank as a companion. For all Zayn knew, this sort of thing was part of the arrangement.

But the woman in the bed provided a complication, if a minor one. Wishing he could face change like the rest of his class, as a quick modification to Frank's face would keep any unexpected waking from being a problem, Zayn put a No-Look enchantment on his hood after pulling it up. At the very least, he could escape without being identified.

A laptop sat amid a scattering of papers on a desk near the bed. Moving each paper as if he were disarming a bomb, Zayn examined their contents as he set them aside. A lot of the papers were mundane, but he found half a map of the square surrounding the dragon well, complete with arcane diagrams. Unfortunately, he couldn't find the other half, which suggested it'd been a misprint. If Frank couldn't keep a kitchen clean, he certainly couldn't operate a new piece of technology like a computer.

Zayn brought the computer to life, cringing when it audibly announced it was turning on. The shape in the covers stirred slightly—freezing Zayn—but quickly returned to an unmoving state.

When the request for a password came up, Zayn cast a quick spell that highlighted the most commonly touched keys. He grabbed a pen and paper from the desk and wrote them down.

R. E. H. M. N. O. F. Shift. A. M. T. U.

The group of letters made him scratch his head. He'd expected a special character or number in the list, which would suggest that the common ones involved his password. If the laptop were new, or he stayed on it for long periods of time, pounding out emails or prose, it would confuse the spell, but he didn't have a sense that Frank would do that.

Zayn focused on the letter U, which seemed like a strange

common letter. The letters at the front, R and E, seemed quite reasonable. He thought about words related to the theater that involved a U, but none came to mind.

It wasn't until he noticed a picture of Frank standing with Sinatra in a black-and-white photo before the earlier version of the Frank Orpheum Theater that he realized what the password was.

FrankOrpheum

It took two tries because he didn't capitalize the first time, but then he was inside.

Only a narcissist would use his own name as a password, which explained a lot about Frank, but not why Priyanka was interested in him. Unless she was using him like she did everyone else.

Zayn had brought up the file manager and was looking for the rest of the map when he heard a husky voice from behind him.

"Frank, dear, I thought you had to go," said the woman from the bed.

A pang of raging desire washed through him, as if he'd been doused with the hormones of a thirteen-year-old boy. The craving hit so unexpectedly, so deeply, that he knew it for sorcery.

Zayn shifted his voice into a New Jersey accent. "I'm Frank's assistant, Eddie. He asked me to come by and print out a few things for him."

He felt the woman move from the bed to directly behind him in the blink of an eye, setting off his alarm bells. Anything that moved that fast was supernatural, which meant he could be in trouble. Zayn tried absorbing her pheromones, but the imbuement couldn't grab hold, which suggested she was humanoid.

"Why don't you turn around so we can talk?" said the

woman in a husky voice that sounded like silk dipped in hundred-year-old whiskey.

Zayn held himself fast to the desk, fearing what would happen to his self-control if he turned around. Her voice felt like hooks being set into his brain. He almost shifted into the Veil to avoid her, but since he didn't know what she was, that choice could prove worse.

"I'm busy," said Zayn as he tried to reach for the mouse. His hand wouldn't move. "But you can tell me your name."

"That's not how this works," she said, drawing a fingernail across the back of his shoulders, sending glorious shivers through him.

If that's what she could do with a touch through his hoodie, he feared what would happen if she had access to his skin. He'd probably find himself tied to the bed by the time Frank returned.

"Then I'll call you Husky," he said.

"Oh," she purred, "I like that name. Are you sure you don't want to turn around? We could have a lot of fun while Frank's gone. If you're his assistant, I'm sure he won't mind."

The tendrils of her voice wrapped around his mind until he was imagining himself pressing his lips against hers, feeling her naked arms and legs wrap around him in a smothering embrace. He started to turn when he remembered where he was, and bit down hard enough to cause his lip to bleed. The shock of pain was enough to temporarily break her hold, though he could tell that he was vulnerable as long as he stayed in her presence.

"Look, let me level with you. I was supposed to get this done weeks ago. I'm super late, so if I don't get this done, Frank will kill me, and you know how he can get," said Zayn, filling his voice with fear. "Do you really want him to come back and find out that I didn't finish the job because of you?"

He could almost hear her pouting, imagined her lower lip bunching up, her foot softly stomping on the wood floor.

"Fine, you're no fun, Eddie. If that really is your name," said Husky.

The worst of the desire faded, leaving him to focus on the computer, though he kept his guard up in case she decided that it was worth the risk.

It wasn't difficult to find the files. Frank didn't appear to have guile when it came to computer security.

After the files printed, he grabbed the papers, pausing before he left.

"Thank you, Husky."

"Piss off, Eddie," she said.

Zayn left the house, quickly disappearing into the night. He returned to the Honeycomb. His room was empty with everyone else out for the night, and spread the papers across his bed.

The map and diagrams proved what he'd thought all along, that they planned to use the well to generate enough faez to trigger the wish spell. What confused Zayn was that in the diagrams, they had a little person icon at the center and beneath it was the name Ernie.

"Does Ernie know the spell? Is that why they want to make friends with him?" Zayn asked aloud.

But that didn't make sense, since a spell of that complexity couldn't be learned by a single person. And Ernie was a sweet kid, but he could barely muster a single Five Elements spell, let alone one that was considered impossible.

Yet the fact that both Frank and Priyanka thought it was real suggested that he had to take it seriously. But it was clear to him there was a fundamental fact about the spell that he was misunderstanding. It felt like the answer was staring him in the face.

"If I don't understand it, I can't use it," said Zayn.

His communications with Aurie about their next date had been misses mostly, which meant he couldn't rely on her for information about the book *Impossible Magics*. He doubted she would steal it for him anyway, which meant he was going to have to do it the hard way. He would have to break in and steal the book from Semyon Gray, the patron of Arcanium Hall.

Chapter Sixteen

Thirteenth Ward, March 2018

Not a typical session

On a rare Sunday morning when Zayn knew that Frank wasn't home, he met Keelan for a sparring session at the abandoned skate park. His cousin was sitting on a railing when he arrived.

"I didn't think you were going to show up," said Keelan with his arms crossed.

"I said I would, so here I am," said Zayn.

Keelan held his hand out flat and teetered it back and forth. "You've been pretty flaky this year. I was giving you a fifty-fifty shot. Sometimes it comes up heads and you lose."

The comment about being flaky stung. Zayn pulled off his hoodie and jumped into the skate area, kicking away an old can that was in his way.

"I'll show you flaky," said Zayn, gesturing with the come-at-me sign. "You've only beaten me once, and that was over a year ago."

"I've beaten you more than that," said Keelan, hopping down. "You make excuses when you lose."

Zayn caught the thread of anger in his cousin's voice, which sparked his own. Without waiting for their usual bows to start, he attacked, bringing Headlong Zipper, which forced Keelan into an immediate retreat.

To keep from getting trapped against the curved wall, Keelan did a backflip onto the upper section, which broke Zayn's attack lines. From the higher elevation, Keelan blasted him with a force bolt, hitting him in the shoulder when he didn't move fast enough.

"I thought we were sparring only, no magic," said Zayn, rubbing his arm.

"And I thought we bowed first," said Keelan.

"There aren't rules in real combat," said Zayn, firing a force bolt at Keelan's legs that he easily jumped, landing back in the lower area, bringing a double kick.

Keelan avoided a double Bomb Run and countered with a move that took Zayn completely off guard. He brought a spinning heel kick, which Zayn ducked, but when Keelan came back around, he threw a glowing purple ball of crackling energy into Zayn's chest.

The electricity slammed into him, turning his muscles into rocks. Zayn stiffened and fell backwards, hitting the concrete like a flat board. Keelan gave no quarter, leaping into the air for a chest-stomping blow, barely missing when Zayn rolled out of the way and onto his feet.

With stars in his eyes and knees wobbling, Zayn blocked his cousin's attacks, barely keeping out of the way while watching for the ball of electricity again.

"Is that what the Lady taught you?" asked Zayn as he countered with Flying Rickshaw. "I didn't know you were her loyal Watcher now."

He regretted it as soon as he said it, but the effect was immediate on his cousin, who rage screamed, bringing multiple kicks followed by two stunning strikes and a force bolt.

While rage brought strength, it betrayed one's intentions, and Zayn was able to easily counter the attacks.

In the space after the attacks and countermoves, Keelan said, "At least I still give a shit about my friends."

The flow of battle brought them to the vert wall. "At least I'm not a Watcher."

This time, Keelan kept his emotions in check. They fought tactically, using the appropriate moves for the terrain, flowing between offence and defense.

Zayn maneuvered his cousin into the corner of the skate park to use Headlong Zipper. Keelan did the spinning heel kick followed by the ball lightning, but this time he was ready, jumping over both rather than avoiding the kick.

"I guess Priyanka's teaching you something," said Keelan.

Sensing he was being baited again, Zayn switched tactics, using a spray of flame to keep his cousin from getting too close. Once he had him set up, he feinted a Singing Rocket but instead of force blasting the ground to make his jump higher, he ricocheted it off the concrete, catching Keelan in the knees.

His cousin went down, and Zayn followed stopping with his fist an inch away.

"I win," said Zayn.

Keelan stared back, jaw pulsing. "You don't have to be a dick about it."

Zayn couldn't understand where the attitude was coming from but he knew he wasn't faultless either. He offered his hand to help Keelan up, which he took after a moment of hesitation.

"What's going on, cuz?" asked Zayn.

Keelan gave him a long look. "How can you not know?"

"Varna?" he asked, receiving a nod. "Sorry. I guess I've been busy with my stuff. I forget how much is going to change for you at the end of the year."

"You have no idea," said Keelan, glancing away. "I don't get to run off with the patron solving supernatural problems in the greater realms."

"If it makes you feel any better, she's given me no indication that I'm going to get to work with her after the year's over. As far as things are now, I'm persona non grata."

The muscles in Keelan's forehead relaxed. "Really? I didn't know that. Sorry."

"It's okay. It's been a messed-up year. I'm sorry about what I said before. That was shitty of me," said Zayn.

"Me too," said Keelan, hanging his head. "I guess I thought we'd get to hang out more this last year. Go out with a bang. But it's like I've barely seen you and we only have a few months left."

"I'll try to make it up to you," said Zayn, but he knew it would be difficult. He was still planning to break into Arcanium, and he was nowhere near finished. He thought about asking for Keelan's help, but there were too many aspects of it he didn't want to have to explain.

"Wanna spar again next week? Back to the usual rules?" asked Keelan.

"Yeah, we can try. Let me see if I can fit it in," he said, though he planned to be staking out Frank's house next weekend. He was afraid he'd miss a chance at the wish spell.

Chapter Seventeen

Fifth Ward, Apr 2018

A thief in the castle

The spring brought heavy rains, and Zayn spent most of his time at the house in the seventh ward, preparing for his intrusion into Arcanium Hall. He'd been reading every blog or article he could find about the bookish building, focusing on current and former members to see if they let something slip in their descriptions about day-to-day life that might give him an idea of the building's protections.

The place itself was shaped like an ancient castle crossed with Notre Dame. It was called the Athenaeum. From what he could piece together it was one of the more heavily guarded halls due to its extensive magical library.

He'd considered using Aurie to break in, but each time he formulated a plan, he found his heart wasn't in it. Try as he might, he knew if he went that route and she found out, she'd never forgive him. And though he knew that any relationship with her would end in tragedy, it would pain him if she thought poorly of him.

When the night of the break-in came, thunderstorms had moved into the area. Streaks of lightning cascaded across the sky, illuminating the Spire in an eerie blue-green glow. Zayn was gathering his gear in the living room while Marley licked his hind leg on the loveseat when his teammates burst through the door. He quickly shoved his gear into his backpack before they could see what had been scattered on the table.

"There you are," said Keelan, wearing an aqua button-down. "We're going out tonight, and you're coming with us."

The others were similarly dressed for a night on the town. Zayn didn't know about the other halls, but he felt like Academy students were best suited for a good time.

Zayn zipped the backpack closed and threw it on his shoulder. "I was going to get some studying done at the City Library."

Skylar put a hand on her hip, tilting her head to the right. "You're a good liar, but you're not *that* good a liar. You're planning something."

"I swear if you're going to do a heist without me, our friendship is off," said Vin, crossing his arms.

Zayn's stomach tightened. He hated lying to his friends and family, and if it weren't for the fact that Semyon Gray was out of the city for the opening of a new library in Paris, Zayn would have considered delaying his intrusion for another night. But this was going to be his best chance, and he was running out of calendar.

"Seriously, I've got work to do."

Portia sidled next to him and looked up with her brown eyes. "We don't see you anymore, *buen amigo*. It's like you're avoiding us. Don't you know we only have a few months together?"

"I know, I know," said Zayn, his heart aching with the way

they were looking at him. "I swear I'll come out with you next week, but I just can't, really, I can't."

Keelan put his hand on Zayn's shoulder. "You know, when the semester is over, it's over. Vin and Skylar already have jobs lined up, Portia's going to Mexico to help her dad open a new restaurant for a few months, and you know where I'll be."

The news that two of the team had jobs and he hadn't known about it stung. *Have I been that far out of it?*

"Nice," said Zayn, "and congrats. Did you get the jobs you wanted or can you tell me?"

"Top secret," said Vin with a wink.

It was common for Academy students to get jobs they couldn't talk about due to the sensitive nature of their employers. No business or government liked to admit they'd hired a potential assassin.

Portia poked him in the ribs. "What about you? Any leads?"

The question caught him so off guard that he almost forgot to lie. He'd been so focused on the wish and preparations for his return to Varna that he hadn't considered anything else.

"Priyanka's lining something up for me," Zayn mumbled, which could have been true, but since they weren't talking, he didn't know.

As he headed towards the door, they stared at him like pets who didn't want their owners to leave. He backed away, hands in the air.

"I swear. We'll go out, soon," he said.

"I thought you said next week," said Skylar, eyebrow raised.

"Next week. Yes. Next week," said Zayn, nodding enthusiastically.

When the door closed, he let out a big sigh and headed towards the nearest station. He planned a visit to the City Library, in case they followed him. They were clearly aware that he had other plans. While he rode on the train in a half-filled car with the people that had no choice but to be out in the rain, he searched his gear and person, finding three separate tracking bugs. He left them where he found them. When he got to the library, he would shed them in one of the private study rooms.

Zayn stayed in the City Library until after midnight, preparing his gear and layering enchantments. When he left, he left as himself—another unfortunate result of not being able to face change—and headed towards Arcanium, which was in the fifth ward, not too far from his location.

A steady rain pounded the city, sliding from Zayn's shoulders due to his protective enchantments. The weather made it easy to see if anyone was following him, but it was harder to move about unnoticed since there were no crowds.

Zayn approached Arcanium from the west, away from the drawbridge that went over the moat. It was rumored there was a great beast that lived in the waters, but Zayn suspected that was a manufactured lie to keep curious swimmers away and increase the touristy value of the area. Nearby shops sold "Cressie" plushies of a giant squidish creature with big luminous eyes.

He chose the west side because it had the fewest windows in Arcanium or the surrounding buildings that might offer a random glimpse of what he was about to do.

With only a ten-foot start, Zayn leapt the thirty-foot-wide moat, landing on the thin edge between the moat and the building. Then he climbed the outer building, using the gargoyle rainspouts as convenient handholds.

He climbed past the crenellations onto the flat roof near

a greenhouse. Zayn waited to see if he'd been spotted before moving. He'd stolen a hall pin from an Arcanium student two days ago, but every hall changed their wardings from time to time for security reasons.

When no one came to investigate, he used the stairwell into the west wing. He had no idea where Semyon's offices were located. The few blog posts he could find mentioned something about a waterfall, which suggested that it was in the lower section of the Athenaeum, but other than that, he was blind to the layout.

The hallways were empty, but without a map of the building, he had to keep moving, checking side rooms and passages for stairways. He found a small reading area with a coffee maker and a fireplace that still had coals. Empty cups and plates filled with crumbs lay scattered across the tables. Zayn imagined a group of Arcanium students busily reading and chatting in the cozy space between sips of coffee or chai, laughing in all the right places. In his mind, he saw Aurie curled up on a comfy chair in pajamas and a big sweater, book held against her chest as she told them a funny story about her classes that day. He saw himself sitting across from her, occasionally sharing coy glances in their burgeoning relationship, all things that could have happened if he hadn't been born in Varna.

"What are you doing up, DeShawn?" came a voice from down the hallway.

A girl with short hair was walking towards him. She'd just walked out of her room. He recognized her. It was Pi, Aurie's younger sister. There was something about the diminutive girl that suggested she was tougher and more resourceful than she looked.

Zayn made a little handwave, along with a sleepy head nod, and moved in the opposite direction. He hoped the dim lighting and the lateness would complete the illusion.

"Hey, slow down. I had a question for you about our lexology class," said Pi.

Her bare feet padded faster after him. His stomach tightened. He really didn't want to have to knock her out, but he couldn't risk being identified. That he couldn't face change was becoming a major liability.

Zayn reached the corner first, and as soon as he went around it, he shifted into the Veil.

"DeShawn, hey, stop...oh," she said when she realized he was gone, head rotating every direction. "Merlin's tits, where the hell did you go?"

She stood two paces away. He held himself perfectly still, not breathing, not even blinking.

The frown on her lips and creasing around the eyes suggested she suspected something was wrong, and Zayn silently willed her to leave so he could return to the real world. The Veil shifted around him with a hazy, dream-like quality. Already a few seconds in, his back prickled with concern. The denizens of the realm were slowly noticing him, and in a place like the Athenaeum that was filled with magic and history, the area was teeming with them.

Zayn pulled a small BB from his pocket, placed it on his fingernail, and expertly flicked it down the hallway to ping off the far wall, causing Pi to lurch in that direction.

As soon as she took a few steps, Zayn moved past her and around the corner, coming out of the Veil. With silent speed, he sprinted away, hiding himself behind the bookshelves in the reading nook.

Pi returned a few minutes later, clearly still looking for DeShawn, though he suspected she'd given up on the illusion that it'd been him. It would be easy for her to confirm it in the morning, but by then he'd be long gone.

After a half hour, he deemed it safe to move again, but this time he kept his sensing imbuement maxed. He wanted to know if a fly was beating its wings around the next corner, and when he detected a slight vibration beneath his feet, he knew he'd found the waterfall.

A spiral staircase led to a limestone grotto shimmering with reflected light. The stone was wet with slick spray and with no obvious egress. He'd expected a grand doorway, or something appropriate for the patron of an original hall. He hadn't been expecting a secret entrance. His impression of Semyon from Priyanka was that he was the type of patron that kept his door open to all students, but maybe he'd misread him based on her biases.

It wasn't until he noticed the stones beneath the surface of the water leading into the waterfall that he knew which way to go.

"I hope there's not a password to get through here," said Zayn as he stepped onto the first stone.

The path was solid, but Zayn slowed as he neared the raging waterfall, which slowly parted revealing a way forward. His pleasant surprise at the skillful magical effect was followed by terror as an oily tentacle grabbed him by the ankles and dragged him into the water.

Zayn managed half a breath before he was plunged beneath the surface and wrapped by two more tentacles until he was suffocating within the creature's embrace. The beastie squeezed him, crushing his flesh and bones. Only his imbuement-hardened body kept him from dying in those first few moments.

The creature dragged him deeper and deeper into the depths, and Zayn had a moment of mute surprise that "Cressie" was real, but he'd have no story to tell if it killed him.

Fighting against the coiling tentacles quickly used up his

oxygen. While he was skilled at extending his efforts with his imbuement, air was the one thing he couldn't do without, and slipping into the Veil wouldn't help him.

With his arms trapped against his chest, he used his hands to scrunch the bottom of the hoodie up, exposing his sides to the slimy flesh of the tentacles. His fourth imbuement didn't work *through* the water, but since they were skin to skin, he hoped the contact would be enough to facilitate it.

When he pulled in the essence, he choked on its richness before shifting it through him, until he attempted to take control.

The beastie resisted him at first, but his fear and terror fueled his faez until it was no longer trying to crush him. When the uncoiling came, he almost blacked out, but fought through it to stay connected to the creature.

With his consciousness fading, Zayn pictured himself out of the water and pushed that feeling into the creature. He felt they were moving through the water, but he could no longer tell which direction, and was too busy holding onto that last bit of oxygen. As far as he knew they were going deeper into the watery doom.

Then as the last dots in his vision connected, he was flung out of the water to land on the hard stone. He lay there, sputtering and coughing, realizing only faintly that he was inside the waterfall.

Lying on his back, Zayn probed his ribs with his fingertips, finding at least one was cracked.

"Now I know how sausage feels," he said.

Beyond the inner room was a mahogany doorway with no handle. While he recovered and shed the water from his clothes with a simple spell, Zayn examined the door for protections. Semyon had left clever enchantments, but nothing Zayn couldn't handle. He suspected that Semyon expected the creature beneath the waterfall to do most of the guarding for him. The enchantments on the door were probably only to keep curious or larcenous students away.

A typical professorial desk dominated the room, complemented by twin bookshelves and an assortment of trinkets scattered around the room. Zayn was particularly impressed by the glass ball on his desk swirling with pink mist. He didn't know its particular name, but he knew scrying magic when he saw it. He suspected it was similar to Priyanka's Starwood Mirror.

His heart leapt a little when his gaze fell upon *Impossible Magics*, seated on the shelves between a pair of thick leather tomes. The book was fragile, practically falling apart in his grasp. The edge had been blackened by fire and the binding had broken long ago. Zayn wondered why Semyon hadn't rebound it until he realized that the author was Invictus himself.

The mercurial head patron was famous for hiding spells and enchantments in simple items. Semyon would know best that this book shouldn't be tampered with.

A brief review of the table of contents revealed that *Impossible Magics* was a catalog of magics deemed uncastable due to the difficult nature of the potential spells. The list included things like raising the dead, stopping or manipulating time, and traveling to distant galaxies. Each entry was a meandering thought-scape from Invictus about how such a thing might be accomplished, sometimes with fragments of spell ideas or lists of ways that he might narrow down the possibilities.

The way Zayn read it, Invictus seemed to be working through the problem as he wrote. It was a little frightening to see his staggering genius unfold on the page. They were lucky Invictus had a mostly benevolent outlook for the human race.

The last entry in the book was for the wish spell. He read it three times, word by word, looking for clues, but the section essentially told him nothing more than he already knew. The last line, in Invictus' thoughtful prose, indicated he thought the spell possible, but he gave no hint to how or why.

Sitting behind Semyon's desk with the priceless book in his lap, Zayn couldn't help but feel disappointed. He already knew that the wish spell was possible, and that it actually existed, but he didn't know its nature, or how it might be cast.

Spells were like computer programs. A spell that could theoretically do anything was impossible because its complexity would make it so difficult to learn that no one could do it. The whole reason that different spells were created was to address each problem separately, and that took a human brain to do, which meant that the wish spell couldn't be an artifact like the pink glass ball or the Starwood Mirror.

"A human brain," he muttered, thinking.

Zayn paged back through the book, looking for dates. Invictus wasn't consistent with recording when he'd made his entries, but there were enough that Zayn guessed the part about wishes had been written in 1991 or 1992.

"Oh no," said Zayn.

Those dates were meaningful. If he'd thought of how to create the wish spell then, it would be right before Ernie was born. Zayn knew his exact age due to his research at the group home.

"Is Ernie the wish spell?" Zayn asked aloud.

It would make a lot of sense. Maybe Ernie wasn't autistic, but the spell had taken up the rest of his mind, leaving it difficult to concentrate. That would explain why Frank and Priyanka were watching him.

But how to trigger the spell? Would it be as simple as asking him, or something more?

Now, he understood why Priyanka had disguised herself as Raziyah to join Ernie in the Second Year Contest. The games were a crucible that would make them fast friends, or at the very least, teach her what levers she might pull to get Ernie to do what she wanted.

Which meant he was woefully behind when it came to influencing Ernie. The only thing he'd accomplished was maneuvering Aurie, her sister, and their friend Hannah into the same group to protect him, but that left him no leverage.

Zayn rubbed the back of his neck. He knew someone who might give him an insight, but after the last trip, he'd thought it best to avoid her. As strong as his feelings for Aurie were, his desire to keep her safe from his curse was greater.

Except he didn't have any other way to get to Ernie, and he needed that wish if he was going to stop the Lady.

Would it matter if his intentions were purely business? Would the curse count that against him?

He knew he would have to chance it. The stakes were too high not to.

As Zayn checked the time, he knew he had to leave. He thought about taking the book for Brodarian, but decided against it. Semyon wasn't his enemy, and he wasn't a thief, despite the price on the book. But there was information he needed for his plans in Varna. He assumed that the Brodarian could get it for him, but he'd need something valuable to trade. He opened the book to a few random pages, nothing he thought was too dangerous, and snapped pictures with his phone. He hoped it would be enough to earn what he wanted.

He was going to leave by the waterfall path, a prospect he wasn't looking forward to, when he remembered that patrons often had access to the Garden Network in their private spaces. Zayn couldn't get in that way, but he could certainly get out.

He found the obsidian stone in a back room near Semyon's bedroom.

Zayn paused before touching the portal, looking back in the direction of Semyon's office.

"Invictus put the wish spell in Ernie," said Zayn, shaking his head.

"What an asshole."

Chapter Eighteen

The Spire, Apr 2018

A reveal and a revelation

Zayn had contacted Aurie a few weeks before about a second date, reminding her that he'd shown her a unique view of both himself and the city. When the fateful day came, he wasn't expecting to turn up at the Spire, in one of the upper chambers in an area normally forbidden to students.

He stayed in the shadows before revealing himself. His intention had been to inoculate himself so his feelings wouldn't get the best of him, but as he watched her mill about the wood-floored room, hands clasped behind her back as she bit her lower lip, a shock of warmth crackled through him.

Her wide luminous eyes, glancing up and to the right, seemed to be considering the possibilities of the night. A hint of a grin made a dimple on her right cheek, and Zayn couldn't help but imagine laying a soft kiss upon it.

His heart grew so large in his chest that he almost fled, worried that his feelings for her would compromise his intentions. But he knew no other way to acquire the information he needed about the wish, so he scuffed his foot as he came forward to let her know he was approaching.

"Zayn," she said, as if she were tasting his name.

He let his gaze bounce around the room as if he were seeing it for the first time before coming back to her. "How did you get access to this place?"

"It doesn't matter," she said. "We're not staying."

"We're not?"

To his surprise, Aurie opened the window. A brisk wind billowed into the room, throwing her hair around her face. There was something cinematic about the way she stood with one foot perched on the edge of the windowsill that not only made his heart leap with desire, but gave him a glimpse into the raw nature of her power.

After slipping off her sneakers and socks, she stepped onto the ledge, hanging on with one hand, swaying back and forth.

"You can climb in those, right?" she asked, wearing a sly smile.

Zayn looked down at his dark jeans, black button-down shirt, and stylish boots, answering her grin with one of his own.

"I can climb in anything."

"Meet me at the top," she said, pulling herself onto the ledge above the window.

To his surprise, she climbed out as if she weren't thousands of feet in the air.

Zayn leaned out the window, looking up. "Are you sure about this?"

"Are you afraid?"

"Fear isn't a bad thing," he called upward. "Keeps you safe. Keeps you from doing stupid things."

"It's not stupid if you're prepared," she said. "I *know* you can climb, or you wouldn't be in your hall. But since you seem to lack the proper motivation, I'll wager you that the first person to the top gets to make the other do whatever they want."

The dare hit him right below the belt. Whatever thoughts of self-control he'd had before had been banished. Memories of that hungry kiss in the Undercity came back triple.

"You won't stand a chance," he said.

"I'll see you at the top," she said, and took another pull upward.

"I never said I agreed!" he shouted into the wind.

"Too bad!" she yelled over her shoulder.

As soon as she was out of sight, he removed his clothes, stuffed them into a small sack that he kept for moments like these, and transformed. Shifting into the body of a giant spider disoriented him, but he welcomed the change because it got his mind off of Aurie.

He was more focused on the climb. Whatever she'd done to her hands and feet so they'd stick to the glass, he didn't have the same benefit. While a spider's feet were made for gripping, that advantage lessened the bigger it got, and the wind outside the Spire was brutal.

With the bag captured in his mouth, Zayn ventured outside the window, right into the wind. The first gust nearly tore him from the glass, forcing him to press his body as close as possible. He scurried horizontally around the back to avoid the wind and to keep Aurie from seeing him, though he suspected if she did, it would keep anything extracurricular from happening.

As far up as they were on the Spire, there was still a long way to go. Zayn made the journey carefully, keeping his body low, making sure the maximum amount of feet were gripping the glass.

By the time he made the roof, he was quivering with exhaustion, not physical, but the emotional exhaustion of knowing that one misstep, or an unexpected gust of wind, would turn his date tragic.

Zayn had come up on the side opposite Aurie, so he was able to change and get his bearings before approaching her. The top of the Spire was fifty feet in diameter. A metal tower at the center rose into the clouds with alternating red and white beacon lights warning away low-flying planes. The clouds were restless like an upside-down sea in a storm.

When he was ready, he found Aurie peering over the edge at the city beneath.

"This view is amazing," he said as he put his arms around her. She leaned back into him and they shared a closeness that made the hairs on the back of his neck stand tall. She smelled both sweet and musky, a combination that had his head spinning.

"I didn't know this place was up here," he said after a time.

"Not many do. There are names carved into the concrete around the rim, some with years. Students have been coming up here for a long time," she replied.

Zayn pointed to the left into the fifth ward. The Stone Singers Hall was lit up like a colorful flower. The massive concrete petals were usually open during the day and closed at night, but it appeared there was an occasion happening. Using his imbuement he could hear music rising up from the Stone Singers Hall.

"You can see every hall from here," he said.

"If you know where to look. I found about thirty-one and then I gave up."

She pulled away and slipped the knapsack covered with buttons off her back. Zayn eyed her curiously, examining then flicking a button reading "I Heart Dusty Tomes" with his fingernail.

She ignored him and opened the empty sack and after maneuvering her hand around, pulled out a couple of bottles of chilled water.

"Nice trick," he said, poking the canvas with a finger. "I thought that thing was empty."

"It is." She held it up. A mist swirled inside the canvas bag.

He wouldn't have believed it had he not seen her pull the bottles of water from the empty bag. Like the day she'd made that group of girls' clothes fall off with one word, her display of power made him a little apprehensive.

"You've got a portal in there."

"It's not as impressive as you think. Only goes back to a trunk in my room where I left a few things for tonight," she said.

He examined the construction of the miniature portal while shaking his head. Portal magic was jealously guarded by his patron, and here this second-year student had made a miniature portal in her handbag.

"We embedded runic switches into a titanium wire frame with obsidian chips creating the scaffolding for the portal," she explained as if she was talking about how to brew a good latte.

"Ignoring how you acquired runic switches, how did you come up with this? You're a second-year initiate. A damn good one, but this is mastery work," he said, underselling his compliment, but only because he didn't want to give away how important it was.

"Are you done admiring? Or did you forget that you lost the bet?" she asked, lips parted slightly, tongue resting on her teeth.

The sudden switch knocked his thoughts askew. "Um...I

am ready to submit to your wishes."

"Good," she said, placing a single finger into his chest. "Jump off the tower."

"What?"

"Jump off," she said, letting the corner of her grin grow wider. "Or are you afraid?"

He glanced around him, suddenly worried. "I don't understand."

"I won. So you have to do as I say. I want you to jump off the tower," she said.

At that moment, a gust of wind battered them both, streamers from the clouds whipping past the tower. He smelled a storm in the distance.

"Fine," she said, shoving the canvas knapsack into his gut. "If you won't jump off, I will."

Before he could say a word otherwise, she sprinted to the east side, and in one leap, cleared the safety wall. His heart went right up through his neck, blowing his thoughts to smithereens.

Zayn had reached the edge about the time she came flinging back up. She hit the concrete and tumbled onto her knees and side, laughing as if the world were laughing with her.

"What the fuck," he said, hands trembling at the shock. "You gave me a heart attack."

She let him help her up. Kissed Zayn on the cheek as a reward before pulling away.

"Let me guess," he said, slowly recovering. "There's a reverse gravity field surrounding the tower."

She nodded enthusiastically. "Your turn."

He handed over the bag and turned to get a running start at the western side.

"No, not that way," she said.

"Now you're just messing with me," he said.

"No, really. The enchantment's weaker on that side. I'm not saying you'd fall, but let's not chance it," she said.

As he made the short sprint towards the edge, he had a fleeting thought that this was all a trick, and he was jumping off the Spire to his death. By the time his feet were flying over the edge, his mind exploded with adrenaline until he was a bundle of excitement. The terror spiked at the moment the enchantment grabbed hold and flung him back towards the roof, where he landed on his feet.

"I can't believe I just did that," he said, holding his hands out, fingers splayed, as if he were trying to keep the world in one place.

It reminded him of his first year with Instructor Allgood, who'd brought them to the parkour course, when he'd pushed too far and ended up in convalescence.

Before she could approach him, he leapt again, howling in victory as he flew. After he repeated it a few times, he approached her.

"I'll never ride another rollercoaster again. That was sick. Sick, sick, sick. Jump with me," he said.

He reached out to her and she stepped inside his grasp, bunching the front of his shirt in her fists. Before he could do anything else, she latched onto his lower lip with her teeth, gently, but firmly. Thoughts of resistance melted away. He tucked his arm around her neck, cinching her closer.

While he'd been jumping, she'd pulled a blanket from her room and laid it on the concrete. She pushed him down, straddling his leg, putting her fingernails against his neck. A distant part of him screamed that the reason he'd come here was to learn about Ernie, and that falling for her would only put her in danger of his curse, but rational thoughts were annihilated by her probing tongue in his mouth, and the way her fingers dug into his side as if she were trying to tear him apart.

Clothes came off. She scratched and nibbled on him, leaving him quivering with excitement.

"Did...you?" he asked.

"I cast the proper spells," she said, looking down on him with hair dangling in her face.

As the sky roiled with the coming storm, so did they, rising and falling, skin cracking with electricity. Thunder rumbled above them as they pushed and pulled, hips grinding, mouths hungrily attacking each other.

When they were finished, they collapsed and rolled onto their sides, cradling each other.

As the endorphins from their experience slowly faded from his mind, they were replaced by a growing worry. He was smitten beyond anything he could comprehend. In a different life, he'd be thinking about her as his lifetime companion, but that could never be for him. To fall for her would only endanger her.

What have I done?

He'd contacted her to find out information about Ernie, but thought the date would be ordinary enough that he could bring it up: small talk about the Second Year Contest, and the like. He hadn't expected to be swept off his feet, literally and figuratively.

"What will you do after you graduate?" she asked suddenly.

He'd come here because of the wish, and ultimately Varna. The question reminded him how much he'd allowed his feelings to betray him. He closed his eyes tightly and shook off the question.

"I'd rather not talk about it."

"What is it?" she asked, her gaze searching him. "You can talk to me."

"I want to. I really do. I've really been enjoying this," he said honestly. There was nothing more in the world that he wanted to do than confide in her. At one time, he'd at least had Keelan to talk to, but since he'd become a Watcher, they could no longer speak about the important things. And being with her reminded him of his loneliness. He'd been on this quest so long that he'd forgotten about his own needs and wants. He'd forgotten because he had to, because the Lady had taken those choices from him.

She kissed him, but he was lost in his thoughts, so he didn't quite kiss back.

"Are you worried about the wish spell?" she asked.

She was looking at him like she saw right through everything. The question punched him right in his soul.

"What are you talking about?" he asked.

His mind roiled with confusion. How did she know about that? Her earlier display of power, the portal in the bag, everything screamed that he'd completely misread the situation. He hadn't brought her here for information, she'd done that to him.

Who was she working for? Was this because he'd broken into Arcanium? Or was she a plant by Priyanka all this time?

Part of him worried that she *was* Priyanka in disguise, given the portal bag and the way she'd climbed the Spire, but he'd contacted Aurie rather than the other way around. But there were other ways to compromise someone. His whole body chilled with concern.

He should have realized it sooner. Instructor Pennywhistle had given him the clue during the face changing class. Hypnotism. Frank Orpheum was a master at it. He could have hypnotized Aurie to question him. It was also the way they were going to get Ernie to use the wish spell to make Priyanka the head patron.

Aurie pushed herself into a sitting position, completely

oblivious to her nakedness, which only further deepened his suspicion that she was not under her own control.

"Back when we first met, you mentioned a project you needed help with. You asked about a book called *Impossible Magics*, but you never asked again about it," she said.

He sat up and crossed his legs, which gave him a chance to formulate his thoughts. He'd kept his imbuements muted before, but now he needed them.

"I figured since you didn't mention it that Arcanium didn't have a copy."

"Are you sure you're not looking for a wish spell?" she asked, drilling her gaze into him.

"Of course not," he said.

"Then why did you ask Lady Amethyte about it?" she asked, clearly expecting that this was a killing blow by the rising heat in her face.

But for Zayn, having switched out of the postcoital bliss and into verbal warfare, her question explained everything to him. Had he not already suspected her allegiance this question might have wrong footed him, but he was able to withstand the blow, especially because it proved two essential points to him. The first was that he knew why his teammates had seen him in the city outside the Glass Cabaret when he'd never been there: because it wasn't him. Priyanka had likely been impersonating him. Clearly they doubted him, so rather than test his loyalty they used his likeness. They'd probably done the same with Lady Amethyte, who was the maetrie Queen of the Ruby Court. He didn't know how she fit in, or how Aurie had learned this, but it spoke to the girl's power and connections. But secondly, unless Priyanka was playing a game within a game, it proved that Aurie wasn't compromised by his patron; otherwise, she would have never asked that question.

"No. I don't know how you know about that, but no.

That's not what that was about. I told you. There's a project I'm working on. Lady Amethyte was answering some questions for me," he said.

Aurie sighed. "Zayn. There's no reason to lie to me. I know you're looking for the wish spell. You work for Priyanka Sai. I know she put you up to this. I've wanted to believe in us all along, but if you're not going to be honest with me..."

He squeezed hands into fists beside his head, suddenly realizing how this was going to end. She was being honest with him, about her questions, her feelings for him. Which made his involvement with her even more dangerous. She was getting involved with Priyanka's schemes, and it wouldn't end well for her.

"I'm telling you. It's not what it looks like. I can't explain why, or what it is that I'm doing, but trust me. This isn't for *them*," he said honestly, wishing he could tell her everything.

"Zayn, you can tell me. I'm...well, I like you a lot. Whatever's going on, I can help," she said.

Zayn grabbed his clothes and started pulling his jeans on.

"No, you can't. I mean, you can, but you can't," he said, instantly regretting his moment of indecision. "Stop talking about this."

"See!" she said. "I can help. You said so."

He looked at his palms, realizing that by coming on the date, he'd endangered her. His stomach twisted with the realization of what he had to do to save her from his curse.

"No. I shouldn't have come. We shouldn't be doing this. I don't want...I don't want..." He paused, looking straight at her. "I don't really want you. I've been using you. It's a game at the hall. We have to pick a girl and seduce her. Make her believe that we like her."

She reacted as if she'd been slapped. "You don't mean that."

"Are you really that naive? I told you I'm Priyanka's assistant. You're a second year. Don't you think she would know exactly what I'm doing all the time? I needed something from you and now I don't. It's over. You can go back to your pathetic hall."

He sensed the faez bubbling up in her, as if she were going to lash out at him with magic. He worried what that might mean given her level of power.

"Zayn. What is going on? I don't believe any of this," she said.

"It doesn't matter if you believe it. It only matters that you leave. Go back to your hall. Forget about me. Worry about your silly contest, and figure out who your real enemy is," he said.

A bolt of lightning slipped past the Spire, blinding Aurie. He used the distraction to slip into the Veil.

Aurie looked around, lips bunched with distress. He stayed too long in the Veil, watching her as she collected her things with tears welling in her eyes, his feelings twisting into an unrecognizable mess.

He'd doomed her. He could feel it in his bones.

Long after she left, he whispered into the wind.

"What have I done?"

Chapter Nineteen

Eighth Ward, May 2018

You're getting sleepy

A few days later, Zayn was in class with Instructor Pennywhistle. She'd long ago given up on Zayn learning the arts of imitation, so she'd had him practice mimicking voices while the others worked on their transformations.

At the end of class, after everyone else had left, Zayn went up to the instructor, who was collecting her notes from a desk. She glanced at him wistfully. It always made him feel like he was a terminal patient when she looked at him like that.

"What can I do for you, Zayn?"

"I wanted to apologize that I've been a terrible student all year," he said.

A light snort of breath came out of her nose. "You might be my worst student of all time. You're lucky that we don't have grades or you wouldn't be graduating. It'll just be a tool that you won't be able to use."

Not being able to face change made him feel like he was

defective. In the history of the Academy, no student had ever been unable to transform, at least in some small ways. He'd never managed to even grow his nose by a single millimeter.

"On the plus side, this sense of self that blocks face changing seems to extend towards a resistance to hypnosis," said Instructor Pennywhistle.

"Yes, about that," said Zayn. "I wanted to know if you could teach me how to hypnotize. I thought it might come in handy."

The instructor stood tall. "Why of course, but I'm not sure how useful it'll be. Hypnotism, even the magical type, can be tricky business. It's not like you can sneak up on someone and then hypnotize them to get them to do what you want. Typically if you have that kind of access, you don't need hypnotism."

"I understand," said Zayn. "But I'd still like to learn."

Pennywhistle put her back against the desk and crossed her arms. Her mouth wriggled as if she were wrestling with a question. Eventually, she gave up and said, "The key to hypnosis, and we're talking the magical kind, not the stage trick stuff, is that you're inducing a state of extreme relaxation. Think of it as that the waking mind is calmed, allowing the deeper consciousnesses to be in control, like a guided daydream. Using magic helps push that consciousness deeper, giving the speaker more influence. But keep in mind that at no time will the person do something against their morals or constructs of personal values."

"What about someone like Frank Orpheum? Didn't he hypnotize a whole stadium of people?" asked Zayn.

"Those things are still true for Frank. Now, he might find it easier to hypnotize people, he's been doing it for a long time, but he has to follow the same constraints," said Pennywhistle.

Zayn imagined that was another reason for Priyanka to

create Raziyah, so when it came time for Ernie to use the wish, he would have a friendly person to bestow it upon.

"Enough lecture, let me show you the charm and talk you through the script, and then you try it on me," said the instructor.

It was simple enough. Using the spell felt like petting the person, coaxing them into sleep.

"Now close your eyes and inhale deeply and hold it for three or four seconds and then exhale slowly...again breath in deeply and exhale slowly..."

Zayn continued, talking through the hypnosis script. In some ways, the mundane parts of it felt like a spell.

Instructor Pennywhistle went under easily. Her chin dipped towards her chest when the hypnosis had taken hold.

"Nod your head if you are relaxed," said Zayn, receiving a sleepy nod from her.

"Tell me, Marilyn, do you typically remember when you've been put under hypnosis?" he asked.

"No," she said, then added, "typically."

A twinge of guilt hit him in the stomach. He felt bad that he'd tricked her like this. He'd remembered from his attempted hypnosis session with her that she'd said those that could change easily were most susceptible, and while he wanted to learn the technique, he also needed confirmation.

"You're feeling quite pleased to see me after all these years," he said, glancing over his shoulder. "It's hard to believe that I graduated twenty years ago."

"It is..."

Her dreamy voice told him she was deep under, but he wondered how deep she would stay.

"You don't look any different, Marilyn, while I've gotten older. I have a little gut now. It's hard to believe I survived all those years ago," he said.

"Yes...I'm sure..."

"Do you remember the time around the one-hundred-year anniversary of the Second Year Contest?" he asked.

She nodded.

"There's a weird thing that I've been thinking about all these years. It's not a big thing, since it's in the past, but I was curious. Are you curious?"

"Yes..."

"It's about Priyanka. You're one of her oldest friends, right?"

Pennywhistle hesitated before answering, "Yes..."

"Why are Priyanka Sai and Frank Orpheum friends? They seem so different," he said.

"Frank was her student," said Pennywhistle. "He wasn't a very good one, but after graduating, he went on his own path."

He knew it was true as soon as he heard it. It made a lot of sense, and explained why she trusted Frank with her endeavor despite their apparent differences.

"Do you trust Frank?" he asked.

Previous answers had that dreamlike quality to them, but this time it came out hard.

"No."

Zayn sensed she was waking, and he should probably bring her back out, but he needed to know.

"Why?"

The words hissed from her lips in a sneer. "He only loves himself."

His first instinct was to worry for Priyanka, but then he realized that was foolish. She'd been around longer, and had known him as a student. She surely knew that much about Frank and was using that to her advantage.

"You are slowly waking, Marilyn, coming back to current time. When I count to three and snap my fingers you will be awake, and you will remember nothing. One. Two. Three."

At the snap, her chin came back up and her eyes were open. She blinked twice, tilting her head.

"Have we started?"

A smile rose to his lips. "We just finished."

"Oh, good," said Pennywhistle. "It seems you're a natural. Is there anything else you need?"

"No, that was it. Thank you," he said.

"My pleasure," she said. "I'll miss you when you're gone. Despite being a terrible face changer, you're a great student. I hope everything goes well for you after you graduate."

The way she looked at him suggested she knew about Varna, but that wasn't a surprise. He assumed all the instructors knew.

Zayn gave her his best smile, the one that hid that his life was balanced on a razor's edge.

Chapter Twenty

Enochian District, May 2018

A wish gone wrong

The last weeks at the Academy of the Subtle Arts came rushing in like a tsunami, obliterating everything in their path. It was funny how time did that, stretched in times of difficulty, then sped up when events grew larger than the mind could hold. The city of Invictus was enraptured by the Second Year Contest, and his class, Academy and otherwise, were preoccupied by what they were going to do after their final year. Everyone but Zayn, whose future seemed like a horizon he couldn't see past.

Zayn knew his only chance to convince Ernie to use the wish spell for him would be to hypnotize him, but he couldn't figure out a way to befriend him. If he'd figured it out earlier, maybe he could have used Aurie to get to him, but he'd ruined that opportunity on the Spire.

He spent his time watching Frank in the Enochian District, knowing that whenever it happened, he would be involved, so it was to Zayn's surprise that he saw Aurie and her teammates approaching the house.

From his vantage point in the nearby abandoned house, he watched as they split up into two groups. The first was comprised of Aurie, Hannah, and Ernie, who gathered near the front of the house. The second group was Pi, Raziyah, and Rigel. They moved around back, using the alleyways to stay hidden. A pit formed in his stomach as soon as he saw what they were going to try to do.

"Oh, no," he said. "This isn't going to work."

As powerful as the Silverthorne sisters were, they were no match for who they were up against. Through the upper windows, he watched Frank receive a message on his phone and then move to the open window, produce a whistle from his pocket, and blow on it. Zayn was a little confused until he saw the doors on the surrounding houses burst open and the neighborhood fill with his thralls. Then Frank in demon form headed to the first floor.

Zayn punched his open hand. They were walking into an ambush, and they had a traitor in their midst. Priyanka alone could take the five of them.

Slipping into the Veil, Zayn leapt out the window, landing on the second-floor roof next door, then ran along the wall. He bounced between the two walls, landing softly on his feet at ground level before returning to the real world. Pouring what he could into speed, Zayn ran to the back, hoping to warn Pi away from their foolishness, also aware that this put him at odds with his patron.

When he rounded the corner, Pi caught him off guard with a force bolt at the ankles, knocking him from his feet.

He raised his hand in a gesture of peace as she approached. "I'm not your enemy. You shouldn't have come here."

But the murderous look in her eyes suggested that she didn't know he was on her side, and he had no opportunity to tell her, especially with Priyanka lurking nearby.

Zayn threw up a flash spell, then slipped in the Veil, disappearing from her sight.

An explosion at Frank's house put a stone in his gut. He sprinted towards the front, only to hear two more explosions from the back. He worried what that might mean for Pi. He hated to see Aurie's sister get hurt, but it sounded like she was trying to fight Priyanka.

Zayn made it around back just when a larger explosion shook the ground and blew out every window for a block. Things had gone south quickly.

Zayn looked down upon a fallen figure. Aurie's sister lay at the center of a small crater. Her limbs were tangled. Blood leaked from her nose and ears.

His patron was also down, but he had no doubts that she would recover. Within seconds, the dark-haired woman stirred. He watched her stumble to the crater to check Pythia's pulse. The soft shake of her head told him what he needed to know. She was dead. Zayn tried not to let that bother him.

Priyanka's shoulders hunched with sadness at the fallen girl. He was so busy thinking about how Aurie was going to feel when she heard the news, that he barely got himself hidden again before Priyanka shot a glance his way. He didn't think she'd seen him, but it was close. Even after getting blown up, Priyanka had the senses of a demon cat.

Inside the house, a battle of elements raged. Aurie was battling Frank Orpheum. Zayn wasn't surprised that she was holding her own against him. The dramatics patron wasn't used to head-to-head battles, preferring subterfuge as his main weapon, which was why he'd teamed up with Priyanka to find the wish spell. But Aurie was the strongest mage he'd ever met.

Around the time his patron got to the back door, the battle ended, and a minute later, the big blonde girl on rollerblades went through the third-floor window.

Zayn moved through the surrounding houses, which wasn't hard since the walkers had flooded into the street. Orpheum had kept the whole population of the district subdued with his hypnotism trick. Zayn climbed onto the second-story roof, making it up the vertical incline as easily as walking across a room. Hannah was alive, but unconscious. He lifted her, and carried her into a nearby building, hiding her in an abandoned house.

If he could get inside, maybe he could get Aurie out too. He shouldn't be so stupid as to risk it, but he'd been the one to get them into this mess.

Through the downstairs window, Zayn spied Priyanka and Orpheum talking. They had the kid Ernie. It was strange to think that Invictus had put the wish spell inside that kid. Messed him up pretty good to have that much magic swirling around inside of him. Zayn didn't have the starry-eyed ideals about Invictus that other people did. The head patron had done some pretty shady stuff, and dooming this poor soul into carrying his pet spell was as shitty as it got. Almost like making him a slave to the magic.

But Aurie was still inside the house. If he could get her out, then maybe he could salvage something. He crept up the wall and through an open window into a room on the second floor.

Zayn fell apart when he found her.

Slumped against the wall, Aurelia Silverthorne stared into vacant space, the awful lines of betrayal on her face. He knew she was gone as soon as he saw that openmouthed gape.

Blood had pooled around her. Zayn almost couldn't believe it. He'd seen death before. Known it from his very hand. But this was someone he'd cared about, maybe even loved.

It'd never been his intention to fall for her. He had only gotten involved to spite Priyanka. He'd hoped they would protect Ernie from his patron, but he hadn't counted on Aurie's ambitions.

The night on the Spire came back to him. Lying with her as the storm tickled their skin with electricity, moving together, cries of passion on their lips. Now, dead. *What have I done*? That moment had been the happiest of his short life.

He wanted to march downstairs and confront Priyanka. *Do you know who you murdered*? he'd say. *Aurie was kind, curious, brilliant. She was fierce, protective of her friends, understanding of her enemies. She was the best of us. And you killed her.*

But he knew he wouldn't because in a way, he'd killed her too.

Zayn wiped the tears from his face and stared at them like traitors. He hadn't cried for real in years. *Is this what I've become? I'm no better than Priyanka with all her deceptions. If I hadn't mentioned the book, or fixed the sorting contest to get both Aurie and Pi into the group, then this would have never happened.*

He closed her eyes with his fingertips, lifted her mouth shut. She was so soft. As beautiful as a sleeping angel. He crept back to the window. They were all dead, or would soon be.

The wish was as good as gone, and even if he could overcome Priyanka and Frank, there was no way he could pry the spell from Ernie. If there was any good he could accomplish, it was to save the girl Hannah, who was at least alive.

Reluctantly, Zayn left the house and retrieved Hannah from the place he'd hidden her, then crept back into the house where he'd seen the Garden Network, took the portal to Golden Willow, and left her in the emergency room along with a note that read: *Contact Semyon Gray, tell him to go to the portal in the Enochian District.*

The realization that Aurie was dead hadn't truly sunk in. Not only her, but her sister and their friend, Rigel. Only Hannah and Ernie had survived, and Zayn wasn't sure if using the wish wouldn't destroy him too.

Zayn took the train back to his house in the seventh ward. He hoped to find his teammates so he could bury his face in their shoulders. He'd gotten a bunch of people killed, including someone he'd had strong feelings for, and it'd been for nothing. Frank and Priyanka had won. He'd needed the wish to fix the poison problem in Varna, but that opportunity was gone. Not only that, but once Priyanka took control of the Halls, it would make the Lady of Varna the hidden hand behind the throne. Things couldn't get any worse.

By the time he made it back to the house, Zayn was contemplating leaving the Halls and taking one last trip around the world before his poison supplies ran out.

The living room lights were on suggesting one or more of his teammates were home. Zayn hoped it was Keelan. He needed family in this dark moment.

When he opened the door, he came face-to-face with an unhappy Frank Orpheum. The door closed behind him, revealing his patron, Priyanka Sai. Thoughts of escape left the moment he felt the tip of a blade press into his back.

"You little shit, you screwed me," said Frank, sneering.

A pit opened in Zayn's stomach. Why were they here and not using the wish?

"I don't know what you're talking about," said Zayn.

"That girl and her sister," said Frank. "You're the one that got them involved. I saw you in the house, carrying the girl with roller skates who crashed through my door. You did this. You took my victory from me."

The moment he said "my victory," Zayn understood that he'd been wrong about who was in charge. It was Frank, not Priyanka. And did that mean the wish spell had gone awry?

"You have her hypnotized," said Zayn, glancing over his shoulder at the blank stare on Priyanka's face. "I didn't think that was possible."

"We've had a thing going on and off for years. I've been sneaking small amounts of a suggestive into her drinks. Not enough for her seers to notice, but enough over time to break down her defenses. I kept my leash loose, so as not to give it away, but that day is over," he said.

"It was you that wanted to be head patron," said Zayn. "You just let her think that it was her who would take control."

"Who better to be head patron, than me?" asked Frank with a preening smile. "I would give them someone to love. Make their miserable existence worth something." His smile turned to ashes. "But since you've ruined that, it's my turn to ruin you."

Frank's eyes turned hazy as he waved his hand at Zayn, who felt a tickling at his mind as he tried to take control. When Zayn's expression didn't change, Frank scowled.

"You seem to be immune," said Frank. "No matter. There are other ways. Pri, knock him out."

Before he could move, the back of the dagger smacked him on the head. His world dissolved into blackness.

Chapter Twenty-One

Harmony, May 2018

Lost in the mist

Zayn woke with a headache. His hands and feet were bound behind him in a suicide hog-tie. The rope went around his neck as well as his hands and feet, so if he tried to break the rope, he'd strangle himself.

It took him a moment to recognize the soft moss and oppressive fog that surrounded him. The air was cool and soothing, but that would mean little when the mystdrakons found him.

Harmony.

A dangerous place, even if he wasn't bound. Frank had sent him here to die.

When Zayn turned his head to see what was nearby, the rope burned his neck. Nothing but pale emptiness.

Even if he could escape, there was no way to get back home. Priyanka had never taught him the password to Harmony, or how to leave. This was her private sanctuary.

At least Frank hadn't had her kill him outright. He imagined that would have broken his control since it would have gone against her moral code, to murder him in cold blood. But taking him on an expedition and leaving him? That was a gray area.

As for killing Aurie and the others, while she would have never done it on her own, Zayn could imagine that her flexible morality would allow it if she thought it was for the greater good. Priyanka more than anyone knew the danger that the Hundred Halls was in without its head patron.

But none of that mattered for Zayn.

He was stuck in a hostile place without a weapon, hogtied, and with a headache the size of New Jersey.

It could be worse. I could be dead. Think, Zayn. What do I have that I can use?

He considered transforming into a spider, but the change would only strangle him. The rope was too tight.

He tried fidgeting with the ropes, but Priyanka had made it so he couldn't move a muscle without causing himself pain. It was like a Chinese finger trap. The more he struggled, the tighter it got around his neck.

Zayn expanded his senses, trying to paint a picture of his surroundings. He thought it was completely devoid of other creatures until he caught the soft squeal of a fledgling mystdrakon about fifty feet behind him.

Great, mystdrakons.

The only thing he did think he could do was to roll on his side and pull away the moss until he exposed the jagged volcanic rock beneath. Maybe then he could saw through the ropes, but that would take time, time he wasn't sure he had. While the mist currently hid his location, as the day went on, the sun would burn it off, leaving him exposed.

He'd heard rumbles of a storm in the distance but he

knew from his previous visits that the clouds often didn't make it over the mountains.

His only defense was the fourth imbuement, but it wasn't like he could control the creatures forever. Eventually he'd get tired and they'd have him for a snack. He was already hungry, dehydrated, and cramping from his awkward position.

What he needed was a herd of hellarmor beasts. If they were nearby, the mystdrakons might not bother him. Since the first was out of his control, Zayn started working the ropes. He rolled onto his side, using his hands to pick away the moss to expose the volcanic rock beneath.

Around the time he finally had the rock exposed enough that he could work on the rope, the mist had burned off and Zayn could see the slight rise where the mystdrakon nest was located. The two adult mystdrakons, probably a mated pair, ambled from their nest, probably to set off on a hunt.

Zayn stopped working, fearing even the slightest movement would draw their notice.

The larger mystdrakon started meandering in his general direction. Without the mist, he was exposed.

Then a fortunate tremor announced itself through the rock. A hellarmor beast herd.

Come on. Come this way. Come this way.

At first the hellarmor beast herd was too far away for him to use his imbuement. He needed them to cross his path so he could pull them closer. But the vibration seemed to cool the mystdrakon's interest in exploration. It hunkered down on the moss like a lion waiting in the high grass.

Zayn thought the hellarmor beasts were walking in the opposite direction, but then they turned slightly, which brought them to the edge of his range.

Exhausted as he was, it took a monumental effort to reach them with his imbuement. He couldn't affect the larger ones at this range, but he managed to catch a calf and make it veer in his direction. The matriarch of the herd tried to nudge the calf back onto the path, but Zayn forced it to hurry ahead on its stubby legs.

Heh, stubby legs. Even a calf is as big as an SUV.

The vibration grew to a rumble. Zayn worried he'd done his job too well and they might trample him, but he managed to still the calf at a spot fifty feet away.

With the mist burned to a faint wisp, Zayn got a look at the hellarmor beasts for the first time. They were bigger than he expected, and more armored. His initial impression that they were tougher versions of a stegosaurus was not far off. Their bodies were covered in gray plates like a pangolin. All of them except for the calf he'd lured.

The appearance of the hellarmor calf drew the notice of the mystdrakons. He sensed they were focused on the mostly unarmored youngster. Its plates were patchy, especially around its neck.

Zayn weaved his imbuement to sample the mystdrakons, but not take control. Now that they had the calf's scent, he planned to send it the other direction. If they attacked or not, it didn't matter to him, because he thought he could cut through the rope by the time they got back.

Before he could nudge, the bigger mystdrakon sped across the mossy plain, hitting the calf at full speed, sending a spray of blood across the herd. The mystdrakon had hit like a cruise missile.

The herd erupted as if a bomb had gone off.

One moment, the beasts were milling about, waiting for the matriarch to signal they could move again. The next moment their honks and hoots filled the air.

The calf had been killed instantly, but the hellarmors went into a rage.

Priyanka had called them ill-tempered. She should have called them berserkers.

Zayn had seen more self-control in a bull-riding contest.

Hooves smashed the mossy stone around the first mystdrakon, which had gotten more than it asked for. A mid-sized hellarmor beast trampled through the mystdrakon nest, killing the younglings and triggering the second to fly into the herd.

During the chaos, Zayn worked feverishly at the ropes, sawing against the rocks, even as the effort squeezed his neck. He realized it was going to be a race between breaking free and unconsciousness, but he didn't have a choice. The longer he was on the ground, the more likely it was that he would be trampled.

The second mystdrakon had latched onto the mid-sized hellarmor, finding a gap between its plates from an old wound. The two spun around in combat not twenty feet from Zayn's location.

Zayn barely avoided being trampled when a second hellarmor charged, knocking the mystdrakon off. Before it could speed away, they smashed it with their hooves, spraying blood and musk in a wide arc that landed across Zayn's back.

The pungent oils filled Zayn's nose, making it feel like his sinuses were on fire. Then he remembered what Priyanka had said about injured mystdrakons creating a frenzy as others tried to get at the high calorie fuel source.

He'd been sauced with mystdrakon juice.

As the ropes broke away from his hands, he sensed other mystdrakons in the area called by the broken glands. Zayn yanked the rope from around his neck, freeing himself before the others arrived.

A quick count told him at least a dozen mystdrakons approached.

Covered in gland oil, Zayn sped from the mossy plain,

leaving the battle behind.

The larger source of fuel drew most of the mystdrakons to the battle with the hellarmor herd, but a few turned towards him. Zayn weaved his imbuements as he ran in a jagged line, dropping into the Veil at points so the mystdrakons couldn't easily track him.

His caution saved his life when one blew past him as he shifted left.

When he hit the jungle, Zayn checked behind him to find that the battle had ended, and the mystdrakons, more than a dozen now, were on his trail.

With no time to rest, he ran in hopes that speed was his best defense. But it was a long way from the mossy plain back to the Aerie, and if he survived, he'd have to deal with Priyanka.

Zayn paused at the river and tried to scrub the gland oil from his skin and clothes, but it was as sticky as paste. He'd probably have to use alcohol or another solvent to remove it.

He stayed ahead of the mystdrakons, mostly because the day had grown warm and that had kept them from moving too quickly, but that time was coming to an end. The storm that had bunched up against the distant mountains was boiling over, sending its squalls into the jungle behind him.

When he reached the pole path, he checked behind him to find that nearly two dozen mystdrakons were following. Muscles pushed to their limits, Zayn made his way through the maulapine territory. He was too exhausted to control them, so he used his speed alone. Once he got to the stairs, the protections Priyanka had put on them would keep him safe, and he could decide what to do about her.

But as he moved through the final section of jungle, the storm raced over the valley, blocking the sun and bringing a chilling rain. The mystdrakons that had lingered at a distance used the atmospheric cooling to surge after him.

Zayn sprinted across the final poles as a pair of mystdrakons, younger ones, rushed up the last hill. He didn't think he was going to make it.

A last push got him to the stairs before they caught him. The lead mystdrakon smashed into the barrier, screeching as the protections zapped it.

While the painful blowback had dissuaded the maulapines from further incursions, it did nothing for the mystdrakons, who were drawn by the gland oil. The second mystdrakon hit the barrier at full speed.

Zayn barely got out of the way as it screamed and wriggled up the stairs towards him, the magics of the barrier burning its scaly body. His nose choked with the smell of burnt flesh, and then an audible pop filled the air, and the sizzling stopped, suggesting that the mystdrakon had broken the barrier.

"Oh, no," said Zayn.

There was nothing to stop them now. Zayn made the journey up the stairs before the other mystdrakons arrived. They wouldn't be cautious like the first.

Priyanka was waiting for him when he reached the Aerie. The dagger in her fist told him everything he needed to know.

"There's no time for this," said Zayn. "We need to leave."

When she twitched, he blinked into the Veil, diving out of the way of the blade that skinned his arm.

He rolled onto his feet.

Priyanka had him dead to rights with a second blade in her hand when a mystdrakon burned up the stairs, hitting her in the chest. The two crashed into the building, blowing through the huge windows, sending glass everywhere.

Zayn thought she'd been killed until he heard her rage scream, and the head of the mystdrakon came flying back out of the building.

More mystdrakons flew up the stairs. Zayn leapt onto the roof of the Aerie, running to the back of the building.

Priyanka killing the first had scattered more gland oil around the house. This drove them into a frenzy. The creatures tore through the building, snapping and crashing into everything.

From the peak side of the house, Zayn spied at least twenty mystdrakons. Their pale dragster bodies weren't built for running long distances. They would sprint, then pause to let the rain cool them.

Spread about the grounds, the gland oil from the first mystdrakon encouraged the creatures to attack each other. Their thrashing took down the western half of the Aerie, the steel girders collapsing.

Zayn wasn't sure where Priyanka was. He hadn't heard her since she killed the first one. Probably she'd escaped the house to the portal back to Invictus, leaving him to fend for himself against the mystdrakons.

Only his location kept him from the fray, but when a younger mystdrakon bounced off a boulder and landed on the roof, Zayn backed to the edge.

His reserves were at empty.

When he reached out to encourage the mystdrakon to attack its breathern below, he found he couldn't even make it turn away.

The rain cascaded off his shoulders. A low rumble boomed through the valley. Zayn glanced over his shoulder to the cliff that fell away on the eastern side of the house. The mystdrakon tramped towards him in its bow-legged waddle.

He was only going to get one chance. He put whatever energy he had left into his sensing imbuement, waiting for the right moment.

When Zayn sensed the glands flaring on the hind legs of

the mystdrakon, he jumped straight up.

Like a rocket, the mystdrakon sped right beneath him and over the cliff. When he landed, he turned around in time to see it tumble against the far slope, body broken from the impact.

His relief turned to terror when the middle of the Aerie collapsed, creating a ramp that led to him. Three mystdrakons turned from their battle, facing him. He might have been able to time another jump if it were only one, but not three.

The section of the Aerie he stood on was unstable. It shifted as the mystdrakons approached. He expected it to shift backwards and throw him over the cliff, so he slipped to his knees and climbed down. He needed to find a place to hide from the mystdrakons they couldn't get to. He considered the cliff wall, but his arms shook from the day's efforts and the rain warned him away from attempting it.

Away from the house, on the northern slope, he spied the lid of a cistern. It was about fifty feet away. He slipped into the Veil, but immediately came right back out.

He was on empty.

The three mystdrakons had moved to the edge. Their patient snorting told him that he didn't have long, but if he made a run for it, they would surely catch him.

He needed a distraction. But he had nothing left. No faez, no weapon, not even a scrap of energy.

He was on the verge of collapse, covered in gland oil, with three mystdrakons about to make his acquaintance.

As the first peered over the edge, he looked around him. The eastern section of the building was about to collapse. He only needed to find a way to finish the job and then escape to the cistern before they caught him.

He spied a beam holding up the roof over what used to be Priyanka's office. The beam was bent in the middle where a mystdrakon had run into it.

Zayn kicked the beam with everything he had as the first mystdrakon prepared to drop on him.

The structure shifted, flipping the creature onto its back next to him. It wriggled as its jaws snapped near the back of his legs.

Zayn kicked again, and the roof shuddered. He gave it a third kick right as the mystdrakon behind him gained its feet.

As the whole building fell, Zayn dove forward, right ahead of the mystdrakon's jaws, barely avoiding his legs being bitten off.

The final section of the Aerie collapsed, crushing one mystdrakon and throwing the other two over the cliff.

Zayn ran to the cistern, expecting the quick snap of teeth before he reached it. He'd never run so slow, but it was all he could do.

When he got to the lid and couldn't lift it, he almost laughed.

Then he realized it was latched, and turned the handle to the side.

Back at the house, two mystdrakons had noticed him. He'd probably have been dead if they hadn't been speeding around the house in bursts, but since they had, they moved towards him in an awkward trot. He lifted the lid, shoving his body through the gap as they approached. He grabbed the ladder and let the lid fall on top of him.

Two seconds later, there was sniffing above him. Zayn clung to the ladder, hooking his arms around it and letting his knees bend. He wanted to lie down, but he could smell the water beneath him. He didn't bother with the dark seeing spell as he didn't care if he could see anymore.

After a few minutes of sniffing the two mystdrakons left. The rain stopped a little later, and sunlight peeked through the gap at the edge of the cistern lid.

He waited until he couldn't sense the mystdrakons anymore before climbing down and cupping water into his mouth. Once he was sated, he left the cistern.

Evening was approaching, but the heat from the sun had forced the mystdrakons to flee the Aerie. Zayn didn't bother moving from the top of the cistern. He fell asleep on the metal plate.

He woke in the hesitant light of morning, his tongue sticking to the roof of his mouth, and surveyed the carnage. The Aerie had been demolished. A few steel beams stuck defiantly into the air, but the rest had collapsed or been thrown down the cliff.

Zayn went in search of food, picking through the destruction to find the remnants of the kitchen. When he lifted a beam, he found a lifeless arm sticking out.

Priyanka.

A quick check of the pulse proved she was alive, barely.

Zayn carefully examined the area before moving anything so he didn't accidently crush her.

When he'd freed her from the rubble, he carried her to the cistern before returning in search of food. It took about two hours of excavating before he found the pantry. He carried what food he'd recovered back to Priyanka, set aside some for her should she wake, and filled his belly.

He was uncomfortably aware that she might kill him when she awoke, but he felt like he didn't have a choice. He couldn't stay in Harmony forever. The lack of poison would kill him eventually. He needed Priyanka. Hopefully it was the Priyanka he knew, not the one controlled by Frank Orpheum.

She didn't wake until two days later.

He used the time to build a shelter, using broken beams and a net from a closet. It was better than thinking about how everything had gone wrong, or that Aurie was dead.

Zayn was coming back from foraging when he found Priyanka cross-legged beneath the shelter.

"You're awake," he said, waiting for a sign of which version he was talking to.

Priyanka blinked. A little frown tugged at the corner of her lips.

"I'm sorry, Zayn."

She looked close to tears.

"Is this the real you?" he asked.

She nodded. "I killed Rigel. He was a good kid."

His gut squeezed at the thought she hadn't mentioned Aurie, or her sister.

"You weren't under your own control," he said.

"That's no excuse," she said, her jaw pulsing. "That I was willing to kill for the head patron job tells me how far I've fallen."

A stab of anger went through him. "Rigel wasn't the only one you killed."

She looked up at him. He realized his hands were fists at his sides but he didn't care. She'd killed Aurie.

"Oh," said Priyanka. "You don't know."

"Don't know what?"

He suddenly felt dizzy.

"She's alive. Aurie. Her sister too, though she was just resilient," said Priyanka, glancing askew.

An overwhelming feeling came over him. Tears burst from his eyes, streaming down his cheeks.

"What? She's alive? They're alive? How?" he asked, the questions tumbling from his lips. He collapsed to his knees.

Priyanka's face bloomed with a broken smile, the kind held together with laughter and madness.

"Ernie saved her. He used the wish to bring Aurie back," said Priyanka, her eyes glistening.

Zayn put a hand to his mouth. "What? You can do that?"

"She hadn't been dead very long. He used the wish to bring her back. It saved more than her life," said Priyanka.

"After that, is that when you and Frank came for me?" asked Zayn.

"Semyon showed up. He kept Frank from doing anything more. That's when Frank sent us here." Her laughing smile cracked, turned hard. "Oh, no. Frank. Before we parted he said he was going to take care of them. He knew a way to do it without anyone knowing. I think it had to do with the Second Year Contest."

They left Harmony, heading straight to the Spire when they returned. They didn't make it a block before they saw the papers splashed with the double news.

FRANK ORPHEUM DEAD

And beneath that in a subheading

SURPRISE LAST PLACE TEAM HARPERS WIN SECOND YEAR CONTEST

"I guess that saves me the trouble of killing him," said Priyanka, staring at the paper through the glass.

"Why do I get the feeling those two things are connected?" said Zayn.

Priyanka's eyes creased. "I think I'm going to have to keep an eye on those sisters."

"Hey..."

A smile broke on her face. "Nothing bad."

"What now?"

"We should get back to the Honeycomb. Everyone's probably wondering where we are." She raised an eyebrow. "Which will stay a secret, right?"

"Of course," said Zayn.

Priyanka looked into the city. “On second thought, you head to the Honeycomb. Let them know we’re okay. You can tell them we had a problem in Harmony that we had to take care of, nothing more.” She sighed. “I need to go pay my respects.”

Priyanka left him on the corner. Zayn’s heart was still tumbling in his chest. He’d barely gotten used to the idea that Aurie was alive.

Chapter Twenty-Two

Seventh Ward, May 2018

Last goodbyes

The semester wound to a close without any further troubles and a palatable excitement in the air, as everyone was moving on to their new lives soon. Keelan had organized a graduation party at the house in the seventh ward. Zayn had been content to quietly help. The events in Harmony had taken a lot out of him.

When the rest of the class arrived, they only took up the living room. Half their first year hadn't made it to the end, the majority leaving the Academy due to their inability to continue the vigorous and morally ambiguous schooling. A few like Chen and Elana, who had died in the Eternal City, were given a place of honor with their photos displayed on the wall.

Zayn sat on the loveseat with Marley in his lap, the callolo purring as he scratched the back of his neck. He was going to miss the cat-like creature. Uncle Larice had agreed to care for the callolo, so he'd have a home.

He was thinking about how much money to leave the bodega owner to pay for treats when Skylar threw herself into the spot next to him, handing him a drink.

"You've been rather quiet, well, this whole semester. I barely feel like we hung out," she said.

Skylar had been growing her hair out, something about the requirements of the new job, but she hadn't given specifics.

"Yeah, it was a strange one. Since we didn't have team activities, and we spent a lot of time with our mentors, it was kinda lonely," said Zayn.

Skylar searched his face. She put a hand on his arm and squeezed.

"Are you going to be alright?" she asked.

"What do you mean?"

Her lips parted slightly. "We've known each other nearly five years, and this whole time there's been the looming specter of Varna behind you and Keelan. You've never once explained it, but it's not like I haven't heard the rumors. The blood of Varna runs deep in the Academy, though no one will explain why."

Zayn lifted one shoulder. "It's probably best it stays that way."

He hated not being able to explain it to his teammates, but it was his burden. He didn't want to get them killed too, there were too many people already weighing on him.

Skylar sighed. "Alright, fine. But don't you go leaving without saying goodbye. Part of me fears that once we leave here, we'll never see each other again."

"I hope that's not true, I really do," said Zayn, nodding, but their shared expression betrayed the truth of their profession. This was probably the last time they'd see each other.

He caught a glimmer at her shoulder and wrinkled his

forehead to examine closer. “Did you ever figure out that cloak?”

Skylar’s grin grew bigger than the whole room. “I did.”

“Do I get to see what it does?” he asked.

“Maybe later, after things have wound down,” said Skylar with a wink.

As the party went on, it got a little louder. Zayn made sure he talked to everyone, even Eddie, who had been a source of endless entertainment during their five years.

Zayn couldn’t help but think that it’d gone by too fast. It felt like one moment Instructor Allgood was screaming in his face, and the next he was staring at the rest of his life. Part of him wanted to give up his quest against the Lady. He could ask Priyanka to find a him a job, something suitable for his skills. She’d probably use him in her private network. It would be a comfortable existence. He’d be able to do some good in his own small way and experience an unusual amount of freedom.

But he knew he couldn’t do it. Sure, he’d be free, but what about his family? What about Neveah, who wanted to be a chef in Paris, or the twins, who wanted to travel? Or his parents with their dreams?

Was it better to risk death to earn freedom? But then again, was it fair for him to choose for them?

Late in the party, Zayn climbed onto the roof. He wanted to experience the city before he returned home. The constant noise—the car honks, rumble of the trains, random laughing and talking—had once felt foreign, an intrusion. Now, it was as comforting as the din of night insects at the Stack.

When he looked south, he caught a glimpse of the top of a seventy-foot illusionary robot doing battle with a girl in a sailor outfit. There were graduation parties all over the city. The second ward threw the biggest, a place for wannabe mages to rub elbows with the future wizards of the world.

Zayn wondered what it'd be like to have that limitless horizon. To have the expectations of growth and change, not the webby darkness of the Lady's plantation.

When he heard someone climbing onto the roof, he thought it'd be Portia or Vin coming to say goodbye, but it was Keelan, who had a couple of beers in his pockets.

"Hey, cuz," he said, taking the spot next to him and handing him a beer.

They clinked bottles together, took a drink.

"Did it go like you expected?" asked Keelan, a smirk on his lips.

"No. You?"

Keelan chuckled, shaking his head. "Not in the least bit. I should have known it was going to be a strange five years when you won your named coin from Allgood using a sparkly pink dildo."

The image of the sexgiest dancing past the gruff instructor brought a smile to Zayn's lips.

They sat in silence for a long time, staring at the battle in the second ward. Eventually, Keelan spoke again.

"I don't want to go back. I don't want this to end," he said.

The weight of his words pulled on Zayn's shoulders. He didn't dare look at his cousin in that moment, because he was afraid he'd see the purple in his eyes.

"I don't either. If I could, I would stay here with you," said Zayn.

Keelan reached out, took his hand, and squeezed it. His fingers were rough and callused.

"Do you remember the time we went into that cave?" asked Keelan.

"Barely got out with our lives," said Zayn, swirling his beer.

"But we learned something important," said Keelan.

The image of Jesse's desiccated body slumped against the wall came back to him.

"Yes, yes we did," said Zayn.

"I'll never forget it and neither should you," said Keelan.

He took back his hand and the silence resumed its earlier intrusion. After a time, Keelan climbed to his feet.

"Goodbye, Zayn. I love you," he said.

Zayn looked up into his cousin's face. He was going to respond that he'd see him in Varna, but he knew what he meant. When Keelan returned, he'd be different. He'd be a Watcher. He'd be the Lady's.

"Goodbye, Keelan. I love you too."

Chapter Twenty-Three

The Spire, May 2018

An answer and a warning

In the final few days of the year, Zayn was summoned to Priyanka's office. He went alone, having access to the secrets and passwords necessary to join her. He found her in a sitting area at the center of the garden. She looked recovered from the injuries in Harmony, but a weight hung on her brow.

"I've been a terrible mentor," said Priyanka.

"Not at all. The lessons I've learned with you are important," he said.

"In spite of me," she said, frowning. "I tried to kill you after all."

"You didn't do a very good job," said Zayn with a smirk.

Priyanka couldn't help but smile. "I can fix that very easily." She looked into her lap. "So do you know what you want to do next? Since I wasn't myself, we haven't talked about the next steps for you."

His heart climbed into his throat. He'd been dreading this

moment because he didn't know which way it'd go. But after the events in Harmony, he wanted to believe that it was the way he hoped.

Zayn met her gaze. "I need to go to Varna for a time."

She stared back without a hint of expression. "I see. How long?"

Zayn rubbed the middle of his palm with his thumb. "A few months."

"I can give you two weeks," she said.

He cringed. He had an idea how he was going to solve the poison puzzle, but it was going to take time to work out the details.

"I need more than that," he said.

"Three then."

"Give me until the first week of July," he said.

"Independence Day?" she asked, the corner of her lip tugging upward.

"That works," he said.

He met her gaze. It felt like she was willing him to ask a question.

"Yes, it is time, you may ask," she said.

A sense of relief flooded in. "What is your relationship with the Lady of Varna?"

Priyanka smoothed away the wrinkles in her shirt as she collected her thoughts. When she looked back, he felt the weight of her years.

"My relationship with the Lady is much like yours, bound by an unbreakable curse, except I joined in mine willingly," she said.

"You knew what she was?" he asked.

Priyanka nodded. "I thought the price was worth what she had to offer. In that time, I'm not sure I would ever make a different decision. But yet, I've been waiting for someone to come along who might break that curse."

Zayn's face went momentarily numb as she acknowledged what he'd hoped all along, that she was truly aligned *against* the Lady.

"I couldn't, of course, show my hand, or her seers would notice and inform her. I have no illusions about the Lady's relationship with the Academy. She would burn it to the ground if she thought I opposed her," said Priyanka.

"Yet, you're telling me now," said Zayn.

"The trick with the comics last year has confused her seers. She is currently blind to the events unfolding around her. By the time she figures it out, it will be too late," said Priyanka.

"That's why you can't give me longer," said Zayn, understanding.

"Yes."

"Can you help me?" he asked.

"The specifics of my curse, which shall remain unexplained, will not allow it. I cannot offer specific or direct help. Not even information. You must figure it all out for yourself. The curse will not allow me otherwise," said Priyanka, crinkling her eyes.

Zayn thought back to his years in the Academy, revising his assessment of many events. She'd provided help, but not obviously. She'd placed many helpful magics in his way that he might acquire them. She'd been on his side the whole time, but the final path would be up to him.

"I see," he said, nodding. "Thank you."

Priyanka stood up. "You should go. If things go well, I'll see you in a few months."

"What will you do until then?" he asked.

"It's probably best that I'm not around for a while, and it happens that I have a lot of work to do in Harmony. Something seems to have happened to the Aerie," she said, raising an eyebrow playfully.

"Yeah, sorry about that."

Priyanka put her hands on his shoulders and though he was taller than her, it felt like she was looking down on him thoughtfully. She cupped the back of his head and pulled his forehead down. She placed her lips there for a kiss.

When she pulled away, Priyanka's eyes glistened.

"Be good. Be safe. And come back to me," she said. "There's a lot of good you and I can do together. And I...I need help. I've lost my way."

Before he could say anything, she turned away, crossing her arms. He placed a hand on her shoulder before walking away.

When he left the garden, he heard a quiet sob.

Chapter Twenty-Four

Enochian District, May 2018

Some goodbyes are worth it

On his last day in Invictus, Zayn went to the Enochian District. It wasn't in preparation for Varna and it wasn't for school. It was something completely for himself. He didn't know when he'd ever get to be selfish again.

He found Aurie near the dragon fountain.

"Zayn," she said softly as she noticed him.

The last time he'd seen her, she was lying motionless in a nearby house. His heart ached with that memory.

"Aurie."

"Congratulations on graduating," she said.

He bit his lower lip. "You know the last time I saw you, you were dead. I didn't learn the truth until I read an article in the *Herald of the Halls* about your win."

"I'm so sorry," she said, stepping close and putting her hand against his chest. It was warm. "I didn't think about that. That you wouldn't know that I was alive."

"It's okay. I deserved it. I was the one that got you mixed up in Priyanka's schemes. It wasn't an accident that you or your sister ended up in a group with Raziyah," he said.

"That's right," said Aurie. "I always wondered how we both ended up in the same one."

"When I saw you and your friends with Ernie, I knew you would be the best hope for him," he said.

"What about Rigel?" she asked.

"He got unlucky," said Zayn.

"Why? Why were you risking yourself? If Priyanka found out she would have killed you," she said.

"She would have," he said. "But for the same reason you were risking yourself. The only thing I didn't know was that Orpheum had hypnotized her. It's a good thing he's dead, or she'd make him die slowly for that."

When she made a face of not understanding, he added, "I talked to Pi earlier. That's how I knew where to find you. She told me everything. Though you two were the first people I thought of when I heard that he'd died. It's the first time a patron has died, well, since Invictus."

"I feel bad for all his students," she said.

"Some of the older mages from his hall, the ones who are hardened against faez, have taken a patronage role, but the number is tiny compared to the whole industry," he said. "They're just not strong enough to keep it going."

"How's Priyanka?" asked Aurie.

"It's a good thing classes are over. She's in a foul mood," he said.

"What's she really like?" asked Aurie.

He gave her a shrug. "I wish I could tell you for sure, but she doesn't really let people get close to her. The only things I do know are that she's brilliant at what she does, and she's a survivor. I want to believe that she's generally good, but she's practical enough to be brutal if she thinks it's important enough. Why do you ask?"

"I don't know. I spent a year hanging out with her. I'd like to believe that some of Raz was real, though I'm not foolish enough to get my hopes up. I also recognize that this whole thing with Invictus dead has to be coming to a head. The Cabal have too many plots and schemes for it not to. So I'm wondering if she's the enemy or not," said Aurie.

"Give her a reason to be on your side and she might be. Might," he said, thinking about what she'd said at the end.

"What about you? What are you doing now that you've graduated?" she asked hopefully.

"I'm headed home," he said. "I have things I have to take care of back there."

"Why? Why can't you stay?" she asked.

"You know when you found me in the closet, half-naked, and I said I was a diabetic? That was a lie, sort of. I have to take regular injections, or I die."

"What? That's terrible. Is that an exotic disease or something?" she asked, brushing her fingertips across his arm.

"Not a disease. Think of it like my blood is poison, and I have to take the antidote to keep it from killing me. It's not exactly like that, but close enough," he said.

"So you see," he said, "I don't know if I'll be back. There's only one place to get the antidote, and that's back home. I was only allowed to come here to get training, and now that it's done..."

"Oh," she said softly.

He stepped forward and grabbed her hands, squeezing them tightly. Before he'd been afraid to show his feelings for her because of Amber's prophecy. But Amber had told him once that if it were thwarted, then it would be broken. Zayn figured that her being killed and brought back by a wish satisfied those rules, so he was free to fall for her.

"What I said on the Spire—" he started, but Aurie cut him off.

"I know. You didn't mean it," she said. "I knew it at the time, though it didn't hurt any less to hear it."

"I really like you," he said. "In ways that, given my circumstances, I shouldn't."

"Vague much?" she taunted.

"Sorry. I wish I could say more," he said.

"You don't need to," she said. "I can see it in your eyes, whenever you mention your home, that you have a lot to deal with. But if you ever need someone to talk to, I'll be here."

She leaned in and kissed him, wrapping her arms around his neck. She tasted like sunshine. They kissed until some passerby whistled at them.

When Aurie pulled away, she looked wobbly.

"When do you have to leave?" she asked.

"Tomorrow morning, early," he said.

"Good."

"Good?" he asked.

"That means you can spend the night with me," she said, grinning.

"Really?" he asked, excited. "Where?"

"Meet me at the usual place."

He nodded hungrily.

"I think there might be a storm tonight," she said.

He looked skeptically at the sky.

"If not, we'll make one," she said, pulling him back in for another kiss.

Zayn returned to her embrace knowing his last night in Invictus would be his best one.

Part II – The Web

Chapter One

Varna, June 2018

An ominous welcome

The kudzu-choked woods surrounding Varna were a dank and unwelcoming place, especially in the summer. Insects crowded the dark spaces, preying on the uncovered flesh while the heat turned even the sturdiest farmer to a jelly-spined porch dweller.

It was no wonder the Lady had chosen a place like Varna, Zayn mused as he zipped through the backroads towards his birthplace. No one would choose to live there of their own free will. The circumstance of birth and the curse of her poison had created a sticky web that no one could escape.

He stayed off the main highway, not wanting to announce his arrival since he and Keelan had left Invictus separately. It wasn't that he thought the Lady wouldn't know. He suspected that little happened in the town without her knowledge, but he wanted a chance to see his family in case she'd figured out that he'd returned to Varna to kill her.

The Yakari motor purred beneath his thighs, bugs smacking against his windshield as he zipped around a semi without a load on a winding turn. Zayn goosed the throttle, thinking about one last burst before he hit the gravel roads that would take him to the Stack, when sirens whirled on from a hidden side road.

Zayn slowed, pulling his bike into the grass. He could have outrun the police car, but it didn't matter. As soon as the officer saw who he was, he'd let him go without a ticket.

When Roy Clovis climbed from the squad car, Zayn knew instantly it wasn't an accident that he'd been pulled over. The one-time star running back had trimmed up. He was a handsome guy.

"Hey, Zayn."

"Hey, Mean," said Zayn with a wink.

"No one's called me that in a long time," said Roy, putting his hands on his hips and letting his sunglasses slip to the end of his nose.

"That's because they're afraid of you, or your dad," said Zayn.

"Everyone but you," said Roy, letting a big grin fill up his face.

The big man leaned over and they shared a hug.

"That uniform looks good on you," said Zayn.

"Thanks. It's good to have you back," said Roy. "You staying long?"

"No," said Zayn. "Maybe a few weeks to see the family. Then I'm headed out."

"Academy business?"

Zayn nodded.

In the silence after, Roy danced back and forth, glancing down the road a few times but saying nothing.

"I take it this isn't a chance meeting," said Zayn.

Roy moved closer and spoke under his breath. “You probably shouldn’t have come back. Things aren’t going well around here.”

Zayn’s stomach clenched. He hadn’t heard anything from his family about problems, but maybe they hadn’t wanted to worry him.

“How so?”

“She’s been acting all erratic. People have gone missing, and when we ask about it, we’re told to mind our own business,” said Roy.

“Missing? Like who?”

“At least a dozen, maybe more since no one’s talking anymore. People like Dale Barker, that old cotton farmer who lived up near the sewage treatment plant. Bubba Freeman, the janitor at the high school. Ms. Gardenia from the trailer park.”

“Ms. Gardenia,” said Zayn, heat rising to his face. “Why are they disappearing? Any common thread?”

“They’ve been outspoken against the Lady,” said Roy, glancing up the road again.

“Outspoken? Sure, they flap their gums, but none of them would hurt a fly. What gives?” asked Zayn.

“Everything went south last year. Everyone was always allowed to privately complain, as long as they didn’t cause a fuss. Now people are disappearing left and right. A lot of people are pointing to some comic. Have you seen it? The likeness to Varna and the Lady is uncanny,” said Roy, looking like he was nauseous.

“Nev showed it to me,” said Zayn, feeling a pit in his stomach. He hadn’t thought about how the comic would affect the people in town. He’d wanted it as cover and now she was lashing out at anyone who’d ever expressed an opinion against her.

“Hey, speaking of your sister...”

"No, I don't know when she's going to make tacos again," he said.

Roy blushed. "Not that. I was wondering if she had a boyfriend. I wanted to ask her out."

"Not that I know of," said Zayn with a smile. "But I'll put in a good word for you."

Roy held his hands up. "Don't say anything."

"I won't. But I'll make sure and find a reason to say some nice things about you in her presence," said Zayn.

"Thanks, Zayn," said Roy, putting his hand on his shoulder.

"So what's the real reason you stopped me? I know it wasn't about the disappearing people or a date with my sister," said Zayn.

Roy gave the road, both directions, and the woods a long look before answering. When he spoke it was so low that Zayn had to use his imbuement to hear.

"I've been thinking a long time about why you went to the Academy under all that secrecy. You don't have to tell me if I'm right, but I think I know the reason. You mean to fix things in Varna."

A chill went through Zayn. While the Lady had long ago figured out what he'd been planning to do, and put his loyalty to the test, the comic and her paranoia had probably put him back on her radar.

"You haven't said anything to anyone, have you? About what happened on Ceremony night?" asked Zayn.

"No," said Roy, shaking his head vehemently. "Who would believe it anyway? Everyone thought we were mortal enemies. Hell, they probably still think that."

"Good," said Zayn with a wink. "We should keep it that way, at least for now."

"Anyway," said Roy, stepping back and hooking his

thumbs in his belt. "I thought you should know about what's going down in Varna."

Zayn shared a fist bump with Roy before starting the Yakari back up.

As the deputy backed to his squad car, he yelled, "Don't forget to put in a good word!"

With the news weighing on his mind, Zayn rode the final miles to the Stack. The whole family poured from the courtyard the moment he arrived. He barely had his helmet off before they swarmed him.

Imani reached him first. She was as tall as him sitting on the bike. Her hair was bound in cornrows.

She threw her arms around him. "Zayn! You're home!"

"And you're so tall. Have you been drinking growth potions while I was gone?"

"Mom says I grew four inches this year. She's teaching me algebra. I think I'm going to join the Academy like you when I get older," Imani said breathlessly.

"Whoa there, little lion. Not all at once," he said. "I'm barely getting used to you being so tall. Let's not talk about joining the Academy."

"What's this about my baby joining the Academy?" asked his mom as she approached.

"Nothing," said Zayn, right when Imani said, "I want to join, like Zayn."

Sela put her arms around his shoulders and rocked him with a hug. "Can't you at least give me a chance to enjoy you being home before we start talking about another child in that place?"

"It wasn't so bad," said Zayn, picking her up and spinning her around.

Maceo came up next. "You didn't have to convince her not to drive to Invictus to check on you at odd hours of the night."

"I had premonitions," said Sela, a hand on her chest defensively.

The twins came up next. They wore baggy jeans and oversized T-shirts with painted handprints scattered across the white fabric. One of them had shaved their head to stubble while the other had a short faux hawk. It took him a moment to figure out who was Izzy and who was Max.

"We're working on a performance art piece," said the head-shaven Izzy.

"It's a commentary on the role of magic in the indigenous communities of our country," said Max.

"Sounds awesome, when do I get to see it?" asked Zayn.

"We could do it tonight," they said in unison.

Sela stepped in front of them. "Let's let him relax first before we inundate him."

"How come I didn't get this reception when I got back from Invictus last year?" asked Neveah, hand on her hip.

"Because we thought you were in Atlanta," said Maceo. "And we only get a few weeks with Zayn before he leaves again."

"Love you, Nev," said Zayn, grinning.

"Love you, big brother," said Neveah with her tongue stuck out playfully.

They dragged him back to the courtyard. Sela brought out a tray of summer fruit with flavors that exploded on his tongue. The twins pestered him about his job with Priyanka. The fact that no job existed yet made it easy to deflect.

A few times he caught his parents looking at him strangely, as if they wanted to ask a question, but it appeared they didn't want to spoil the mood.

After a dinner of roast lamb, carrots, and potatoes, Neveah brought a graduation cake from the kitchen. It was in the shape of the Academy badge: a raven with an olive branch in its beak. Zayn's eyes rolled in the back of his head at the first bite.

"It's chocolate, chocolate, my favorite. Thanks, Nev," said Zayn.

Sela cleared her throat. "Ahem. You mean, thanks Mom. Your sister doesn't do all the cooking, and I wasn't going to miss out on making your graduation cake."

"Oops," said Zayn with a grin, wiping an errant hunk of chocolate icing from his chin. "At least we know where Nev got her mad skills from."

Sela squinted. "Nice save. I guess they did teach you a thing or two about diplomacy."

The evening devolved into a philosophical discussion about the nature of free will. His father took the position that since everything could be described with physics, it therefore became an infinite chain of cause and effect, which meant that people lacked free will. The twins, in a skillful response that bounced between them like a ping pong ball, suggested that quantum mechanics added enough variation into physics that it gave people free will.

A few times, they tried to drag him into the conversation, but Zayn was content to listen. He didn't know how many more of these dinners he would enjoy, so he wanted to imprint it into his memory.

When everyone else but Neveah went into the kitchen to clean up, Zayn asked his sister. "What's with the weird looks from Mom and Dad all night? You didn't tell them anything, did you?"

"No way," said Neveah. "But sometimes I think they've figured it out."

"That's not good," said Zayn, looking into the darkness. "Roy Clovis stopped me on the way into town with a similar story."

"Roy?" asked Neveah with a rosy cheeked smile. "I didn't

know you two were friends."

"On the down low," said Zayn. "We helped each other out in high school a few times."

"So you *weren't* mortal enemies?" asked Neveah.

"Yes, but eventually no," said Zayn. "It's a long story that has to do with the Goon."

"He's really grown up," said Neveah, fanning herself.

"He asked about you," said Zayn.

"He did?" said Neveah with a hint of breathlessness.

"I told him you hated his guts though," said Zayn with a shrug.

Neveah threw her napkin at him. "You didn't!"

Zayn broke out in laughter. "No, I didn't. I'm just messing with you. But he wants to ask you out." He remembered what he told Roy. "But don't tell him I told you. I was supposed to keep it a secret."

Neveah opened her mouth to ask a question when Sela came in with a dishrag in her hands and a furrowed brow. "Buford Ash is outside."

"Buford Ash? What's he doing here?" asked Neveah. "I thought he worked at the Gardens."

"He does, or did anyway," said Zayn, puzzled by the appearance. "I'll go talk to him."

When he went outside, Buford was standing next to the security golf cart that he used for driving around the Gardens. Buford was hopping from one foot to the other like his shoes were on fire.

"Buford, hey, what an unexpected surprise," said Zayn.

"Oh, hey Zayn. Congrats on graduating. That's super big," said Buford, who didn't know what to do with his hands. "This is the first time I've seen the Stack. Super cool. I really had no idea how awesome it would be."

"Thanks, I'll tell my parents. Is there anything I can do for you? Seems like a long way to drive the subdivision cart," said Zayn, approaching cautiously.

"It is? Oh yeah," said Buford, reaching into his back pocket, which made Zayn twitch until he saw the envelope. "Keelan wanted you to have this. Said he was supposed to deliver it himself, but he wasn't feeling well."

"Was he wearing Watcher shades?" asked Zayn.

Buford looked away and blinked. "Yeah, I guess he was."

He'd probably been told to deliver the letter, but hadn't wanted the whole family to see his purple eyes when his Aunt Sela told him to take them off at dinner. Zayn opened the envelope and pulled out an invitation:

Come Celebrate!
In celebration of our newest Academy graduates
June 12th, 2018
7 pm
#1 Plantation Way

This invitation entitles you to a plus one.

"What is it?" asked Buford, leaning forward.

"A party," said Zayn.

"For what?"

"For me and Keelan. For graduating," said Zayn.

"Wow, that's awesome," said Buford, eyes wide with wonder.

"I guess so," said Zayn with a sinking feeling in his gut.

Chapter Two

Varna, June 2018

A night to rub elbows and avoid webs

The night of the party came quickly. Zayn spent his days sleeping and his nights working in the old trailer at Doc's junkyard. He didn't even tell Doc, since the old man wasn't getting around as well as he used to. He was using a cane and stopped frequently to catch his breath.

In the trailer, Zayn put up blackout paper so no one could see the light he used to read by. Each night when he was finished working, he put everything into his backpack and hid it in the ceiling of the trailer.

He wore the bracelet Keelan had made him at all times, hoping that would keep the Lady from scrying him while he planned her demise.

But on the night of the party, he left it at the Stack. He wanted no outward appearances that he was anything but her loyal subject. Until this point, the only thing that had kept her from killing him was his work for Priyanka, but even that wouldn't save him if the Lady thought he had resumed his plans.

Which made the party a huge risk, one that he couldn't avoid. In previous years, he couldn't recall a special party for the graduates, though he supposed it could have happened without his knowledge. Even though Zayn worked for the Goon, his employer had never shared the inner workings of the town.

Zayn arrived at the plantation in tailored pants and a suitcoat over a black shirt. He'd never been one for ties, and he'd never lacked compliments for his outfits. He'd borrowed Doc's beater truck for the ride since the gravel roads from the Stack would have made a mess of his black clothing had he ridden his Yakari.

The Watcher at the door took his invitation, asking, "No plus one?"

"My last girlfriend died," said Zayn, deadpan.

He chuckled to himself as he left the Watcher stunned at the front door. The normally stoic guardian clearly hadn't known how to react to the news, and had it not been for Ernie, it might have been truly tragic.

When Zayn walked in, a round of spontaneous applause broke out, leaving him to blush and raise a hand in acknowledgement. The attention brought a rush of endorphins that reminded him of the feeling he got in the middle of a good fight.

The Speaker with her coifed blonde hair and white pantsuit swept in, handing him a flute of champagne. Zayn spied his cousin on the far side of the Grand Room chatting with the mayor.

"Congratulations, Zayn Carter," said the Speaker. "It is quite an accomplishment to survive the Academy with such honors. You and your cousin will be a tough duo to top."

Zayn had to remind himself that despite his revulsion for

the Speaker, he was here for a party in his honor and he needed to be congenial.

"Thank you," said Zayn, bowing his head. "I have the Lady to thank. Her gift gave us more range and stamina than the rest of the class."

He glanced around at the tuxedos and formal dresses. The Speaker caught his eye.

"You're the guest of honor. You get to wear whatever you want tonight. Besides, I imagine you'll start a trend after this. You look smashing," said the Speaker with an appraising look.

"Uhm, thank you," he said, a little taken aback. Zayn took a sip from the champagne to hide his discomfort, but not too much as he wanted to keep his wits.

The Speaker put out her arm. "I want to take you around and introduce you to some people. While it is my understanding that you'll be working for Priyanka, it's good to know the right people in town for when you decide to retire from your patron's service."

Zayn noted that it was a given he would have to return to Varna, signaling that he was merely on loan to Priyanka, not a full participant in his own life.

But Zayn played the part of the gracious guest. The party came with benefits. It gave him a lay of the land on who supported the Lady and remained in her favor. Zayn noted a few prominent citizens that were missing like the Chawala sisters who held charity balls at the high school, and David Boss, who owned the hardware store and made a point of being very pro-Varna in all his advertisements. He suspected that like him, their outward support had been only that—outward.

He nodded and smiled at all the right moments, staying on the Speaker's arm the whole time as if he were a corsage. Years of training with Instructor Pennywhistle had prepared him for this moment. Zayn found himself reflexively matching the deepness of their Alabama accent as he spoke.

He got so used to doing it, he forgot the Speaker was there the whole time until she spoke about it later in the introductions.

"You are quite the polished gem, now aren't you?" asked the Speaker.

"It's hard to turn off," said Zayn, giving her a wink.

"I'm sure it is." She winked back. "If you weren't, well, if you weren't much younger than me..."

"I'm flattered," he said with a pleasant smile, mentally calculating how much longer he needed to stay at the party so he didn't look rude when he left.

When the Speaker's gaze flicked to the left without acknowledging who was approaching, Zayn knew that the Lady of Varna was behind him. It wasn't hard to guess by the way the others in the area had reduced the volume of their voices.

"Good evening, Lady Arcadia," said Zayn before he turned around and greeted her with a deep bow. "It is a pleasure to see you again."

"I doubt it," she said, regarding him carefully as if he were a dangerous animal behind a short fence. "You have learned to wield a velvet tongue, I see."

She wore a lavender gown that accented her eyes.

"No games, Lady Arcadia. I am thankful for the party in my honor," he said, looking up into her stern face. "I realize that my history suggests otherwise, but I have accepted the bargain completely. The work with Priyanka is too important to be sidetracked by petty and shortsighted views of the world we live in."

Lady Arcadia gestured towards an open door leading to the gardens behind the plantation.

"Shall we."

"My pleasure," he replied, noting she didn't offer her arm

like the Speaker had.

The waning moon provided silvery light for their walk, though Zayn didn't need it. He suspected that the Lady didn't either.

"Thank you again for letting my sister pursue her passions in the food truck," said Zayn.

Lady Arcadia looked down on him as if she was deciding how to interpret his statement.

"I do not understand how forcing yourself to live in a tiny box, living in your own cooking grease, and serving food to the random denizens of the outer world can be a favorable thing, but I will take your word for it that she enjoyed the experience. I'm pleased that we can come to an agreement on our relationship."

The Lady paused.

"But please do not mistake my message. I will kill you and your family if I even think you'll betray me. I cannot have dissent."

"I understand," he said.

Lady Arcadia turned on him. Her mouth was a slash across her face. "I don't think you do. It will not be a pleasant death. Not for you, or your parents, or your sister Imani. I will flay them alive if you so much as think improper thoughts about me."

Zayn said nothing, but matched her gaze. After a long, uncomfortable moment, the Lady continued down the path. He'd heard the fear in her voice, which surprised and worried him. Paranoia would bring additional defenses to overcome. His plan was tenuous under the best circumstances. He'd have to rethink it before the fourth.

"How does Priyanka plan to use you? Has she told you that much?" asked the Lady, her earlier severe tone softened.

"No," he said. "But she was preoccupied when we talked

last. She said I would find out when I returned."

"Preoccupied? Has there been a problem?" she asked.

Zayn saw no harm in explaining the current environment in Invictus. The Lady probably already knew about it anyway.

"Frank Orpheum used her, and she wasn't happy about it," said Zayn.

"Did she kill him? Slowly?" she asked.

"No, a group of students did that, but she would have if they hadn't," he said.

"I see."

"May I ask a question about you and Priyanka? For curiosity's sake," said Zayn.

"You may, but I cannot guarantee that I will answer, or that I won't judge your question," said the Lady.

Zayn nodded. "Fair enough. I wondered how long you've known her."

"What relevance does this information have?" asked the Lady.

He heard the warning in her voice and knew he was treading on dangerous territory, but he needed the Lady to think he was above suspicion. He knew that wasn't completely possible, but if he could at least make it seem plausible, it would be worth the risk. His fate, and the fate of the town, required it.

"To understand the sense of history," said Zayn. "One of the things I enjoyed about the Academy was that it's an original hall and that Priyanka is an original patron. It's, well, cool to be a part of that. That she knew Invictus sort of blows my mind."

"He was not a person whose company I enjoyed," said the Lady coolly.

"I've heard he was an asshole," said Zayn.

The Lady made a polite noise. "That would be an understatement. He believed himself above everyone else. That he was smarter than them. I will not miss him."

Zayn wanted to press it further when she stopped abruptly. The Lady regarded him with half-lidded eyes.

"I'm afraid I must leave you now. Feel free to return to the party and enjoy yourself," said the Lady.

Zayn made a polite bow. "Thank you, Lady Arcadia."

When he turned his back to her, he resisted the urge to run. Part of him was convinced that she was going to leap on his back and suck the marrow from his bones.

Zayn found Keelan when he returned from his walk with the Lady.

"Hey," said Keelan.

Purple colored the edge of his irises.

"Hey, cuz," replied Zayn. "Great party."

Keelan nodded. "I wish Jesse was here to see me. He'd be real proud."

Zayn was real glad he was taking a sip from the champagne glass because he was able to hide his reaction. Jesse was the last person Keelan would want to be there. While he'd made his peace with his death, he certainly wanted no part of his father.

"He would," said Zayn, eyeing Keelan for a clue to the comment.

Keelan held out his champagne glass. "Even though we're only cousins, you've always been like a brother to me. Thank you, Zayn."

Zayn couldn't tell where he was going with his comments, so he nodded and took another sip.

Keelan gestured towards the party with his glass. "Did you know a lot of people here are cousins? I found out we're related to Phil Greenwood. Second cousins twice removed or something like that."

"That's interesting," said Zayn.

"Anyway," said Keelan, glancing towards the mayor. "I need to get back. See you around."

"See you," said Zayn, forcibly hiding his puzzlement. He was painfully aware that Keelan had left off the "cuz" endearment that he'd been using for most of their lives.

But what was he trying to convey?

Zayn couldn't make heads or tails of it, except that he was reminding them they were still family. Maybe he felt guilty about becoming a Watcher and not being there for the party at the Stack.

Zayn left the party through the front door. He gave the place a backwards glance as he climbed into the beater truck that Doc had loaned him. If everything went as planned, he'd be back in a few weeks.

Chapter Three

Varna, June 2018

Prep time

The food truck was parked behind the Stack on its own bed of gravel. Flowers had been planted around the space. It was already colorful with the painting of Neveah on the side as the Tacowitch.

Zayn rapped his knuckles on the back door before heading inside. Neveah sat on the foldout cot, red headband holding back her beaded hair, polishing a beaker with a rag. The space had a clean, antiseptic smell.

"I don't know how you keep this place smelling so nice," said Zayn.

"I'm not above a little elbow grease," said Neveah, setting the beaker on the table next to a row of glassware and grabbing another.

"Elbow, I get, but this has to take the whole arm, shoulder, and back," he said.

Neveah's lips were pursed together. She glanced towards

the metal window even though it was closed.

Sensing her concern, Zayn lifted his arm. "I'm warded from scrying. We're safe to talk."

"Are you sure?"

Zayn was about to tell her that Keelan had made it but thought better of it. He was a Watcher now. Anything he did was suspect, and she wouldn't understand that he'd made it for a different purpose.

"We're good. I've tested it," he said.

Neveah rested her hands holding the rag and beaker in her lap. "Are you really going to go through with it?"

"Killing the Lady? I am," he said.

She jawed at the air for a moment before speaking. "Since you've been back, I keep expecting a horde of her Watchers to come rushing into the Stack to take us away to the plantation. I'm scared."

"Do you want me not to do it?" he asked.

Her lips pinched together. "No. I mean, yes, I think you should do it. *If* you have a solution for her and the poison." She shook her head as if she were in pain. "If it were just you and me, and Mom and Dad, it'd be easier. But I worry about the little ones."

"They're not so little anymore," said Zayn.

"The twins are sixteen and Imani is eleven," said Neveah, exasperated. "If they get hurt, if they..."

Neveah stared into the distance with her fist against her mouth.

"I know, Nev, I know. I've been over the risks time and time again. There's always a risk to standing up, of calling out what's right and wrong. There's no easy way to end this. She has everything on her side—the town, the rules, the Watchers, her poison. There are probably things I'm not even aware of protecting her."

Zayn balled his hands into fists, squeezing them as if he were trying to turn coal into diamonds. "But to let her continue like this, keeping the town hostage, keeping us hostage. You should know better now that you've seen the outside world, how much promise there is in freedom. We can't live like this, chained to the Lady for all our days."

When Neveah spoke next, she whispered. "I understand, I really do. And I agree. But I'm still new to these thoughts, the dangers. I'm just worried is all."

"Worried, scared. That's to be expected. If I fail she'll kill us all," said Zayn.

"It's not the killing that worries me," said Neveah, voice low and heavy, "but what happens before that."

"Then be prepared for that possibility," he said, glancing towards her alchemy equipment.

Neveah bit her lower lip before she nodded.

"What else do you need?" she asked.

"Knockout potions, a bunch of them," he said. "Can you do that?"

Neveah reached out and patted the slim tome that Celesse had given her. "I can, but who are they for? I need to know so I can calibrate the recipe."

"The Lady," said Zayn, and when Neveah wrinkled her forehead, he continued. "It's how I plan to circumvent the poison problem. I can't kill her, or the town will die, but if I turned the tables, kept her a prisoner to me, then we could keep everyone in town alive and end the practice of infecting the newborns."

"How are you going to do that? The Lady is a powerful creature, that much I know," she said.

Zayn tapped on his ribs where his fourth imbuement was tattooed. "She's not the only one."

"How many do you need?" she asked.

"Enough to keep her knocked out for a week. You should be able to get more reagents in that time for more, and if I fail then you won't need any at all," he said.

Neveah had taken out a pad of paper and was busily sketching notes.

She tapped the pen on her lips as she looked at him. "I have a few other potions I'll brew for you. You're going to need any advantage you can get."

"Don't I know it," said Zayn, thinking about the Watchers that guarded her. Those were members of the Academy of the Subtle Arts, trained by Priyanka and her instructors. He was going against the best of the best.

"I need a favor from you too, big brother," she said.

"Big brother? I sense an arduous favor brewing," he said.

Neveah batted her eyes. "Who me? I'm feeling quite shamed here."

"What is it, little sister?" he asked, a grin cocked on his lips.

"Roy asked me out on a date," said Neveah, blushing.

"I told you he would," he said. "Do you need help picking an outfit? Skylar taught me a thing or two about fashion."

Her mouth gaped open while she looked down her nose at him. "Really, Zayn?"

"I'm just sayin'," he said, scratching the back of his head.

"I want you to come with me," she said.

"On the date?" he asked, incredulous.

"Yeah," said Neveah, "I know it sounds weird. Roy and I have tried to talk before, but I think we both get so nervous that we clam up. We were both hoping you could come along. Then it wouldn't feel so much like a date and we could just learn to talk."

"I have a lot going on," said Zayn.

"Zayn," said Neveah, gritting her teeth. "Please. This

might be my one and only chance to have a date, before, well, before everything changes. Give me this. Please. Me and Roy like each other but we're terrible at this dating thing."

He was going to make a crack at his sister's expense, but saw the way she held herself. He recognized his relationship with Aurie in her expression. It was that feeling that you didn't trust yourself around the other person, as if they'd unlocked your soul. It was a scary thought to feel so helpless, yet exhilarated by the possibilities.

"I will," said Zayn. "I'll even be on my best behavior. I like Roy. I think you guys will make a good couple."

"Thank you, Zayn."

Zayn leaned over and kissed her on the forehead. "Love you."

Chapter Four

Varna, June 2018

A third wheel is important too

On the night of the date, Zayn drove his sister into town in Doc's truck. To his surprise, she wore a dress, the first time he'd seen her in one since Uncle Jesse's funeral. She'd replaced her red handkerchief with a colorful print.

The whole ride into town Neveah was bouncing her knees and staring out the window.

"We're just getting together for drinks at Bob's Bar," said Zayn.

"I know," said Neveah, but when she looked at him, he saw the vulnerability in her gaze. His sister was a strong woman with her own idea of how she wanted to exist in the world. Seeing her raw and exposed like she was ensured that he'd do everything in his power to make sure their date went off without a hitch.

When they arrived at the bar, Roy was seated in the back corner, wearing jeans and a sport coat over a button-down. He stood when they approached, his eyes never leaving Neveah's once.

"Hey, Roy," said Zayn, sharing a handshake and a hug.

"Hey...Zayn," said Roy, clearly distracted.

Neveah leaned up and gave Roy a peck on the cheek. It looked like it might have fried his brain by the way he stared into space.

They crowded into the booth, Roy on one side, Zayn and Neveah on the other. The two of them sat with their hands in their laps, staring at the table with occasional furtive glances at each other.

Oh, boy, they really do need help, thought Zayn.

"So how's your dad doing? Being sheriff was a lifelong dream for him," said Zayn.

Looking startled out of a coma, Roy said, "Uhm, yeah. He loves it. Though it's been stressful lately." He glanced askew, their earlier conversation serving as the explanation. "But he's surviving."

"Do you live in the Gardens?" asked Zayn.

Neveah spoke up for Roy. "No, they live in their old neighborhood. His dad turned down the Lady's offer."

Zayn looked to his sister. "And how would you know this since you two don't talk?"

They both blushed. "We've been writing letters."

"People still do that?" asked Zayn.

Neveah punched him in the leg beneath the table.

"I'm not making fun. I just didn't think about it. What with magic and technology," said Zayn.

"I don't know," said Roy with a lift of his shoulder. "It's been nice, receiving letters from your sister. I rush to the mailbox every day. I can't wait for the next one. Neveah puts a little of her perfume on each paper."

They shared a grin. Seeing an opportunity, Zayn asked,

"What have you been talking about?"

Neveah tapped nervously on the table. "You know, just, whatever we're thinking at the time, what we'd do if we weren't in Varna."

"I've never been farther than Selma," said Roy, looking exasperated. "But what Nev tells me about her trip to Invictus, I'd really want to see that. The second ward nightly illusionary battles, a concert at the Glitterdome, hell, anything really. It sounds like an amazing place."

"It really was," said Neveah, "even though I saw most of it through the window of the food truck. Did I ever tell you about the ravelles?"

Roy tilted his head. "No, I don't think you did."

"Oh my god, there were these creatures, like something crossed between a squirrel and a raven," said Neveah, hands held expressively before her.

Sensing the ice broken, Zayn stood up. "I'm going to grab us some drinks at the bar. I know this story, so you keep telling."

Neveah resumed her story. The two of them leaned forward, enraptured by each other's presence. Zayn had thought that it would take time to get them to talk, but he was worried no longer. He would stay at the bar for a short time, but find an excuse to leave, forcing Roy to take her home, or wherever they wanted to go.

Zayn stood at the bar, waiting to get the bartender's attention when he heard a familiar voice at the other end.

"...goddamned Lady don't care shit for us..."

Every hair on Zayn's body stood at attention when he heard the words. He quickly surveyed the room, finding Buford Ash sitting at the far end of the bar, an empty mug of beer in his fist, head lolling.

The patrons near Buford moved away as if they thought

he was contagious. Zayn checked the bar to see if anyone had heard him. A couple of Watchers were on the other side, sitting quietly at a table while sharing a plate of ribs.

Before Buford could speak again, Zayn rushed to his side and put a hand on his arm.

"Buford, hey man, how are you?" asked Zayn.

His security guard uniform was disheveled, the top three buttons undone with beer and BBQ stains. Buford tried to focus his eyes, but he was drooping on the stool.

"Zayn?"

"Yeah, it's me," said Zayn, pulling the mug from Buford's hands. "You've probably had enough to drink tonight."

"I have had enough," said Buford, raising his voice. "Damn Lady's taken everything from me."

He tried to put his hand over Buford's mouth, but he'd shouted it before Zayn could stop him.

"Quiet," hissed Zayn. "Are you crazy? You're going to get yourself killed."

"Why does it matter?" asked Buford with sad, puppy dog eyes. "She took my sister. She's the kindergarten teacher. Carol Anne ain't done nothing to nobody."

Carol Anne had graduated five years before them, but she had a reputation for being a sweet lady who would do anything for her kids.

"If she didn't do anything, then I'm sure she'll be okay," said Zayn, who didn't believe it, but he needed Buford to so he didn't get himself in trouble. The Watchers hadn't moved, but they were clearly paying attention.

"Are you on their side?" asked Buford, lip curled with disgust. "You are? They had a damn party in your honor, fucking Lady."

Zayn half got his hand over Buford's mouth, although he fought against him. He hooked his arm under Buford's shoulder, prepared to drag him from the bar and take him to his home to put him to bed, when he found the two Watchers behind him.

"He's drunk," said Zayn, holding Buford up while keeping his hand over his mouth. "I'll make sure he gets home safe."

The sunglassed Watchers stared back stoically.

"We'll take care of him," said the first Watcher.

The way he said it sent chills through Zayn. "It's okay, guys. He's an idiot who drank too much. I can take care of it."

"No," said the Watcher. "He's not an idiot. He speaks his mind and the Lady has made it clear that dissent will not be tolerated. We'll take him from here. Thank you and step aside."

"I will not step aside," said Zayn.

The silence, which had already been balanced on a knife's edge, filled with chairs shifting away from tables as customers fled the bar.

"This is an unwise decision, Zayn Carter," said the second Watcher, taking a step forward.

"He's no harm to you or the Lady," said Zayn. "And it's not dissent. He's a drunk without a filter for his mouth."

"We'll be the judge of that," said the first Watcher. "And despite your reputation, I don't think you can take the two of us."

"I'm not here to fight," said Zayn. "I'm only here to get my friend home. To his bed."

"So this traitor is your friend?" asked the first Watcher.

"He's not a traitor," said Zayn forcefully. "And you're not taking him."

"You can't stop us," said the Watcher.

"Try me," said Zayn.

"You'll have to go through me too," said Roy, standing behind him, revealing the gun he was wearing beneath his sport coat. Neveah was next to him with her arms crossed.

"Just let me take him home," said Zayn, wishing Roy and his sister hadn't gotten involved, "and we can all go back to living in Varna. Peaceably."

"The Lady will hear about this," said the first Watcher.

"I'm not concerned. She knows I'm on her side, but I think she had a couple of overzealous Watchers on her side that I would be happy to make an example of. You can learn firsthand whether or not my reputation is true," said Zayn.

The two Watchers shared a glance before walking from the now empty bar.

As soon as they were gone, Zayn turned on Neveah and Roy. "You shouldn't have gotten involved. I have a certain amount of immunity. You don't."

"You needed backup," said Roy.

"I need my sister and her boyfriend to be safe," said Zayn.

The pair of them looked sheepish, but they took each other's hand.

"You want me to take care of Buford?" asked Roy.

"No," said Zayn, "you two go enjoy yourself. I'll take him home. Stay with him to make sure he's safe."

Roy and Neveah left holding hands. Zayn threw some money onto the bar for the owner, who was nowhere to be found. Buford was nearly asleep on his feet, so he walked him out to Doc's truck. Buford was snoring before he'd put the truck in drive.

The fourth couldn't come fast enough. It was a week away. Zayn hadn't meant to cause trouble, but he couldn't stand there and let them take Buford away, knowing that he would die in a hole.

The whole way back to Buford's place, Zayn couldn't help but worry that things weren't going to work out. The Lady had too much on her side. She held too many advantages. And now because of Buford's drunken mouth, he might not even have his element of surprise anymore.

He thought about moving up his attack so there would be less time for the repercussions of the events at the bar, but he didn't know how to do that without upsetting his plans.

Another week, he thought. *I just have to survive another week.*

Chapter Five

Varna, July 2018

The first part is always the easiest

Morning came early on the fourth for Zayn, who woke in the solemn time after the insects had halted their nightly dirge and before the sun crested the horizon. He climbed from his window and sat on the top of the Stack, looking across the woods.

It might be the last time he'd see a morning, he realized. Zayn stared at his hands. Was he ready to die? He didn't want to, but he knew that death was a strong possibility.

What he didn't have was regrets. Since the day he'd made the promise that he would end the Lady of Varna, he'd dedicated himself to the task. When he'd first conceived it, a large part of him thought it impossible, but now on the morning of that fateful day, he knew that if everything went right, he could finish what he'd started.

He remembered how impossible it'd seemed at the beginning. But it wasn't that it was impossible. It had been a task too large for his mind to comprehend at the time. Humans were flawed calculation machines with limited capacity. Impossibility was just a lack of imagination, but item by item, he'd conquered it.

Sometimes believing was enough to make it possible. Zayn saw why Invictus mused about supposedly impossible magics. They were only impossible because no one had done them before. The technology and magic of civilization—cellphones, ghost taxis, manned ships that had visited the moon and returned—were once considered beyond the realms of men, and now they were common place.

Zayn sensed stirring in the food truck, so he climbed down from the Stack. Neveah was sitting on the cot, bleary eyed with a mug of coffee in her hands.

"It took all night but I finished the knockout potions," said Neveah, nodding towards the row of vials on the table.

"Will they work?" he asked.

Neveah lifted one shoulder. "One drop will knock out an adult rhino. As for the Lady, who knows? It's not like we even really know what she is."

"She's ancient, that much is sure," he said.

"How old do you think she is?" asked Neveah.

Zayn thought back to the first time he'd met her when he had a vision of the Lady on a ziggurat with thousands of worshipers bent at the knees.

"A few thousand years, at least," said Zayn.

Neveah made a low whistle.

"Then you'd better give her a full dose," said Neveah. "How do you plan on administering the potion? It's not like she'll just drink it if you ask."

Zayn snorted. "That's exactly what I'm going to do."

Neveah wrinkled her face.

"Don't worry. I have a plan. Academy secrets." Zayn

paused. “But I’m going to need you to do one more thing for me.”

“Anything,” said Neveah.

“I’m going to make my move tonight during the fireworks celebration at the plantation. When I do, I want you to get the family out of here. Leave Varna. Grab Doc and Aunt Lydia too. Take them somewhere I don’t know about, because if I’m alive, I will tell her,” said Zayn.

“I see,” said Neveah. “What about the poison? We won’t last long without it.”

Zayn handed her a piece of paper with an address. “There’s a large store of poison here. It’s from the Goon. It’s enough to last you a couple of years. Maybe you can brew an antidote by that time, or at least everyone can see the world before the end.”

“Let’s hope we don’t need it,” said Neveah.

“Don’t forget to prepare a potion to drink in case you’re going to be caught. Nothing can happen to the twins or Imani. They’re too young, but that won’t stop the Lady. She’s made that clear enough,” said Zayn.

Neveah’s eyes grew watery. “I’ll brew them. But I don’t want to have to use them. I can’t imagine telling them to drink such a thing.”

Zayn held his sister’s shoulders, stared her directly in the eyes. “Think about what the Lady would do to them. Think about that when you’re brewing and if we get to that moment.”

Neveah shook her head and looked away. “I don’t know why it got so real right now.”

“Because we’ve grown up with the danger.” He checked the time, the sun would be rising soon. “I have to go. I’ve got a few more errands today.”

Before he left, they embraced, staying in a hug for a few minutes.

When he climbed into Doc's truck, a surprise tear streaked down his cheek. He quickly wiped it away. He didn't have time for that.

Zayn arrived at Miner Explosions and Fireworks right when the owner was opening up the building, which was in the next town over. Varna didn't have a fireworks vendor. It was the rare exception that a non-Varna member was allowed in the town.

Zayn had changed into a suit like the Watchers' and wore a pair of sunglasses. He also had a satchel over his shoulder.

The owner, Gregg Morrow, flinched when he strolled up. Clearly the owner understood the danger presented by the Lady. Zayn imagined that they'd threatened him early on to ensure his silence, and since he lived in the next town over, he'd probably heard the rumors about Varna.

"Good morning," said Gregg with a forced smile. "Last-second check on the festivities?"

Zayn modulated his tone. "There need to be a few changes."

"Changes? No problem. You're the customer," said Gregg, holding the door open for Zayn.

When they stepped inside and Gregg had his back to him, Zayn placed an enchantment on him that would make him more susceptible to hypnosis.

"You've had a long night, haven't you? You're feeling rather sleepy," said Zayn.

Gregg sat in his drafting chair before a map of the plantation grounds that showed the plans for the fireworks display.

"It was a long night. I never sleep well before this event," said Gregg, his eyes growing heavier.

Zayn continued with the spell until Gregg was under. Then he opened up his satchel and handed over the items inside with explanations on how they would be used.

He might have been able to get away with not hypnotizing Gregg, and relying on his fear of the Lady and her Watchers to ensure his compliance, but he didn't want to take a chance, and he didn't want Gregg to mention the additions to the show.

Zayn left before Gregg's other employees showed up. The changes would go easier if they thought they came straight from the boss.

He didn't go to the Stack afterwards. As much as he wanted to see his family again, he drove to the Goon's old place. The building had been boarded up years ago. Zayn had no intention of going in, but it was in a region that few people drove past, so it provided a good spot to wait out the day.

Vines had grown up around the building, turning it into a green box. The yard, which had once been meticulously kept so the Goon could see anyone sneaking onto his property, was covered in waist-high weeds.

Zayn broke the chain holding the gate and parked the truck on the weedy gravel road. He spent the time mentally walking himself through his plan and reviewing the maps of the plantation he'd acquired. He didn't know where the Brodarian had gotten them, but Zayn didn't care as long as they were accurate. The pictures from Imp*ossible Magics* should have ensured that.

But even the maps didn't show everything beneath the plantation. Zayn knew as much because he'd been below with the Lady. It appeared the lower sections had been expanded since these maps had been made. The maps Uncle Jesse had found years ago showed the area was littered with cave systems.

When evening came, Zayn changed into his favorite black clothing, gathered his equipment, and layered protective enchantments. He drove to an old forgotten road on the backside of the plantation and hiked through the undergrowth until the white building was within sight.

Then he waited.

Over the next hour, the town arrived at the plantation grounds. The car doors closing and laughing excitement filtered through the trees to Zayn's location.

Hearing them made his heart rate soar, so Zayn spent the time meditating, focusing on his breathing until he heard the first boom announcing the firework show would be starting soon.

Zayn checked his watch at the second boom and moved closer to the back building in sight of the side door that he planned to go through.

When the final boom marked the start of the display, Zayn set his watch. He'd memorized the timing list for the fireworks, and knew exactly when his distraction would start.

The night sky above the plantation was filled with the colorful display and accompanied by patriotic music that matched the syncopated explosions. A few of the fireworks had been coded with magic, so illusionary dragons or lions came bursting forth along with the sparks, but the Lady preferred the traditional displays, so there were few of those innovations.

Hovering behind a copse of old-growth trees, Zayn was preparing to move when he saw the form of a Watcher wandering from the back of the building. Zayn's hackles went up when he realized it was Keelan.

It seemed too much of a coincidence that Keelan would happen to be walking past right at the appointed time. His gut screamed that he should abandon his plan, that the Lady had figured it out.

But Keelan didn't stop. He kept strolling as if it were a normal patrol.

Maybe it's just the Lady's paranoia.

The delay put him behind schedule. Nothing terrible, but

he'd planned his intrusion down to the second.

Zayn slipped into the Veil and sprinted to the side of the building. When he came back out, he was safely behind a tall manicured bush near the side garden.

As his watch counted down, Zayn stripped off his clothes, stuffing them into his specially made backpack. He wouldn't have time to remove them later.

The explosions from the display had a nice, soothing rhythm timed with the music blaring on the speakers. For the really big ones, there was scattered applause.

Zayn knew the moment that his distraction had begun. A few screams carried over the plantation. He imagined the confusion as the smoke filled the viewing area, covering the families seated on their foldout chairs. At first, they would think it was part of the show, but then as the forms surged out of the mist—illusions created by the distraction cubes—they would be frightened.

Zayn hated to think that someone might get hurt in the chaos, but he needed a distraction worthy enough to bring the Watchers that patrolled the inside out onto the grounds.

As the initial screams turned to general pandemonium, Zayn ran to the side door, quickly disarmed its locks, and slipped inside. He stood in the side chamber off the Grand Ballroom.

When the sound of pounding feet approached, Zayn slipped back into the Veil until they were past. Then he moved into the shadows and transformed.

Maneuvering into the specialty harness was difficult, but he'd practiced it a dozen times to make sure he could do it within the required time. Wearing a backpack designed to fit a giant spider allowed him to move faster than if he were carrying it in his jaws.

Zayn scurried up the wall, taking to the ceiling for the

remainder of the journey. The high ceilings provided ample places to hide when Watchers came rushing from below to help quell the chaos.

When he found the appropriate hallway, the one with the illusionary wall that led below, Zayn paused, apprehensive about the next step.

It was the one part of the plan that he'd formulated on faith. He knew about this barrier from the last time he'd been below. Since he couldn't study it beforehand, he had no idea how it worked. But Priyanka knew about the barrier, and had gifted him an imbuement that allowed him to change into a spider.

When he was sure no more Watchers were coming, Zayn crept towards the illusionary wall. He remembered the feeling of passing it last time. It'd tingled across his skin like the barrier at the Bastille. If it didn't like him, he could be held in suspension or killed outright. He'd only been allowed through last time because he'd been supervised.

Zayn paused before the wall, front legs hovering in the air. A secondary explosion from outside startled him into movement.

He went through the illusion without incident.

Zayn changed back to his human form, dressed, reset his protective enchantments, and flexed his arm where the blade was hidden. He had no intention of using it unless everything went wrong. One way or another an end was coming.

Zayn took the dark curving staircase leading downward to the Lady.

Chapter Six

Varna, July 2018

Through a tangled web

Zayn crept down the steps, his senses bristling. He was halfway to the bottom when the sound of footsteps approached, but he was in human form, and couldn't retreat back through the barrier safely. It sounded like at least three people, which meant there was no room for him to use the Veil and slide out of the way.

As the footsteps rounded the corner, Zayn pushed his hands against one wall and his feet against the other, and walked up the wall until his back was against the ceiling. When the three Watchers ran beneath him, he slipped into the Veil just long enough to avoid their sight.

When they were past, he hopped back down, heart thundering in his ears. He'd already been in the Veil too long. He couldn't rely on it much more or he'd compromise himself.

At the bottom of the steps, there were three different passages. Zayn took the center one, which led to the Lady's library, where he assumed he'd find her.

The sound of footsteps, this time solo, forced him into a side passage. Not wanting to rely on the Veil again, Zayn found a stainless steel door that whooshed with air when it opened. The inner threshold was built like an airlock, which seemed odd to Zayn.

The room was filled with what looked like incubators connected to tubes in which a familiar yellowish liquid drained into stainless steel pots. Large oxygen bottles ran tubes to each box. Zayn couldn't see what was in the glass boxes and he wasn't sure he wanted to know. The room was at least fifty feet deep with dozens of the incubator setups.

When he was sure the footsteps had passed, Zayn returned to the passage. He found the library, stepping silently across the luxurious carpet.

On the far side of the shelves, he heard the Lady speaking to a Watcher.

"...do we know what caused this interruption?"

The Watcher cleared their throat. "No, ma'am. But we'll find out. A few questions to the owner will surely reveal why the display was changed."

"If he won't answer then he may need to visit my chamber for a real questioning," said the Lady.

"We'll take care of it," said the Watcher, who hurried up the passage, past where Zayn was lurking.

Looking through the shelves, Zayn spied the Lady. She wore lavender robes. Her hair was bound into a long black-and-silver braid that fell down the middle of her back. She strolled around the room with her hands behind her back, deep in thought.

The dagger in his arm itched as if it wanted to be freed. Zayn ignored the pull, reached into his pack, and produced a pair of potions. After he downed the first, his body buzzed as if it contained a nuclear furnace. Every hair on his head felt alive, and even without tapping into his imbuement, Zayn felt like he could throw a car over a building. Neveah hadn't been exaggerating when she'd called it a hero potion. Zayn swore he could hear the Lady swallowing from across the room.

Gripping the knockout potion in his hand, Zayn opened up his fourth imbuement. His first taste was revolting. It was like drinking the rot after a body had been stored in the earth for a long time. It felt like drinking hate.

Zayn reached out to capture the Lady at the same time he stepped into view. There was no reason to hide once he had her in his grasp.

She fought him for a moment, but then fell under his command, her tall form stiffening.

Zayn wasted no time, rushing to her side, handing her the small glass vial. He kept his grip firm, not wanting to chance an escape.

"Drink it," he said.

The Lady of Varna, tall and regal as a queen, reached out with a trembling hand and took the potion. She fought him but he left her no room for free will.

"Drink it," he repeated.

Her purple eyes betrayed her fear while her trembling hand lifted to her lips. She placed the glass against her bottom lip and hesitated there.

"Drink it now," he said, pouring his will into her.

A noise came from the Lady that left him cold. Low laughter fell upon him as the fear turned to amusement. Zayn clamped down on her with his imbuement only to find his grip easily broken.

The Lady dangled the knockout potion before him between her fingers.

"Did you really think this would do anything?" she asked,

before dumping it onto the carpet.

Standing within a foot of the Lady, he reached for the dagger in his arm, but she grabbed him by the wrists. It was like being held by the deep earth. He couldn't move his arms even a millimeter. Zayn tried to kick her, but she twisted his arm, causing a frightening amount of pain that left him immobile.

Then he heard the sounds of many feet approaching. But it wasn't the footfalls that stilled his attack, but the familiar screams of his sister.

Within moments, a group of a dozen Watchers entered the room. They had Maceo, Aunt Lydia, and Neveah in their grasp. Neveah was putting up a fight, requiring three Watchers to hold her. He could see the effects of the hero potion raging through his sister.

"Where are the rest?" asked the Lady.

"She attacked us before we could get them," said one of the Watchers holding Neveah as he strained. "They got away."

His father had a stoic expression while next to him Aunt Lydia was squirming against the Watcher.

"I don't understand, why am I here? I've been loyal. My son is a Watcher. Where is my son? Where is he?" asked Aunt Lydia, tears flooding down her cheeks.

The Lady of Varna held him within spitting distance, a toothy grin on her lips.

"Did you really think you could kill me? While you were cleverer than any before you, I still saw through your subterfuge. I haven't been alive for this long without a healthy amount of skepticism when my enemies claim their friendship. In fact, it's usually a sign that they're plotting against me."

A cold, helpless feeling overtook Zayn. "It was only me. Please leave the others alone. I understand you'll want your revenge, but leave my family alone. They've done nothing."

The Lady tilted her head, glancing askew at Neveah. "Are

you trying to tell me that she didn't make those potions you carry in your bag? The one you tried to feed me? I'm not stupid. I don't know everything that happened in Invictus, but I know for a fact the two of you killed Watcher Sabrina. I will not forget or forgive that. As for the rest of them, it is my unfortunate opinion that even if they promise that they will do nothing, they will eventually be tempted by revenge given what I'm about to do to you."

The hidden blade burned in his arm, waiting to be released, but she held him fast. No matter how he strained, he couldn't move.

"What I don't understand is Priyanka's role in this," said Lady Arcadia. "It might be time to end our relationship. As valuable as her teaching has been to create my loyal Watchers, there are far too many risks being introduced. I think I could train them myself much better and without the specter of betrayal looming."

Cold fear burned down his spine at the thought of Priyanka's death. Without her protection from faez, his friends would go mad. He hadn't considered that his decision to kill the Lady would affect them.

"Now for the real fun," said the Lady as she threw him across the room.

Zayn hit the wall and nearly blacked out. The impact rattled his bones.

Before he could climb to his feet, she kicked him in the head. He hadn't even seen her move.

Only the years of sparring with Instructor Allgood and Keelan had saved him from a broken jaw. Spots filled his vision as she threw him down the hallway, catching up to him with another brutal kick to the ribs when he landed.

When Zayn tried to fight back, she slapped him back down, moving in a blur. He'd fought the dragon Akhekh before, and the Lady was nothing like him. Zayn was sure that she could have killed Akhekh without breaking a sweat.

"Stand up, Zayn. Stand up and fight," she taunted.

But he barely had time to climb to his feet before she was on him again. He felt like a child against her.

"Then kill me," he said between blows.

The dagger burned in his arm. He wanted to pull it free, stab her, but she seemed to know exactly when he would try, and threw him again.

"You're going to die, Zayn Carter. That much is true. But it won't be me to deal the final blow," she said.

Zayn avoided the full blow of the next hit, spinning away rather than being thrown. It gave him an opportunity. If he couldn't save the town, he could at least kill the Lady. Everyone would die, but at least they would be free from her. It would save Priyanka, his friends, and the family that got away.

Abzu, the Hidden Blade, tore from his arm, leaving his flesh intact, but feeling like it'd ripped the muscle and sinew in half.

"Ahhh," screamed Zayn, climbing unsteadily to his feet to face the Lady.

She blurred towards him. Zayn stabbed to where he thought she was moving, but she hit him cleanly. He fell much further than he thought he should. He landed hard, knocking the breath from him.

With the blade in his fist, he struggled to his feet. The world spun around him. It took him a moment to realize he was in a larger cavern with a natural well at the center. Old bloodstains and scars marked the stone.

Lady Arcadia stood above him on a ledge, surrounded by her Watchers, who held his father, sister, and aunt. The cave was an arena, he realized. He saw blast marks on the stone and manacles on the wall to hold prisoners.

Zayn knew who he would fight the moment Aunt Lydia cried out his name.

"Keelan, no!"

But Keelan ignored his mother and let the Lady whisper in his ear. When he was finished listening, he vaulted into the arena, landing with a puff of dust around his boots. His eyes had been swallowed by purple until even the white had disappeared. The Lady had him completely under her control.

"No," said Zayn. "I'm not killing you."

He tried to throw away Abzu, but it was stuck to his hand. He'd been warned that once it was freed from his arm, it had to take a life.

"For a weapon that was made to kill me, it has spilled the blood of my enemies more than any other," said the Lady. "And now, you will take your cousin's life."

"No," Zayn said as Keelan approached. "I won't kill him."

Zayn shuffled to the side, using the hole in the center of the cavern to keep Keelan away.

The Lady snapped her fingers at the Watchers holding his family. Uncontrollable screams erupted from them, turning Zayn's will to water.

"Stop, please. Kill me if you must, but not this. I won't kill my family," Zayn shouted at her as he shuffled away from his cousin.

"Then watch them die slowly when I feed them to my children," said the Lady. "You can't run forever."

Before Zayn could try running up the side of the cavern, Keelan leapt the well. He attacked relentlessly with fists and fury. Despite his imbuement and the hero potion, Zayn barely kept up his defenses.

He slammed his cousin with a force bolt for space, only to catch a glancing blow from a purple electricity ball. The left side of his body seized up, which Keelan exploited with punishing attacks to that side. Zayn felt like he was fighting with a wooden arm for a half minute until the feeling came back.

It didn't help that Abzu remained in his right fist, which kept him from using advanced magics. He didn't want to kill his cousin either, which meant the weapon was useless.

But that didn't stop the blade from hungrily whispering in his head. Abzu required blood, and while it wanted the Lady's, it would happily accept anyone's.

The battle with Keelan kept Zayn from assessing the situation other than how to stay alive for another moment, but over time, as they flowed through the arena, bouncing off the jagged rocks, leaping over the well multiple times, he got a picture of his audience.

The Lady stood at the center, surrounded by four Watchers. Against the wall, his family had been chained, and each one had a Watcher by their side, ready to deliver pain should the Lady require it.

The battle had at least given his family a respite from the torture, but that delay was only temporary. Zayn had no idea how he was going to escape Keelan, then somehow kill the Lady. Even if she didn't have four Watcher guardians, he'd been able to do nothing against her.

He didn't want to believe that all hope was lost, but the prospects of his survival were bleak.

It's not impossible, he told himself. *I just need to break this down into smaller problems to solve.*

The first issue was his cousin, who looked completely under the Lady's control. He caught her twitching along with Keelan's movements as if she were holding his puppet strings, which also explained why he wasn't fighting in the Academy style.

Zayn needed to break her hold on Keelan. Then maybe the two of them could solve the next problem.

When Zayn dove out of the way of another seething ball of purple electricity, he scooped up a handful of rocks. Then using a counterattack to disguise his motion, he zipped a marble-sized rock at the Lady's head.

The projectile whizzed past as she ducked, but the momentary loss of control let Zayn complete his real plan, which was to hit Keelan with a stun bolt right in the side where his Watcher tattoo was located.

When the purple fled his eyes, revealing the brown beneath, Zayn said, "Keelan, quickly, we need to attack her. Take her out together."

Keelan put his hand against his temple as if he were recovering from a bad migraine. He shifted his jaw around.

"Keelan, come on. Together we attack," said Zayn.

He was about to sprint up the wall on his own when he heard Lady Arcadia.

"I had my fun, but now it's time for your cousin to finish the job. If you don't, Keelan dear, I guarantee that I'll make you watch while I tear the rest of her limbs off."

"Keelan, don't listen—"

His cousin didn't wait for him to finish, bringing a Headlong Zipper, which Zayn countered with Cascading Frog. The battle fell into the rhythms they'd developed at the skate park.

"Keelan, stop," he said, between blows.

But his cousin didn't hold back his attacks like they had on the sparring grounds. The little grunt at the end of each attempted blow, the piston force of the imbuement, signaled the deadliness of the fight.

Because Zayn didn't want to hurt his cousin, he fought awkwardly, using the hilt of his blade to block blows, retreating whenever he saw openings to counterattack.

He tried several times to get through to his cousin, but Keelan kept coming.

"Why are you doing this?" he asked as he blocked a Towering Triple.

Zayn didn't think he'd ever get an answer, when Keelan said under his breath, "We both have to die."

Keelan glanced to the prisoners above.

"No," said Zayn, shuffling backwards, avoiding a force bolt. "Together. We can fight her together."

Keelan shook his head as he kept coming, kept throwing blows, kicks, force bolts.

As the fight wore on, the burning in his arm grew until his right side was a forest fire. Abzu filled his head with thoughts of blood, which Zayn resisted, but how much longer would he be able to?

If only I could run away, thought Zayn. But if he did, they'd torture his family until he came back.

When Zayn tried to shift in front of the well, Keelan brought Headlong Zipper. It wasn't the right attack for the circumstance, but it caught Zayn off guard. He threw a Gorilla Shield in response; it was the best defense in the situation, requiring a feint to the middle before bringing both arms up for a block.

But rather than respect the feint, slowing his attack, Keelan threw himself forward and impaled himself on Abzu. The blade sunk into his chest, right up to the hilt. His cousin collapsed against him.

"No," said Zayn, feeling like the world had gone dark. "I didn't mean to. I didn't want to."

He was faintly aware someone was screaming above him, but all Zayn could see was the light fading from Keelan's eyes.

His cousin pressed against him, lips moving.

"It was the only way," he whispered in his ear.

"No, you can't die," said Zayn, clutching him, holding him up.

"But I must and so must you," said Keelan.

His cousin pushed something small and cool into his hand.

"No, please don't die. I don't want you to die," said Zayn, holding onto Keelan, pressing against him as if holding him up would prevent him from dying, but the blade had gone in right beneath the heart. The blotch in his shirt was growing, spilling warmth against Zayn's chest.

His cousin was growing colder by the second, the hungry blade draining his life.

In the barest whisper, Keelan said, "I had to die. She knew something, that I was, it would have compromised..."

"No, you can't..."

Zayn couldn't believe it. He'd spent his life with Keelan, playing on the tracks together, having black walnut wars in the woods behind the Stack, swimming in Doc's old pond. He was more than his cousin, he was his brother, his best friend. The person he couldn't live without.

"Jesse was right...they're a weapon..."

Keelan's eyes half-closed, fluttered once, then snapped awake as if he'd remembered one last thing he had to say.

"The tears. Find your allies." Keelan coughed, blood leaking from the corner of his mouth. "I'm sorry, cuz."

In a surge of final energy, Keelan pulled away. A blade appeared in his hand. He brought it down, shoving it right through Zayn's ribs and into his heart. It was like he'd been stabbed with an icicle.

"Keelan..."

The whole world went cold.

Lips numb with shock, Zayn could only mouth at words.

Then Keelan pushed him into the well.

Zayn died before he hit bottom.

Chapter Seven

Varna, July 2018

Get a life

Long before Lady Arcadia had left the old world, before humans had come out of the shadows, before agriculture and stone working, the earth beneath the plantation at the center of Varna had been filled with limestone. Over the countless millennia, the acidic water that fell from the sky dissolved away the limestone creating the caves that littered the central region of Alabama.

It was in one of these holes that Zayn fell, a steep shaft that ended at hard rock. Sometimes the bottom was filled with cool, clear liquid, but the water table had fallen, leaving enough water to keep the stone moist but not enough to flow.

Zayn's lifeless body lay at the bottom as a hovering magelight descended the shaft. Death was revealed by the pale blue light casting across his open eyes, as if the impact had surprised him. The Lady of Varna stood for a brief time, musing over the final fight as fading sobs echoed into the cavern.

The Lady stared at the fallen form of Zayn Carter, content that she had once again thwarted an attempt on her life. But it had been too close. The pair of them had weaved a masterful deceit and she'd almost detected it too late. How the younger one had been able to join the ranks of her Watchers while holding hate for her in his heart would be a puzzle she would have to uncover before she allowed another to join her ranks.

Of the family, she would feed them to her children at the proper time. For now, she only wanted to retire to her residence away from the others and consider what she needed do about Priyanka Sai. Their arrangement had lasted longer than any other, but its time had come to an end. Killing the Academy patron would be complicated, but the Lady was certain it could be accomplished without too much collateral damage.

The Lady slipped away from the well, her faithful Watchers trailing behind her, not one of them giving the hole in the ground a second glance.

Had she lingered a little longer, or had one of her Watchers been listening as they marched away, they might have heard the sudden inbreath of shock from the bottom of the well.

The gift that had been given by the Queen of the Veil, the magic that had weaved itself around his chest waiting for the right moment had finally triggered, shocking his heart back to work and flooding healing magics into his body.

The energy stored up in his nerves from the impact shot through him. Zayn's mute cry tore through his throat, his fingers digging at rock, tearing fingernails.

Memories blasted through his mind as he rolled onto his side, body shuddering with the spasms of rebirth.

"Keelan, no."

It took a few minutes before he could move again. When he'd died, his muscles had begun to harden and now his blood had to pump away the waste.

He climbed to his feet, nearly passing out. Zayn leaned against the rocky inner wall of the shaft until the feeling left him.

With his head against the stone, he noticed something shiny near his left foot. A small darkly colored bottle in a crevasse in the wet stone.

Zayn recovered it, remembering that Keelan had given it to him before he'd knocked him into the well.

"A gift from Petri," Zayn reminded himself.

In the eyedropper bottle were Petri's tears. She'd said they would help find something that was lost.

"Find your allies," said Zayn, remembering his cousin's last words.

But what did that mean?

He had no allies. He'd come alone with only the potions from Neveah in support, and now she was being held by the Lady along with his father and Aunt Lydia.

He needed to rescue them, but there was no way he could attempt it in the shape he was in.

Zayn shoved the bottle into his pocket and made the slow climb up the wall. He could have used his imbuement, but after he fought the Lady at full power and lost, he didn't feel like relying on it.

He paused at the top, unsure if he wanted to go this way. While he had the element of surprise, he had no way to kill the Lady. The best he could do was to free his family and escape the plantation, but he knew that was unlikely as they would be guarded by numerous Watchers.

Zayn peeked over the edge and almost lost his grip when he saw they'd left Keelan's body near the edge of the well. He scrambled to him, cradled him in his arms, tears flowing freely.

His cousin's blank stare looked up at him from his lap, strangely peaceful. The blade had been removed, probably by the Watchers. He couldn't imagine the Lady touching it. Zayn caressed Keelan's forehead as if he could feel the embrace through the barrier of death.

"You knew this would happen," said Zayn, lower lip trembling. "Didn't you?"

Zayn leaned his head back and stared at the rocky ceiling. The things Keelan had said to him in the past changed meaning based on what he'd said in those last moments.

I had to die. She knew something, that I was, it would have compromised...Jesse was right...they're a weapon...

He didn't know completely what his words had meant, at the moment, but he could feel the truth drawing in around him.

Zayn wanted to lay his head on Keelan's chest, remember his best friend, but then he heard the sound of voices approaching. They'd probably come to take his body away.

He resisted the urge to close Keelan's eyes, lest the simple gesture give him away, and slipped over the edge of the well, quickly climbing down using his imbuement for speed.

At the bottom he realized he had a serious problem. It wouldn't just be Keelan's body they would be retrieving. A Watcher or two would surely climb down to get his.

Zayn crouched under the overhang that led into the side passages. The wet stone suggested an answer.

He wasn't an expert at illusions, but he was skilled enough to create the impression the bottom had filled with water. Zayn constructed the idea in his mind, before drawing the scaffolding in the air with faint trailers of faez fading from his fingertips. When he was finished, the illusion folded over the construct, creating the appearance of water at the bottom of the well.

To maintain the fabrication, he only had to hold the idea in his mind and let faez trickle in.

It took a few minutes before the Watchers examined the well, but their exhalations of surprise reached him as a hollow echo.

"It's filled with water," said the female Watcher. "What the hell do we do now?"

"Climb down and get him. It can't be that high," said the second.

"If the well flooded again, his body's sure to be floating through the deep tunnels. No way am I swimming through that to find his body. Let's just tell her what we found. She'll understand," said the first.

"Understanding is not something she does," said the second. "Especially after an attempt on her life. I saw the way she looked when she headed back to her rooms."

After a long pause, the first said, "She'll have to accept it. It's not like we can breathe underwater."

Zayn almost missed that one of the Watchers had dropped a stone into the well. He made a *bloop* noise with his mouth a second after it hit the ground, then waited with his breath held to find out if his subterfuge had been accepted.

When he no longer heard the two Watchers, he waited another five minutes before releasing the illusion.

Zayn pulled the bottle of Petri's tears from his pocket.

"Find your allies," he said. "But I lost the one that mattered most."

Zayn tilted his head back and squeezed the tears into his eyes. The cool water refreshed. He blinked away the excess tears, waiting for an effect.

Within seconds, a ghostly light formed about ten feet ahead of him in the low passage, shining faintly off the glistening walls. Zayn turned his head right and left to find that it stayed in the same place. When he took a step forward, the light surged ahead.

Once he realized he needed to follow the light, he crouched down and moved through the low passage. After twenty feet, the floor sloped down, allowing Zayn room to walk, but then his progress was stopped by dark waters. He'd reached the water table, but the light had disappeared into it, glowing faintly a few feet beyond the surface.

"Are my allies a bunch of sightless fish? Or maybe an alligator that got flushed last year?"

As he prepared himself to swim through the watery tunnel, he remembered how Keelan had rescued him in the Bastille from the glass guardians. His heart ached that he wouldn't be able to rescue Keelan in turn.

A pain that went from his chest down to the balls of his feet had him burying his face in his hands. Sobs slipped from his squeezed lips as he tried to hold it back, push away the memory of Keelan's chest bumping against the hilt of the dagger. Zayn clenched his hands into fists, pressing them against his eyes.

He wanted to curl into a ball and grieve for his cousin, to forget everything else, let the pain wash over him, but he still had family alive, and he wanted to keep them that way.

When he had regained his composure, Zayn prepared to hold his breath for a long time. When he had gathered enough oxygen, he pushed into the water, using the ghostly light to guide him.

The passage twisted and turned, splitting twice, but he confidently followed the guide until he crawled back into a dry cavern. After banishing the water from his clothing with a spell, he followed the ghostly light through tunnels that slowly led upward.

At one point, he reached a juncture where the tunnel split. A breeze kissed his wet skin from the left, but it was to the right that the ghostly light had gone. There was also a smell coming from that direction that raised his hackles without indicating the reason.

But the direction was clear and he went right, which led him another two hundred feet before bending upward into a vertical shaft.

He heard voices as he climbed. Zayn was concerned that the Watchers had figured out he wasn't dead and had moved to cut him off when he realized he recognized them.

"Maybe something happened and he can't get to us," said Vin. "We should go in search of him."

"The message from Keelan was clear. We're supposed to come here and wait," said Skylar.

"But what if there's one of those spider people in the way?" asked Portia.

"Then I would have killed them," said Zayn as he exited the shaft.

His heart filled with joy at seeing his friends in the low cavern. A shared surprise kept them apart for a moment.

Then Portia wrinkled her forehead and asked, "Where's Keelan?"

Before he could form words, his face cracked with tears. He shook his head and croaked out, "He's dead."

Then Zayn crashed into the three of them. Instinctively, they crowded around him, capturing him within their arms, holding him against the storm.

He bawled for what seemed like an hour until he could recover himself enough to face them.

"What happened?" asked Skylar, eyes searching him.

Zayn opened his mouth to speak but his brain raced in multiple directions as he tried to formulate what to tell them.

Eventually he was able to ask, "What did Keelan tell you?"

Skylar lifted a shoulder in a half shrug. "Not much. Only that our help was needed."

"What about your new jobs?" asked Zayn.

"Our jobs can wait. We're a team," said Vin. "We came right away."

Zayn knew that leaving their mystery jobs wouldn't be well received. It was likely that they'd lose them.

"Thank you. I...I can't tell you how good it is to see you," said Zayn. "I'm...I'm lost."

"Well, that makes the four of us," said Portia. "You and Keelan have always been so secretive about Varna and the danger that clearly remained for you both."

Zayn took a deep breath. "I didn't want to tell you because that would have put your lives at risk."

"But that's why we joined the Academy," said Skylar. "And why we were the best damn team to ever exist there. Because we were willing to die for each other. And we damn well did a few times."

"Maybe you'll understand more after I explain," he said.

It took about a half hour, but he gave them the history of Varna and the Lady, the promise that he'd made to Keelan and himself to kill her, and what had gone wrong.

After he finished, they were dead silent for a full minute.

Eventually, Vin crossed his arms and said, "I can't believe it. I really can't believe it."

"That I went on a heist without you? I'm sorry, Vin," said Zayn, repentantly.

"No," said Vin, blinking. "That you made that promise when you were, like what, twelve years old? I was busy at that age memorizing *Les Misérables* to sing into the mirror in my bedroom."

Skylar looked equally stunned. "Yeah, that's pretty heavy. And the poison that you have to take. I always imagined it was something weird, but not that. Not a deadman's switch for a whole town." She shook her head. "Even your little sister

Imani?"

Zayn nodded, feeling relief that they understood why he'd never told them.

Portia came up to him, motioned for him to lean down, and captured his face in her hands. She stared straight into his eyes and said, "We are here for you now. Whatever you want us to do. We'll kill that murderous bitch."

Portia kissed each cheek then let him go. Zayn felt like he'd either been marked for death by the Godfather or witness to a deadly serious vow.

"Thank you. Thank you for coming to my rescue, but I hope you understand the odds are not in our favor. She made me feel like an insect when I tried to fight her. The Lady is thousands of years old, which means her power has only grown. I fear I don't know how we can beat her."

"That's why we're here," said Skylar. "You don't have to have all the answers any more. Plus, we have Keelan."

Hearing his cousin's name put a spike through his chest. "What?"

"You weren't the only one planning a hit on the Lady it seems. Somehow he managed to hide his betrayal from her until his death." Skylar lifted a bag from behind the rocks. "He left us this. We didn't understand what it was until you arrived."

"Right before, right before the end, he told me that he had to die. That she knew he had betrayed her, but not how," said Zayn, rubbing the spot in his chest where the blade had gone through his ribs. Petri's healing magic had closed it up, but he knew he would have a scar there, and maybe an ache that would never go away.

"I'm so sorry, Zayn. I know you two were close. We got to spend five wonderful years with him, but you and he were like brothers your whole life," said Skylar.

Zayn put his hand over his mouth, dug his fingers into his cheeks until the pain subsided. His friends waited until he could speak again, their eyes glossy and wide.

"He was telling me the whole time what was going to happen. I just didn't understand. On the train to school this past summer, he said, *sometimes even the best plans fail.* He *knew* the Lady was onto me, but couldn't tell me or she'd have known. He prepared for this moment."

"What's in the bag?" asked Vin. "Maybe he left us instructions."

Portia dug through the contents, revealing them one by one. "Here's a map of the cave system and the lower levels of the plantation, some bracelets, the leftover potion of ambrosia, a half dozen deception cubes, and a group photo of a bunch of people in suits and sunglasses."

"Watchers," said Zayn, taking the photo. "Must be like a company photo or something. And those bracelets." He held up his arm. "They block scrying. Everyone put one on. If he left them for us, there must be some active measures that the Lady has."

"Anything else? Like a plan on how to kill her without killing Zayn and his family?" asked Vin.

Zayn shook his head. "He couldn't leave anything like that. She would have known if he had. He could have put these items in a bag, because that could be for anything. But as soon as he wrote the words, she would have known. We're going to have to figure it out ourselves."

"You've spent your whole life trying to figure out how to defeat her poison and we're going to do it in a few short hours?" asked Skylar.

"Actually, I think Keelan left me clues to that too, but it didn't make any sense until I saw a room filled with incubators and the Lady mentioned feeding my family to her children."

Zayn paused, thinking about Neveah, his father, and Aunt Lydia. He hoped they were still alive. "Keelan had been trying to tell me something about my uncle Jesse and cousins, and I think that has to do with the spiders. You see there are the Lady's spiders, purpura domina aranea, which are everywhere around here. They can grow bigger than most, but no one knows why. There's also another species, achaeranea magicaencia, the magic eaters. I'd forgotten that they were related."

"Can we use the magic eaters to kill the Lady?" asked Vin.

"I don't think so," said Zayn. "Not directly anyway, because you can't control them. They're dangerous to everyone, and she'd probably just run away rather than fight them."

"Then what?" asked Portia.

Zayn paced back and forth, trying to figure out what his cousin was telling him.

"Wait, I think I understand. I should have figured it out earlier because of the Goon." Zayn slammed his fist into his other palm. "The magic eaters devour faez and grow larger. But the Lady's poison is like low-grade addictive faez. That's how he made that damn drug, he used her poison. They're cousins. Purpura domina aranea and the magic eaters, which means those aren't just her spiders, she *is* those spiders. Somehow she must be an advanced version of them."

"Wait," said Vin. "You're telling me we're facing a spider Pokémon? I don't know if I should be excited or terrified."

Despite the grim mood, Zayn couldn't help but smile, as did the others.

"The incubators were for her spiders. That's how she produces so much poison for the town. She must collect, or raise, or do something to gather that many larger ones," said Zayn.

"Are her spiders solitary hunters?" asked Portia.

Zayn snapped his fingers. "Yes, you're right. They're solitary, where the magic eaters are community spiders. Her spiders must kill each other when they get bigger. She's the alpha predator of her species. It still doesn't explain the weird stainless steel airlock door though."

"But now you have a solution to the poison. You can use the spiders once she's dead," said Portia.

"That's right," he said. "But how do we kill her?"

"That's easy," said Vin. "You do what you do in any situation you find a spider in any location."

"What's that?" asked Zayn.

"You burn it to the ground. Not to cinders, but ashes. Nuke the entire site from orbit, it's the only way to be sure," said Vin, completely serious.

"I can't really argue with that logic," said Portia.

"Didn't you say there were oxygen bottles in the incubation room?" asked Skylar.

As soon as she said it, everyone's eyes widened. "We can trap her in there, ignite the bottles, and whammo, there's no way she can escape that."

"I'll do it," said Zayn. "If you can get her in there, I'll ignite the bottles."

Portia punched him in the arm. "No suicide missions. We don't need your sacrifice anyway. We can use a trigger from one of these deception cubes."

"But how do we get her to go into the room?" asked Skylar.

Vin was staring at the photo. "Who is this lady in the white pantsuit? Is she important? Would the spider lady listen to her?"

"She's the Speaker," said Zayn. "She speaks for the Lady of Varna, and after her, there's no one more powerful."

Vin waved his hand over his face, which morphed into the Speaker's sorcery smooth one.

"How's this?" he asked in his voice, which sounded strange coming out of her face.

"You need to work on the voice, but you look perfect," said Zayn.

"I think we have a plan," said Skylar.

"Not completely. We need to save my family, and I don't even know where they're at," said Zayn.

"I'm the best scout, and fighter," said Portia with a cocky head tilt.

"I'll go with you," said Skylar.

Vin held up a distraction cube. "Any use for these?"

After Zayn thought for a moment, he said, "I know how we'll use them. Give them to me."

"Then we have a plan," said Skylar.

"A plan," said Portia, putting her hand into the middle.

Zayn stacked his on Portia's, followed by Vin and Skylar. They looked each other in the eyes.

"A plan," said Vin.

Zayn nodded grimly. "For Keelan."

Chapter Eight

Varna, July 2018

The unexpected heist

Using the map, they arrived at the room with the well. The way was long, requiring several sections of climbing that would have taxed a champion athlete, but the Academy students with their imbuements made them easily.

Portia signaled the team in their secret language, and went ahead to scout. It was the middle of the night, which in normal circumstances, would mean that everyone was asleep, but they didn't know Lady Arcadia's physiology, so they had to assume she was awake.

After Portia confirmed the way was clear and the location of his family, they would move to the incubation room and set up their trap. Once the trigger mechanism was set to explode the oxygen bottles, Vin would lure her into the trap disguised as the Speaker.

While Portia was gone, Zayn stood at the spot where Keelan had died, examining the dried blood coating the stone, a patina of death. He'd been too late to figure out that his plan had been compromised. He hoped he wasn't too late to save his family.

A signal from Skylar indicated someone was approaching, forcing them to hide in the arena. Zayn took position behind a rocky outcropping, while Vin climbed down the shaft. Zayn didn't see where Skylar had gone, but he noticed a particularly deep shadow along the wall.

"...told you that she wouldn't be happy," said the Watcher that Zayn had heard earlier at the top of the well.

"But how do we find the body if it's flooded?" asked the other Watcher.

"At least you were smart enough not to ask her that question," said the female Watcher.

The two Watchers, an older pair that Zayn didn't recognize, climbed into the arena in their suits with sunglasses tucked into their front pockets. If they meant to climb into the well, they would find Vin, who had moved below the edge. Zayn glanced to Skylar's pocket of shadow to find it had moved.

As the male Watcher approached the well, he said, "Did you hear they found the rest of his family? Caught them north of Selma in a rental moving truck. I almost feel sorry for them. Don't they know you can never outsmart her? She sees everything."

A gaping chasm opened up in his stomach. Doc and his mom. Izzy and Max. Imani.

He couldn't fail them.

What the Watcher said also confirmed that Lady Arcadia was the seer. Maybe it had something to do with her spider physiology.

Lady Arcadia, he thought. *I need to stop thinking of her as the Lady and rather as a creature that I'm going to kill.*

The picture of the comic rose up in his mind. *The Spider*

Queen Must Die!

As the pair of Watchers moved to the edge of the well, Zayn prepared to attack. They couldn't let these two escape to warn the others.

The man peered over the edge, preparing to climb down when a hand reached up and yanked him into the hole. The woman Watcher reacted quickly, turning towards the ledge, and Zayn burst from behind the rock to cut her off.

He kicked her in the side before she could leap up. She rolled into a ball and came up firing, a crackling stun ball of electricity flowing towards him.

Zayn jumped it, but the change in direction gave her an opportunity to bound up the wall. He thought she was going to escape until the shadows opened like a gaping maw and swallowed her with a mute scream. A moment later, the Watcher's body came tumbling out to crash onto the floor with a blank stare.

As Vin climbed from the well, a smirk of victory on his lips, they heard an exclamation from above. Another Watcher stood on the ledge, looking down at them and the fallen woman.

"Oh shit," said the Watcher, a dark-skinned woman with short hair.

"Catch her!" cried Zayn, but she had a head start.

Skylar was closest. The cloak of shadows around her shoulders flowed like a dark river before her, allowing her to run unaided to the ledge. But there was no way she was going to catch the Watcher before she warned the others. Their plan had failed before it had started.

When Skylar reached the top, she stopped and put her hands on top of her head as if she'd run a long race.

Zayn didn't understand why she'd stopped until he saw Portia join her with the escaped Watcher hung over her shoulder.

"That was a close one," said Zayn.

"Too close," said Skylar. "Good thing you came back when you did."

Portia nodded grimly. "I found the jail."

Zayn's heart leapt in his chest. "And?"

"It's guarded by eight Watchers. I can take one easily, two if I must, but eight is too many, even with Skylar's help."

"You'll have to figure something out," said Zayn. "If anything happens, she'll instruct them to kill her prisoners, or use them as human shields. We have to take her and the Watchers out at the same time. And even if we manage to kill her, I don't know where their loyalties will lie. Some people joined her willingly, because it meant they were given a position of power. They might be very angry with us if we kill their golden goose. We need to sneak them out through the tunnels before they figure it out."

"What about the rest of your family? I heard what they said about catching the others," said Skylar.

"We can't worry about that now," said Zayn. "Let's keep to the plan."

"But the jail guards," said Portia, frowning.

"Figure it out," said Zayn. "Sorry, I told you it wasn't going to be easy."

Portia glanced to Skylar before nodding. He knew how she felt. The chances of them succeeding were infinitesimal, but there was no way he wasn't going to try.

Vin held up the bag that Keelan had given them. "What about the ambrosia? Who should get it?"

Everyone pointed at each other, which made them chuckle as a group.

"You take it, Vin," said Zayn. "Yours is the most critical part. If she figures you out, you're going to need a little extra to get away."

He checked the time on his watch. "Okay, mark time from here. Twenty minutes."

The others nodded.

Portia and Skylar left through a different passageway. The maps from Keelan had shown that the whole complex was much larger than Zayn had expected, but he should have guessed as much. She'd been in the town for centuries and she had to house and feed many Watchers for her defense.

When Zayn turned around he was confronted with the image of the Speaker in her white pantsuit and coifed cobra-like blonde hair.

"You gave me a heart attack," said Zayn, his heart racing from the surprise.

"Good," said Vin-Speaker, in her exact dialect. They'd worked on it in the lower cavern until it was perfect. It was quite remarkable how quickly he'd dialed into her voice having never heard it, based solely on Zayn giving him hot and cold directions.

While the other two had slunk away through the shadows, using their stealth and shadows to stay out of sight, Vin-Speaker strode down the middle of the passageway with Zayn at his side. Vin had placed the illusion of the Watcher they'd killed over him, but had cautioned him not to speak because he wouldn't be able to match the illusion.

They were tested not long after leaving the arena. Two male Watchers, younger ones that Zayn recognized from his school years—Austin and Sawyer—approached from the opposite direction. They both stiffened when they saw the Speaker. He caught side-eyed glances at him, suggesting they thought his pairing with the Speaker meant he was in trouble.

Zayn was prepared to pass them when Vin-Speaker said, "And what is it that you two think you're doing right now?"

They both stopped short, heads bobbing up in surprise.

"I, uhm," said Austin.

"We're headed to the cells for our shift," said Sawyer, looking at his shoes.

Zayn couldn't figure out what Vin was doing, but he had no way to communicate, since he was as powerless as the other two.

"I need you to do something else for me," said Vin-Speaker. "The rest of the Carter family will be arriving later today, but I'm concerned about renegade elements in the town disrupting it."

"Renegades? I thought we'd taken care of everyone?" asked Sawyer.

"The conspiracy goes deeper than we first thought," said Vin-Speaker. "In fact, I want you to grab at least two others, and take them to the edge of town. Wait there until they arrive to guard them on the way back in. Make sure nothing happens to them."

Sawyer and Austin shared a conflicted glance.

"But ma'am, I thought no one was supposed to leave right now?" asked Sawyer.

"Are you refusing my order?" asked Vin-Speaker.

"But the Lady...she had...earlier," said Sawyer, looking pained.

"Things have changed," said Vin-Speaker. "Need I remind you that she sees what no one else does? Events have changed and we must change with them."

The doubt that had risen to their eyes was dispelled by the comment. They both nodded enthusiastically before returning the way they'd come, hurrying as if to distance themselves from Vin-Speaker.

"That was dangerous," Zayn said under his breath.

"I wanted to test the illusion before I spoke to the Lady,"

said Vin-Speaker. “And now there are four less Watchers in the building.”

Zayn checked the time when they reached the incubation room. The delay had cost them a few minutes.

He got the shivers when he looked into the first incubation chamber, finding what he’d feared, a purple-tinged spider as large as a housecat. The critter had been fitted with a contraption around its stinger that squeezed every few seconds, milking the yellowish poison from its large body.

“Well, that’s nightmare fuel for the next, oh, let’s say, rest of my life,” said Vin-Speaker, his lips curled.

Zayn examined the oxygen tanks that were feeding the incubation chambers. The higher concentration seemed to make the spiders lethargic.

Zayn unhooked the tubes from four different incubation chambers, letting the pure oxygen vent into the room. He set the trigger device beneath one of the chambers, setting it for a time nine minutes away.

“Alright,” said Zayn. “The next step is up to you.”

“Where are you going to be when I return?” asked Vin-Speaker.

“I’ll find a spot to hide,” said Zayn.

“If you don’t think I can get out without alerting her, then trap the both of us in here,” said Vin-Speaker.

“No way,” said Zayn. “We’re getting out of here alive, all of us. Just get her in here.”

Before he left, Vin-Speaker crimped a couple of lines on the incubation chambers, forcing the yellowish liquid to build up. When he was finished he stood before the door and tugged on the front of his pale white suit coat.

“I have a feeling this is going to take the performance of a lifetime,” said Vin-Speaker.

“I’ll nominate you for an Oscar,” said Zayn, holding his fist out for a bump.

"First step in the EGOT," said Vin-Speaker with a grin, which was creepy to Zayn, since it was her face, but his expression.

After Vin-Speaker strolled away with the confidence of a head of state, Zayn realized they'd forgotten about one small detail. If they killed all the spiders, there wouldn't be enough poison to keep the town alive. He doubted harvesting the small ones in the forests would be enough.

On the way to the incubation room, they'd passed a lounge area. Zayn propped the door open and dragged an incubation chamber into that room. The boxes had wheels on the back legs, making moving them around easier. He managed to move three chambers and their oxygen tanks into the next room before he ran out of time.

Zayn hid in the lounge when he heard Vin-Speaker and the Spider Queen coming down the hallway. Their low conversation reached him faintly through the closed door. He checked his watch to see they were three minutes away from ignition, which would mean Vin-Speaker had time to kill.

"...it certainly looks like sabotage, though I cannot confirm it," said Vin-Speaker.

"Do you have any ideas who might have done it?" asked Arcadia as she passed the door where Zayn was hidden.

"Austin and Sawyer were in the area when I arrived. I sent them on an errand until I could determine their innocence or guilt," said Vin-Speaker.

"You think other Watchers have also conspired against me?" asked Arcadia.

"It would explain your visions," said Vin-Speaker.

The silence after his comment made Zayn's hands ball into fists with worry. He had no idea how much the Spider Queen shared her abilities with her Watchers. He hoped that the Speaker was one that received extra access.

"Yes, you're probably right, I still sense danger in the web..."

They passed beyond his hearing. Vin-Speaker had another two minutes and ten seconds to get her into the room and then slip out.

It seemed like the plan was going to work. Zayn wished he could communicate with Skylar and Portia so he could find out if they were going to be successful. He didn't know if he could handle losing his sister, father, and aunt after losing his best friend.

Zayn took a deep breath, preparing himself for an end that he thought would never come.

Then he heard a new set of people approaching. When he recognized the real Speaker's voice, his whole body went cold.

"...I definitely did not give you permission to leave the plantation. We shall find the Lady and have a long conversation about disobedience," said the Speaker.

"Yes, ma'am," said Austin and Sawyer in unison.

"Danielle said she had headed to the incubation chamber," said the Speaker. "Though she thought I was with her, which does not make a lick of sense."

Zayn froze with indecision. Once they stepped into the incubation chamber, the ruse would be exposed. He had to find a way to stop them before they reached it.

Chapter Nine

Varna, July 2018

Only the shadow knows

Walking within the shadows always made Skylar feel ultra-powerful. It was like the shadows obeyed her commands, or at least one particular shadow. As the cloak flowed around her, making her nearly invisible in the dim hallway, it whispered to her like an excited child.

whatwillwedonext

iwanttosmotherthem

flyflyflyflyletsfly

"Quiet," said Skylar.

"Who are you talking to?" asked Portia, who seemed to move unseen through her own private method. It almost seemed like she blinked from one spot to the next.

"No one, or myself, I guess," she said when she realized her first comment sounded crazy.

When Petri had given her threads of moonlight to weave into her cloak of shadows, she hadn't expected it to give the fabric an intelligence, but given the strangeness of the Eternal City and the way the very city seemed alive, she shouldn't have been surprised.

They reached the area near the jail cells. Through a barred door, a central chamber held eight Watchers, who were currently playing a game of poker. The hallway had multiple cameras so no approach was unseen.

"There's probably a panic button," whispered Skylar.

Portia nodded. "There most certainly is."

"So we need to get through a locked and barred door, keep them from hitting the panic button, and kill eight Watchers," said Skylar.

"It must be done," said Portia.

Skylar checked her watch. They had eight minutes. "Ideas?"

Portia chewed on the inside of her cheek while her right eye twitched with thought. Zayn was the best improviser of the group, but he was in the other part of the complex. They had to figure it out on their own.

"Can we use the Veil?" asked Portia.

Skylar pointed to the faint runes etched on the ceiling. "Blockers. They know better."

"What about your cloak? Can you make it to the door unseen?" asked Portia.

"Probably," said Skylar. "Depending on how much they're paying attention."

"If you can get the door open, I can take care of the Watchers." Portia paused, a wicked grin rising to her lips. "At least for a few seconds. Then you'll have to find the panic button and keep them from hitting it."

"Here goes nothing," said Skylar, letting the shadows cover her until the world turned dim.

She didn't want to give herself away, so she moved slowly,

creeping along the wall. If they were paying attention, they'd see a pool of shadow that shouldn't be there oozing forward. The hallway was only twenty feet long, but it took Skylar a full five minutes to reach the end.

With two minutes left to go, she examined the door for physical and magical protections. She could avoid the enchantments, but the door was held with a bar across it, which made lock picking impossible.

Inside the guard chamber, the Watchers were laughing. Chips were being thrown against each other in the middle of the table.

Skylar let the edge of her cloak slip through the crack at the bottom, guiding it with thought. The fabric climbed the inside of the door, grasped the bar, and lifted it from its moorings.

Before she finished the job, Skylar glanced back to Portia hiding at the far end, nodding to indicate she needed to be ready. The next few seconds would be crucial, so Skylar flooded her imbuements with faez, readying for battle.

When the bar fell and the door opened, Skylar felt Portia *whoosh* past her, appearing suddenly on the table in the middle of the poker game with three throwing knives in each hand. As the Watchers, six of which were seated at the table, grabbed weapons, Portia flung blades in a spinning arc.

The other two Watchers were seated on opposite sides of the room, each at a desk with a monitor. They both looked up at Skylar, who sensed them about to hammer the panic button. She hadn't expected a redundant alarm system on opposite sides of the room making neutralization nearly impossible.

But impossible was what they'd been sent to do.

Skylar sent her shadow cloak to the left, while she went right, kicking through the monitor and into the chest of the Watcher before she could reach the alarm. She knocked the woman right out, before turning to the mayhem at the center of the room.

Portia had killed two Watchers in the first second of battle, and wounded two more, but the tide had quickly turned. Guns and blades appeared in their hands.

Mentally noting that the other alarm hadn't sounded, Skylar leapt at the Watcher about to aim his gun at Portia's back, driving her knife into his neck before he could pull the trigger.

As Portia backflipped over a sword thrust, Skylar kicked a chair into the Watcher to her right, interrupting him from his unprotected attack, while throwing her knife at the Watcher on her left about to bring her weapon around. The blade went right through her hand, and she dropped the gun.

With half the Watchers down, the odds shifted in their favor. Skylar flipped the table, spilling chips into the air like a volcanic explosion, then using it like a shield, dove beneath it, coming up beneath the Watcher on the other side to drive a new knife into his gut.

Facing down two Watchers, Portia moved in a stutter step, in one place at one moment, then appearing five feet away as if she'd teleported, right between them. With a blade in each fist, she slammed them into the Watchers' chests.

The last Watcher turned to flee. He made it halfway to the door before six knives found his back.

"Who got that kill?" asked Skylar, her right hand hanging in the air.

"I put more knives in him," said Portia, holding up four fingers.

"Fair enough," said Skylar.

Portia furrowed her forehead. "Where's the eighth?"

Skylar made a soft whistle and her cloak released its victim. They appeared in a pool of shadow, eyes vacant with death.

Pulling a wetnap from her pocket, Skylar wiped the blood from her hands and face. She went into the jail section with a handful of keys she'd recovered from a Watcher. There were six big cells.

"We're here to rescue you," said Skylar to frightened looking prisoners who pressed themselves against the bars.

"Oh my word, thank you," said a chubby guy with a black eye and multiple abrasions on his face. "I thought I was going to die in here. I'm Buford Ash."

As Skylar checked down the hallway, she noticed a few faces she'd expected were missing.

"Are Maceo and Neveah Carter here?" she asked.

"No, ma'am," said Buford. "The Lady had them removed and placed in her private chambers about an hour ago."

The brief thrill of victory turned to ashes in her mouth. Skylar put her hands to her jaw as Portia said what she was thinking.

"She knows."

Chapter Ten

Varna, July 2018

A role of a lifetime

There was an art to throwing yourself into a role, thought Vin as he strolled beside the Lady, chatting about the problems in the incubation room. He didn't know the Speaker, except by Zayn's description, but from that verbal sketch he'd pieced together the outline of her soul.

"Do you have any ideas who might have done it?" asked the Lady beside him, walking with her hands behind her back. She wore long flowing purple robes that matched her lilac skin tones.

Understanding the Speaker meant filling in the unsaid details of their lives, like what kind of socks they liked to wear, their favorite foods, until breathing through them became second nature. Vin had surmised that the Speaker was proud of her position in the town, but wary that she could be replaced at any moment. She would be deferential, but confident; otherwise, the Lady might think her fallible.

"Austin and Sawyer were in the area when I arrived. I sent them on an errand until I could determine their innocence or guilt," said Vin-Speaker.

"You think other Watchers have also conspired against me?" asked the Lady.

"It would explain your visions," said Vin-Speaker, not knowing where the idea had come from. Zayn had suggested that the Lady employed seers, but as the words had flowed from his mouth, Vin thought otherwise.

He interpreted her silence as thoughtful consideration. "Yes, you're probably right. I still sense danger in the web."

When they arrived in the incubation room, Vin subtly checked the time to see he had a few minutes to kill.

"The air is different in here," said the Lady.

Vin feigned sniffing. "I sense that too. There must be a leak. I'll take a look." He gestured towards the pinched poison lines. "Those were like that when I found them."

Vin stood at the oxygen tanks, examining them as if he were truly looking. He'd purposely picked one that wasn't disconnected and near the open door. He planned to slip outside and close it at the last moment. He didn't know if the door would hold in the explosion, but it had been sturdily made.

"Treachery is a terrible thing," said the Lady, straightening the pinched line and shaking her head. "My poor babies. I'm sure that feels terrible."

The Lady opened the lid on the incubation chamber and stroked the spider's back.

Though inside he was crawling with revulsion, he maintained a stoic expression as he kept examining the oxygen tanks for leaks. It was down to a minute before it would trigger.

"Thank you for showing me this," said the Lady as she strolled towards the door. "I shall have to think on it, but it has been a long night and I wish to retire to my chambers. Send the appropriate persons to fix this."

"I found one," said Vin-Speaker, pointing to an oxygen tank with the line unhooked. He had to keep her in the room for a bit longer. "More sabotage. We should find the rest of the unhooked lines and fix them before something sparks the oxygen. I'll take the front of the room, you take the back."

Almost as soon as he said it he sensed something was wrong. She wasn't moving. Instead, she stared back at him with a smile that put a stab of worry in his gut.

"A masterful performance, whoever you are," said the Lady. "If I hadn't know you were an imposter, I would have been fooled."

She reached down and plucked the trigger mechanism from beneath the incubation chamber, deftly disarming it with a flick of her fingernail.

"By the skin of my teeth," she said, showing him a predator's smile.

A growing realization filled his gut. "You knew this whole time."

"My dear, don't you know that spiders use webs to detect danger?" The Lady held her arms above her head and gestured around her as if there were an invisible web. "My psychic web surrounds me, protects me, warns me. You never had a chance."

Vin moved to escape, but the Lady was there, grasping his wrist before he could move even an inch. Zayn had been right, she was more powerful than anything they'd ever faced.

"Will you satisfy my curiosity and let me see who you really are?" asked the Lady.

Seeing there was no harm in it, Vin let the illusion fall, revealing his true form. The Lady placed her hand against his cheek as she stared at him with her alien purple eyes.

"You look quite delicious," she said.

In a last fit of desperation, Vin summoned fire to trigger the excess oxygen in the room. But she snapped her fingers and his spell dissipated like smoke.

"You have no idea who you're dealing with," said the Lady, pulling him along by his wrist. "Come, I promise it'll be over quickly."

Chapter Eleven

Varna, July 2018

Further complications

Without a way to disguise himself like the others, Zayn stepped into the hallway.

"Looking for someone?" asked Zayn.

The three turned slowly as if they expected a trick. The Speaker's eyes widened until they were as big as moons. Her normally reserved expression cracked with confusion.

"But...I saw you die," said the Speaker.

"I did. But now I'm back. So you can either get out of my way or die where you stand," said Zayn.

The Speaker's face blotched with rage. "What are you waiting for? Kill him!"

The two Watchers sped towards him. They moved like race cars, their fists and feet blurring into action.

But Zayn was ready. While he was taunting them, he'd ramped his senses, examining them for clues. Sawyer's left knuckles had more calluses than his right, suggesting a dominant hand, while Austin had scuff marks on both of his Italian leather shoes.

Zayn shifted forward, moving inside Austin's roundhouse so his knee and upper thigh hit him rather than the flat of his foot. With a flat hand, he deflected Sawyer's left hook into the side of his partner's head.

As Austin reached into his jacket where a gun bulge was located, Zayn rabbit punched him in the throat and beat him to the weapon.

He didn't want to shoot them, as the noise would alert the Spider Queen that something was wrong, so Zayn pointed it at them.

"On your knees, hands on your heads," said Zayn. "You too, Speaker, or whatever your name is."

"You will pay for this," said the Speaker, falling to her knees.

"How very villainy of you," said Zayn, glancing at his watch.

He was expecting the explosion at any moment.

"Come on," he said, willing it to happen.

When the appointed time came and went, a sick feeling filled Zayn's gut. The longer the explosion didn't happen, the more he knew that everything had gone wrong.

Zayn wasn't surprised when the Spider Queen appeared in the hallway with Vin before her as a human shield.

"While I don't relish having to pick a bullet out of my body, it won't bother me that much. Put the gun down, or I'll tear his head off right here and let you pick through his brains," she said.

Zayn thought about shooting Vin and turning the gun on himself, but he couldn't do that. Not while they still drew breath.

"Damn you," said Zayn, switching the safety on and letting the gun drop.

"No, it is you that is damned. Damned to failure," said the Spider Queen. "Grab him and hold him tight so he doesn't try anything dodgy."

Austin and Sawyer took his wrists, but he wasn't putting up a fight. He couldn't win this battle.

"Get the others. I want to execute them all and get this over with. It's gone on far too long," said the Spider Queen.

An ache of defeat went into his bones. His head dipped down, the pain of letting his friends and family down warping his expression.

"Don't worry," said the Spider Queen. "I'll make it quick. You're far too troublesome to leave alive for too long."

With the agony of defeat wracking his face, he asked, "May I ask a favor? I know I don't deserve it, considering I've been trying to kill you."

The corners of her eyes narrowed. "And?"

"Will you...do it...kill us...in your chambers? I've always been fond of books, and it would be an honor to die surrounded by them and my family," said Zayn.

The Spider Queen stared at him for a long time before finally speaking.

"Take everyone to the arena, and send some of the Watchers into my chambers to search it," she said.

Zayn squeezed his eyes and mouth shut and let his limbs empty until he was barely a rag doll. The two Watchers dragged him down the passageway, his feet scraping the carpet.

Rather than stay above at the ledge, the Spider Queen brought them down to the rocky arena floor.

"Hold him tight, I don't want him trying to escape through the well," she said.

After a few minutes, more Watchers showed up, pushing Skylar and Portia ahead of them with guns trained at their backs. The other prisoners were with them, the ones they'd rescued from the jail cells. Ms. Gardenia was with them, looking ragged and frail. Zayn also saw Buford, whose eyes pooled with tears.

Last to arrive was his family: Maceo, Neveah, and Aunt Lydia. Neveah kept resisting when they pushed her into the arena—defiant to the end.

They were lined up on the far wall. Neveah stood next to Zayn, grabbing his hand. His father had tears in his eyes, but he nodded, as if to say *thank you for trying.* Aunt Lydia was nearly comatose, blankly staring into the distance, already grieving from the loss of her only son.

As the Watchers with guns prepared, Zayn reached out and touched the hands of his friends and family one last time.

"Thank you for trying. I wish it would have worked," said Zayn.

To their credit, his teammates met his gaze, giving him their own nods as if to say they wouldn't have had it any other way. Surrounded by those that opposed the Spider Queen, Zayn faced the firing squad. He kept his gaze locked on the Spider Queen, who stood a head taller than the others. She met his gaze with a smug one of her own.

"Begin firing on my count," she said. "One. Two—"

A strange hiss erupted from the well, releasing mist that billowed into the arena. The Watchers, waiting for her final command, looked back at her as she wrinkled her lips.

"It's nothing," said the Spider Queen. "It's one of those distraction boxes he used during the fireworks. He must have placed one in the well, but don't worry, bullets can't be stopped by mist."

She waved her hand, the scent of sorcery filling the air. The mist sucked towards her hand and disappeared as if it were being bottled up.

"Let us begin again," she said. "One—"

At that a great chittering filled the air, coming from the well. Zayn squeezed his family's hands and said under his breath to the others, "Do nothing."

"Two," said the Spider Queen, and before she could say three, a wave of spiders came flowing out of the well, a brown skittering carpet of insects.

The sudden appearance brought confused reactions from the Watchers. Austin shot into the well, which ricocheted back into the arena, while two others reacted by spraying flame at them, right as the Spider Queen yelled, "No magic!"

But it was too late.

The flame hit the leading edge of the magic eaters, inciting them and filling them with faez, which plumped them up until they were the size of small dogs.

Before they'd left the tunnels, Zayn had set up the distraction cubes in a long chain, setting them to go off after the explosion trigger in a way that would draw the magic-eating spiders into the arena. If they'd been successful at killing the Lady, he would have disabled the cubes. They served as their safety plan.

Even the best plans fail.

Keelan had taught him as much.

As he stood against the far wall, doing nothing but watching, the spiders moved towards the Watchers and the Spider Queen. They'd pulled the spiders towards them through their use of magic.

The Speaker, who didn't understand the danger, tried to blast one with a ball of electricity, only to have it devour it, then leap onto her face.

As the carpet of spiders overtook the Watchers in the firing squad, the Spider Queen fled into the lower areas. Screams filled the air, echoing through the hallways.

Zayn waited until the last of the magic eaters had disappeared into the plantation complex before motioning to the team.

"Down the well, we need to get out of here," said Zayn.

"What about the Lady?" asked Vin.

At that moment, an explosion rocked the plantation. Vin looked to Zayn with his head tilted.

"I put another trigger mechanism in the hallway outside the incubation room. With luck, it collapsed the ceiling. Either way, I don't think we have to worry about her much longer," said Zayn.

"Pull out the ropes—we need to do this the hard way," said Portia, motioning to the others.

It took a while to get everyone down the well. The whole time Zayn worried that the Spider Queen or the magic-eating spiders would come back. He hoped they would gorge themselves on the faez, before dying. He felt bad that he'd sentenced the colony to death from overeating, but at least he knew where another colony lived.

Three hours later, after carefully shepherding everyone through the torturous cave system, they made it out, right when the horizon filled with the pink light of morning.

But Zayn couldn't rest with the rest of his family still in danger. They hiked to Vin's car, piled in, and drove to the edge of town, where they found the rest of his family walking along the side of the road.

Sela had a bump on her head, while Doc and the younger kids looked shook up, but they generally appeared healthy.

"What happened?" asked Zayn after a round of hugs.

"We were driving along, thinking we were headed to our deaths, when the moving truck went off the road and crashed in the trees. It took a few minutes, but we managed to get the back door open. Both the Watchers that had been driving were dead, but I don't think it was the crash that killed them," said Sela.

In his heart, he found it hard to believe, but there was no other reason that the Watchers would have spontaneously died.

"She's dead," said Zayn. "The Spider Queen is dead."

Chapter Twelve

Varna, July 2018

Beneath the plantation

After getting his family back to the Stack and sending Buford and the other prisoners into town to notify the other residents of what happened, Zayn took his team back to the plantation. Though he wasn't sure there would be anything left, he needed to find Keelan's body, and there was also the question of the poison. If any stores existed in the plantation, they needed to find them.

As he approached, his teammates following close behind, Skylar remarked, "It's quite an idyllic looking building."

"Sometimes the prettiest things are rotten inside," said Zayn.

At the columned porch, they found their first dead Watcher. Zayn recognized him as one of the two that had stopped him in the bar. Blood ran from his eyes, suggesting that the Spider Queen's death rather than the magic-eating spiders had killed him.

Before they went inside, three Varna police cars arrived with their lights flashing. Roy Clovis was the first to reach them, followed by his father.

"Hey, Roy," said Zayn, then to Roy's dad, "Sheriff."

Roy looked anxious as he approached. "Is Nev?"

"She's okay," said Zayn. "Back at the Stack. You should come by later and see her."

A big smile rose to his lips. He nodded.

The sheriff moved near the dead body they'd been examining. He hooked his thumbs in his belt. "Is it true?"

"I think so," said Zayn, motioning towards the dead Watcher. "The...she was linked to them psychically, so they died when she did."

Roy and his father shared glances.

"How?" asked Roy. "I assumed she was invincible, living as long as she had. Did you do it?"

"In a manner of speaking, yes, but not directly," said Zayn. "You could say she killed herself."

"Zayn," said the sheriff, pulling off his hat and wiping a sweaty forehead with his sleeve. "I appreciate what you did, but eventually you're going to have to explain every last detail of what happened."

"Be happy to, Sheriff," said Zayn. "But right now I think the most important thing is that we secure a source of poison."

"That was going to be my next question," said the sheriff, grimly. "Otherwise you've killed everyone in this town."

"I did not embark on this lightly," said Zayn. "I have a solution. Let's go inside and I'll show you."

Zayn led them through the plantation, finding a pair of dead Watchers on the way, until they reached the illusionary wall. He'd expected that he would have to disarm it, but he found the magic had been eliminated, either by her death, or the spiders. A light smoke twirled from below, suggesting potential fires.

"What's this goo on the wall?" asked Roy, using a pencil to poke at the pinkish substance.

"Now would be a good time to let you know there might still be dangerous creatures below. If we encounter them, it's best we run as fast as we can back here," said Zayn.

"Run? Why not kill 'em with a spell or something?" asked Roy.

"That would be very unwise," said Skylar. "We should grab some fire extinguishers before we go down."

After everyone found one, they headed below. The bottom of the steps looked like a war zone. The incubation room was a smoking hole in the ground with a few small fires still burning, but they were easily put out.

It was in the main hallway that they found torn purple robes with singed edges covered in pinkish goo. Zayn poked the robes with his boot.

"There's nothing left of her," said Vin.

"After all this time, she was pure magic," said Zayn. "The spiders probably devoured her whole and then exploded when they grew too fast."

In the lounge they found the three incubation chambers. The purple spiders remained, still pumping the yellowish liquid into a stainless steel canister.

"You have got to be kidding me," said the sheriff, pushing his hat to the back of his head.

Roy stood next to him, looking like he was going to be sick. "That's what we've been taking?"

"I mean, deep down, we all knew," said Zayn. "It was how she was able to keep so many of us hooked. There was a whole other room filled with these, but they went up in the explosion."

"Does that mean we're going to have to pick and choose

who lives?" asked Roy with an ashen expression.

"Even if we don't find stores, there's another option. The Lady's spiders, the ones we see everywhere. Those eventually become these big ones. I'm not sure how it happens, but I'd put money on there being a book or two in her library about it. You couldn't find anything about the Lady or her spiders anywhere, because she found them and made them disappear, to here, I bet."

Zayn went straight to her chambers, finding Keelan's body wrapped in a sheet. He was relieved that his cousin was covered. He couldn't take seeing him right then. A final goodbye at the funeral would be enough. Skylar volunteered to take the body.

The rest of them moved through the complex cautiously, finding only dead bodies, pinkish goo, and the occasional twitching spider leg. After an hour of searching, they determined that nothing lived. Zayn was beginning to give up hope that there was a store of poison until Portia found it.

"The secret door was hidden, not by magic, but a clever sliding wall panel," said Portia, bowing graciously when they gave her a round of applause.

The giant cooler held hundreds of boxes of spider poison, each carefully labeled with an expiration date. A quick survey of the materials showed they had enough poison to keep the town alive for a full year, which should be enough time to ramp up production of fresh poison. They also had the three spiders in the incubation chambers.

"I'll put a guard on it," said the sheriff, "until we can get it moved somewhere safe."

"Good idea," said Zayn.

"What do we tell the town?" asked the sheriff.

Zayn massaged the bridge of his nose with his forefinger and thumb. "I was hoping you could take care of that detail.

I'm running on reserves. It was a long night."

The sheriff paused before clucking his tongue and nodding to indicate he would take care of it.

Zayn gathered his teammates and they headed out of the plantation. Roy volunteered to take them back to the Stack in his patrol car.

When they arrived, Neveah went running into Roy's arms. They were still hugging when everyone else went inside.

"Boyfriend?" asked his mom.

"He's a good guy," said Zayn, then he introduced his teammates to his family. The twins took right to Vin, especially when he changed his face to match theirs. Portia and Skylar jumped in to help in the kitchen when Neveah and Roy returned from outside.

Zayn found his mom in the living room away from the discussion happening in the kitchen.

"Is Aunt Lydia here?"

Sela nodded towards the courtyard.

"Does she blame me?" he asked.

She squeezed her lips together until they were white, tears pooling in her eyes.

"It's going to take time. But I think you should go to her," said Sela.

Aunt Lydia was sitting at the center table, her prosthetic arm unhooked. She looked up, flinching when she realized who it was. Zayn almost left, but kept putting one foot in front of the other until he was standing before her.

"May I?" he asked, gesturing to the spot next to her.

Her jaw pulsed, but eventually she held out her hand.

Zayn sat next to his aunt, steeling himself for her eventual outburst. He was ready for anything except for what happened when she threw her arm wide and pulled him against her shoulder. He buried himself against her, wrapping his arms around her in turn.

Sobs came freely. Zayn wasn't sure how long they stayed like that, wrapped in each other's arms, crying. But eventually they pulled apart.

Aunt Lydia reached up and smoothed away a tear from his cheek.

"I forgive you, Zayn. I know you didn't have a choice," she said. "But I still might be angry from time to time. Please know that I still love you. I know he did."

She looked towards the kitchen. They were all standing in the doorway with trays of food.

"A good meal with family and friends will soothe away any heartache," said Maceo. "At least for a little while."

Within moments, the table was filled. Everyone took a seat. Zayn stayed by his Aunt Lydia, who held his hand.

But no one moved towards the food. Zayn sensed they wanted him to say something, but he wasn't ready yet. He reached for his knife, breaking the tension, and they fell into dinner. There would be time later for words.

Chapter Thirteen

Varna, July 2018

Final words

In the days before Keelan's funeral, Zayn found it hard to concentrate. Sitting in the courtyard at the Stack, he kept expecting to turn around and find Keelan there, ready to throw a black walnut or make a quip about being an ice zombie.

While the family adjusted to the idea of not being bound to Varna, Zayn took long walks in the vine-choked woods, enjoying the way the sun beat down on his head. He didn't bother with enchantments to protect himself from the heat, not that it wasn't hot, but it reminded him of being a lanky kid running around with his cousin playing the stupid games you played when you were poor and lived in the country.

One day, he found a couple of old drums with broken glass scattered around them. He and Keelan had made a makeshift slingshot out of rubber bands and a bunch of duct tape wrapped around a coat hanger. They'd taken turns exploding bottles they'd stolen from the garbage dump.

Zayn picked through the glass, hoping to recapture the feeling he'd had spending time with Keelan. In the final years at the Academy, the duties they had with their separate patrons had kept them apart, so his memories felt distant.

He missed the days when they could climb on top of the Stack with a couple of sleeping bags and watch the shooting stars in the middle of summer when the Milky Way was a glittering swath in the deep sky. Zayn always worried about falling asleep and rolling off the Stack, but it never bothered Keelan, who would lean over the edge to spit into the rocks.

Zayn hoped that Keelan hadn't been afraid, going into those last days. It'd been easier for Zayn because he'd gone into the plantation with the expectation of winning—he couldn't have gone in any other way.

But Keelan had known he was going to die. He'd probably known for a long time.

Zayn searched his memory of the time he'd spent with Keelan during the year, reviewing the words passed between them to divine if he had, but realized over time it would only hurt worse to know. Better that Keelan had thought they might both live, at least until the very end.

On the day of the funeral, Zayn wore a suit and tie. Putting it on reminded him of Uncle Jesse's funeral, which was the last time he'd worn a suit.

Neveah caught him in the living room, fiddling with his tie.

"You look like you're twelve years old again, the way you're messing with that," she said, knocking away his hands and fixing the knot so the side didn't bulge.

"In some ways, I wish I was twelve again, then he'd still be alive," said Zayn.

"But then the Lady wouldn't be dead, and we wouldn't be free," said Neveah, lips squeezed with emotion.

"I know," he said, shaking his head then looking away.

"Someday you're going to have to accept that he sacrificed himself for us. I plan on honoring him by seeing the world like I always wanted to," said Neveah.

Zayn smiled wistfully. "Remember when we were having dinner, and Dad asked about what we would do if we didn't have to stay in Varna?"

The memory crossing Neveah's mind appeared on her face with a soft "Oh."

"He wanted to be Jesse, didn't he?" asked Neveah.

Zayn nodded.

"I don't know how he could, after all that," said Neveah.

"He might only have been our uncle Jesse, but that was still his dad. It was complicated. He was an asshole, that much is certain, but without him we wouldn't have won. Uncle Jesse was the one who figured out the spiders," said Zayn.

Neveah stepped back. "Really?"

"Yeah," said Zayn. "I think there's some link between the colony I found in the Undercity and the one here in Varna, and probably the link is Uncle Jesse. Either way, it was his notes that led us to them."

Skylar entered the room, and catching the look on their faces, she turned around. "Sorry."

"No, no," said Neveah, reaching out for her. "We're just reminiscing about Keelan."

"I should leave, he was your family," said Skylar.

"Yours too, by way of the Academy," said Neveah, reaching out and clutching Skylar's hand.

"I miss him," said Skylar, getting glossy eyed.

A car honk saved Zayn from another round of grieving.

Maceo stuck his head through the door. "Doc's here, time to go."

Zayn rode with Skylar, Portia, and Vin in their rental car,

while Roy took Neveah and the three younger kids in his police car. His dad rode with Doc, who wore his favorite scrapyard tie. Sela had been staying with her sister, helping her with the final preparations. They would meet at the grave site.

When Skylar pulled up, there was nowhere to park. "Is there another funeral going on?"

"Probably," said Zayn, who stared absently out the side window. "Roy said there's been a lot of suicides this last week, mostly from the people that had profited from the Lady's arrangement."

Vin leaned forward between the seats. "I don't think that's the case. I see some of the instructors up there."

They found O'Keefe, Pennywhistle, and Noyade dressed in their finest, along with two men that Zayn didn't recognize. Pennywhistle threw her arms around Zayn, squeezing him until his ribs hurt. "I'm so sorry."

"So am I, lad," said O'Keefe. "He was the best damn student I ev'r had. Always trusted him not to muck it up."

Noyade cupped his cheek in her hand, a single tear glistening on her face. "I will always remember him."

"Thank you for coming." Zayn looked around the grave site. "I thought Allgood and the patron would be here too?"

A gruff voice came from one of the people he didn't recognize.

"We're here," said a man who was clearly Allgood.

The second man nodded towards Zayn and as soon as he looked him in the eyes, he realized it was Priyanka.

"I hope you understand why we can't be here as ourselves," said Priyanka.

"Yes, of course, I should have realized that," said Zayn, remembering the Ceremony.

Priyanka leaned into his ear and whispered, "After the funeral, I have to leave again. But I'll be back at the end of the month for you. We can talk more then."

"I'll be here," said Zayn.

He was silently relieved that he wouldn't have to get to work right away. He knew he would need a few more weeks to recover. They all did.

When the services started, Zayn gathered with his family. He held Imani's hand while the preacher spoke about Keelan. His littlest sister had been hit the hardest by his death. She'd adored Keelan because he'd always made time for her when the twins would ignore her. She kept wiping her cheeks with the back of her hand and sobbing.

Aunt Lydia stood on the other side of his mom. She looked worn out from grief, past the stages of crying, at least for now. Zayn didn't think any of them would get over it in their lifetimes. And why should they, since Keelan had given his life for theirs?

He wasn't paying attention until the pastor said, "And now Zayn Carter would like to say a few words."

As he walked to the front of the casket, he caught his aunt Lydia's eye. With her lips squeezed together and eyes filled with emotion, she nodded at him.

Standing at the head of his best friend's casket, Zayn looked out upon the crowd that had gathered to see him put into the earth. It looked like most of the town had come out to pay their respects.

Zayn had a speech in his coat pocket, but he realized he didn't need it. Remembering Keelan was something that would never be hard to do.

"From our family, we dearly appreciate that so many of you have gathered with us to remember Keelan Walker. Like most of you, he was born in Varna, lived in Varna, and expected to die in Varna.

"Varna has been for all of us, a chain around our necks,

a lodestone of fate we couldn't avoid. For some, that chain turned golden, for others, a noose. But not Keelan.

"He saw what had happened to us as a problem to solve, a weight to bear. It was on a day like this when we buried his father, Jesse, that I made a promise to myself that I would do everything I could to end the Lady of Varna. Little did I know that at the time Keelan had done the same, except his path was harder, because he never told a soul, not even me. He knew that the Lady would never be defeated unless someone became one of her guardians, to figure out the final clues to her demise. He did this knowing that the Lady would find out, because she always found out, and that he would have to die."

Zayn looked at the casket surrounded by bouquets of flowers. He wished Keelan could hear what he had to say next.

"But it is not his death that I want to talk about, as important as it may be, but his life. We were cousins, but more like brothers. I don't remember a time when I wasn't hanging out with him, taking part in the walnut wars behind the trailer park, or getting beat up by the Clovis brothers."

The crowd chuckled as Zayn smiled at Roy and his brothers.

"Keelan was kind and generous and smart. If he hadn't been born in Varna, he might have gone to MIT or Stanford and saved the world in a different way. He could be moody when he didn't get the highest score on a test, but willing to help you get your best score on yours. He was flawed and complicated and full of contradictions.

"At the Academy, he was a brilliant student, no surprise there, and quickly earned the trust of his fellow students, the instructors, and the patron herself. He was, among many things, a person who had so much to give, and he did.

"But most of all he was my best friend. The person I will miss for the rest of my life, no matter how old I get, or how far from Varna I travel, because I will carry him with me, always and forever."

With tears in his eyes, Zayn lifted his chin.

"For Keelan."

And the town responded.

"For Keelan."

Chapter Fourteen
Varna, July 2018
The best of teams

Keelan's funeral wasn't the last, and the busy cemetery seemed to raise the temperature in town. There were a lot of fights, a half dozen knife wounds, and one gut shot with a rifle. It took the sheriff hiring extra deputies to turn the tide, paid for by the monies recovered at the plantation, but even then it took weeks for the fever to break.

Roy told them about the many disappearances, usually of folks that had lived in the Gardens. The rest of the town didn't appreciate how they'd used the Lady's power against them. Only his aunt Lydia escaped the quiet wrath, and that was only because of Keelan.

Some of the time in the following weeks was spent trying to figure out what to do with the plantation and all the wealth stored on it. They assumed Lady Arcadia had a large bank account, probably offshore, but no one knew how they might access it. But she had kept a reserve of cash, jewels, and bonds on her property, which the sheriff turned over to the new mayor to use for reparations.

Zayn stayed at the Stack, though he was visited regularly by the sheriff in consultation, or by townsfolk who wanted to thank him for killing her.

When it came time for his teammates to return to their jobs, they met him in the courtyard as he was setting the table for dinner. A cool breeze rustled the holiday lights hanging over the table as the crickets played their evening tune.

"Heading back?" he asked, to a chorus of nods.

"I'd stay for a month if I could. I love your family," said Vin.

"No wonder you risked everything for them," said Portia, hugging him. "They're the best."

"It balances things out for being born in Varna," said Zayn, chuckling. "I hope everyone has a job still after leaving like that."

"Priyanka made sure they understood that we were on hall business," said Skylar.

"Do you know what she's going to have you do?" asked Portia.

"Probably jetting away to exotic locations on ultra-cool heists," said Vin, adding overly dramatic hand motions.

"I've had enough heists for a while," said Zayn.

Vin slapped his hand against his chest in a faux heart attack. "My heart cannot take such negativity."

A pause in the conversation grew until Zayn said, "Man, I am going to miss you all. I can't believe this is goodbye. I really don't know how to thank you for coming to my aid when I needed you most."

Portia punched him in the arm. "Next time don't wait until the shit has hit the fan before notifying us."

"I get it, I get it," said Zayn with a wistful smile. "Next

time, I will."

"Not without Priyanka's permission," said Skylar.

"What? You guys don't think I'd disobey her?" he asked.

"Guaranteed," said Skylar, then added a big sigh. "We've got flights to catch."

Without saying another word, they collapsed into a group hug. Zayn squeezed them as tight as he could. He buried his face in their shoulders and necks.

Then he took them each by the shoulders, gave them a long hug, a kiss on the cheek, and a promise that they should get together on a regular basis to catch up and compare notes from their soon-to-be illustrious careers.

As his friends headed to their rental car, he heard Vin say, "To think, at the beginning of all this, Zayn was the guy who had to get naked on his first day in the Academy."

"And last to get his named coin," said Skylar.

"Using a sparkly pink dildo," added Portia, laughing.

He watched them drive away from the window, missing them already. A little while later, Neveah and Roy came downstairs with a pair of suitcases.

"You're not leaving too, are you?" asked Zayn.

"Sorry, older brother," said Neveah, "I can't stay. Maybe in a few years the town will fix itself, but for right now it's going to be a mess. We're getting out of here while we can."

"You're going with her? What does your dad think?" asked Zayn.

"He gave his blessing. He'd get out if he could, but he feels responsible for the town, at least to keep the peace until things settle down," said Roy.

"Where are you headed? Back to Invictus?" asked Zayn.

A big grin appeared on his sister's face. "Paris. I want to get a job at a top restaurant. Learn how things are supposed to be done for a few years, then maybe open my own place."

"That's awesome. You're going to kill it," he said, sharing a fist bump with her.

He looked to Roy. "What will you do?"

Roy scratched his chin. "Dunno. I guess I get to figure out what I want to do with the rest of my life. Working for my dad was just something to do since I was stuck in Varna. It certainly wasn't a dream of mine or anything. Maybe I'll learn to paint, or be a waiter."

"How's your French?"

"No hables Espanola," said Roy, chuckling.

"What about the poison?" asked Zayn.

"Mom and Dad are going to send it to us," said Neveah. "They're going to help set up the supply chain before they leave in the fall."

"Everyone's leaving? Where have I been?" asked Zayn.

Neveah tilted her head at him. "On long walks in the woods. But I understand. I know you miss him."

"Will there be a town left in a few years?" mused Zayn.

"Maybe not," said Neveah, "and why should there be? This place was her place."

Zayn nodded. When he thought of home, he thought of the Stack, a separate world from Varna, but he could understand how others might think differently.

"I bet no one would stay if it weren't for the poison," said Roy. "But hey, eventually no one will have to worry about it. Any kids born now will be free of her."

Zayn caught the way Roy and his sister looked at each other. He wouldn't be surprised if he was an uncle in a few years after she got established in Paris.

A honk from outside goosed Neveah and Roy into action. She threw her arms around Zayn and kissed him on the cheek. Roy gave him a quick hug too.

"We have a plane to catch, Doc's taking us," said Neveah

over her shoulder. "Come visit us!"

The next few weeks, Zayn busied himself with the poison supply business. The town had gathered a few hundred of the Lady's spiders for poison production, though it would be a while until they were big enough to milk. Seeing the rows of aquariums filled with the solitary hunters gave Zayn the creeps, especially knowing that she'd come from such humble beginnings.

Sela and Maceo told them about their plans once things were in place. Along with Doc, they were going to take the kids on a whirlwind tour of the country, and the Grand Canyon would be their first stop. They didn't want to go too far in case problems came up in Varna.

Aunt Lydia had volunteered to run the poison distribution operations. She seemed to be spending a lot of time hanging out with the sheriff, which was a good sign for her recovery.

On the last day of the month, when the June bugs were thick and the heat kept them in the courtyard, Priyanka Sai appeared at the Stack. She looked thinner than when he'd seen her last, with a few wrinkles around the corners of her eyes.

He'd been drinking tea with his mom and dad. They rose when she entered.

"Please sit," said Priyanka. "It's your house."

"But you're a guest." Sela grabbed a glass. "Can I pour you some tea?"

"Thank you," said Priyanka, slightly exasperated at the deference.

When her glass was full, Sela kissed Zayn on the cheek. "We know you're leaving now. Do try to send word now and then with news. We'll leave information on how to contact us when we embark ourselves."

His parents gave him long hugs. The twins and Imani

were swimming at Doc's, but they'd said their goodbyes that morning. He'd told them that Priyanka would come that day.

"They're very nice," said Priyanka, after they left. She looked different than when he'd seen her last. It took a moment for him to realize she was wearing long sleeves in the middle of summer.

She caught where he was looking and pulled a sleeve back, revealing bright red lines snaking up the inside of her arm.

"Is that from her?" he asked.

Priyanka nodded. "They'll disappear in time, but the recovery has been rough."

She took a long drink from the glass, completely emptying it before setting it back onto the table with a sigh that came from her gut.

"That was glorious. I'd forgotten how much I enjoyed sweet tea," said Priyanka.

"The secret is a pound of sugar per glass," said Zayn, smirking. "So I assume you're here to collect me?"

"I am," she said.

Priyanka stepped close and grabbed him by the shoulders. A wellspring of emotion was behind her eyes. He could see the centuries in her expression, a relief that had been waiting for a long time.

"I can't tell you how proud I am of you. You and Keelan both. I'd been waiting for a long time for a student to come along like you. Someone to challenge the Lady and put an end to her reign. What I didn't know was that there'd be two of you. I wish your cousin would have survived. But since he didn't, I'll make sure that his sacrifice was worth it. Especially with that bitch gone"—Priyanka paused, a twitch of anger on her lips before she continued—"we can really get to business. You're special, Zayn Carter. It won't be easy, but there's a lot of good we can do, you and I."

"I'm ready," he said.

"Good," she replied. "We can leave as soon as you gather your things."

"My bag is sitting by the front door," he said.

"Excellent," she said.

He grabbed his bag and threw it over his shoulder, and they walked out of the Stack. He didn't look back because he was afraid that he'd never see it again if he did.

"There are so many places I want to show you," she said. "You must learn to walk between the worlds as I have, speak their languages, learn their customs, help where help is needed."

Worlds spun through his mind. The heavy blanket that had been covering him was thrown off as they climbed into her SUV. "I'm ready. Where shall we go first?"

"There's a realm filled with lush tropical islands, an archipelago of paradise inhabited by sea-dwelling peoples," said Priyanka, standing at the open door.

"Is there a fascist ruler we need to overthrow? An underwater fortress we need to break into? What will we find on these islands?" he asked.

"Pina coladas."

Zayn wrinkled his forehead. "Pina coladas? I don't understand. Is that like a secret organization or something?"

"No," she said. "It's a drink. I taught the locals how to make them a few decades ago using local ingredients."

"I don't understand," he said. "I thought we had a lot of work to do?"

"We do. I need to finish recovering, we both need a short vacation, and there's a lot I need to teach you," she said.

"But I thought I'd get right to work? Isn't that what my five years at the Academy were for?" he asked.

Priyanka climbed into the front seat.

“That was to get a normal job,” she said. “This is so you can eventually be the patron of the Academy of the Subtle Arts.”

“Wha—”

“Don’t worry, Zayn. You’ve got a few more decades of learning first, but now that you’re not a student anymore, I can really begin teaching you.”

“Really begin teaching me? What was all that in Harmony? Those were some of the hardest tasks I’ve ever had to survive,” said Zayn, blinking. “Which I barely survived, by the way.”

“Oh, Harmony?” She started the car, flashing a wink in his direction as she had her hand on the gear shifter. “That was a warm-up.”

Zayn touched his chest where the scar from where he’d been stabbed in the heart was located.

“Let’s go.”

§ § §

Stay tuned for the first book
in next Hundred Halls series

THE WARPED FOREST

July 2019

Also by Thomas K. Carpenter

HUNDRED HALLS UNIVERSE

THE HUNDRED HALLS

Trials of Magic
Web of Lies
Alchemy of Souls
Gathering of Shadows
City of Sorcery

THE RELUCTANT ASSASSIN

The Reluctant Assassin
The Sorcerous Spy
The Veiled Diplomat
Agent Unraveled
The Webs That Bind

GAMEMAKERS ONLINE

The Warped Forest

Special Thanks

It's hard for me to believe that another series has come and gone. I'm pleased with the reaction to Zayn's story. I think it's my best one to date. While I'll miss spending time with Zayn and his family—Neveah especially—I'm also looking forward to showing you a new hall with its own unique problems. But don't worry, for you Zayn/Aurie fans, their story isn't done, but it's going to be a few years until we come back to them.

Now to the most important part of the book, a thank you to all those people that helped make these stories what they are. People like my wife Rachel who helps me craft the stories that you love, Ravven who conjures the covers from her imagination and skillful craft, my editor Tamara Blaine who fixes my absurd word choices and makes the reading experience more pleasant, the beta readers (Tina Rak, Carole Carpenter, Paula J. Fletcher, and Patty Eversole) who give me great feedback while dealing with an error filled manuscript, to the Vanguard (Elaine Stoker, Jennifer Beere, Lana Turner, Jess Churchfield, Thad Moody, Phyllis Simpson, and Andie Alessandra Cáomhanach) who catch those final gremlins that plague every book.

Your time and effort have helped bring to life this moment of joy in readers' lives. Thank you!

ABOUT THE AUTHOR

Thomas K. Carpenter resides near St. Louis with his wife Rachel and their two children. When he's not busy writing his next book, he's playing soccer in the yard with his kids or getting beat by his wife at cards. He keeps a regular blog at www.thomaskcarpenter.com and you can follow him on twitter @thomaskcarpente. If you want to learn when his next novel will be hitting the shelves and get free stories and occasional other goodies, please sign up for his mailing list by going to: http://tinyurl.com/thomaskcarpenter. Your email address will never be shared and you can unsubscribe at any time.

Made in United States
Orlando, FL
06 August 2024

49985425R00183